THE DEAD HATH NO FURY

A VISCOUNT WARE MYSTERY #5

J. L. BUCK

A Camel Press book published by Epicenter Press

Epicenter Press
6524 NE 181st St.
Suite 2
Kenmore, WA 98028

For more information go to:
www.Camelpress.com
www.Coffeetownpress.com
www.Epicenterpress.com

Author's website: janetlbuck.com

The Dead Hath No Fury
2025 © J. L. Buck

Library of Congress Control Number: 2024952543
ISBN: 9781684923144 (trade paper)
ISBN: ISBN:9781684923151 (ebook)

To Latte, my Siamese cat, and Pippin, my Min Pin puppy,
who've tolerated my working on manuscripts in what they
consider their play time.

Clutching the reins in one hand, his hat in the other, Andrew Sherbourne leaned into the sharp gusts of a March wind and urged General into a gallop. The big gelding responded gallantly even though Sherry knew he had to be tiring. Nor was this pace all that safe in the mist and drizzle. On such a well-traveled road, another rider or conveyance could appear out of the fog with little or no warning.

Yet Sherry felt an urgency—albeit unreasonable—that kept propelling him forward, urging his mount's pounding hooves to ever greater speed. He knew he could not turn back time nor change the events that had shaken his life, so why was he rushing headlong toward London in such inclement weather? Was he truly that keen for answers or merely attempting to leave the truth and its consequences behind him…if just for a while?

After a few minutes, he slowed General's pace to a walk, as he'd forced himself to do off and on, for the past hour. Regardless of his inner turmoil, he had no wish to harm his favorite mount by pushing him beyond his limits.

Hearing the rattle of an approaching coach, he reined General to the edge of the road. A mail coach rumbled by, and moments later Sherry spotted the Wild Boar Inn on the left as he entered the outskirts of the city. His destination was only minutes away.

He drew a deep, shaky breath. Soon now, he would set in motion his best hope for learning how this nightmare had come about, and once he'd accomplished that, duty would take him back.

Chapter One

Lucien Grey, Viscount Ware, heard the lady's maid, Jenny, clear her throat loudly, and he loosened his arms around Lady Anne with a low laugh. She swiftly straightened from the kiss they'd shared and scooted a few inches away as the door to the hallway rattled open. When a house maid entered with a tea tray, he smiled at the relief on Lady Anne's face and leaned over to brush a fair curl back from her flushed cheek.

"It could have been Father," she said softly, her blue eyes glinting with humor. "It is just as well Jenny warned us, or the servants would surely be gossiping."

Lucien laughed aloud this time. "As though they were not already."

He caught a glimpse of Jenny struggling to hide a smile. For the last twenty minutes, she'd been sitting on the far side of the Earl of Chadley's spacious peach-and-dark green drawing room, pretending to concentrate on her mending and fulfilling her duty as chaperone to Lady Anne Ashburn, the peer's only daughter. Lucien suspected she had been carefully watching the door to ensure the earl didn't see anything he should not. Lucien appreciated her diligence as he preferred that he and Lady Anne make any decisions about their future when they wished and without pressure from the earl or the haute ton.

"Whatever the servants think they know, it would be wise if we did not give them cause to talk about us," she said dimpling, sliding another few inches away on the green upholstered sofa and placing her hands sedately in her lap.

He smiled at the angelic picture she presented, the fair curls and innocent blue eyes hiding a curious and adventurous nature. They had been formally courting the past eight months, becoming acquainted outside the harrowing events that had comprised most of their prior relationship. Lucien and his friend/fellow agent Andrew Sherbourne had been spying for England for eight years, the first four under Wellington on the Continent, the last four as members of the Prince Regent's secret spy unit working out of Whitehall in Westminster, London.

More than two years ago, Lady Anne had become entangled with the same villain Lucien was following, discovered Lucien's secret connection to Whitehall, and since then had unexpectedly played an important role in four of his most complex inquiries. She'd almost become another partner—although Lucien was not about to admit it—and had placed herself in danger more than once. It was those risks along with the hazards ever inherent in his work that held him back from asking for her hand. Such risks were not suited to married life—and Lady Anne was well aware of his reservations.

"Tea, my lord?" she asked, interrupting his thoughts and holding out a cup she'd just poured.

"Yes, thank you."

He had barely taken his first sip when she asked, "Have you heard from Lord Rothe? A new assignment, perhaps?"

"Nothing to speak of, particularly to you, my lady." He gave her an amused look. "The nature of spy work is its secrecy, or have you forgotten?"

"Honestly, my lord," she said, tasting her own hot drink. "It is a bit late to pretend I am unaware of what you do for the Crown. Besides, I *have* helped, have I not?"

"You certainly have. That does not mean it should continue." He broke off, wanting to avoid another disagreement on this particular subject. "Moreover, I have nothing to tell. Whitehall has its hands full fighting wars on three fronts, squelching the baseless rumors of Napoleon's death, and stabilizing an economy reeling from the stock market's ups and downs and the recent stock fraud scandal. Not to forget the Luddites. I can only hope that uprising is over now. How can Lord Byron and politicians like Philip Beaumont and Ambrose Wynn support workers who believe smashing machinery will save their jobs?"

"Perhaps they too have been swayed by General Ned Ludd."

"The Luddites' alleged leader? I doubt his existence. He never appears at their protests, and they claim he lives in Sherwood Forest, rather like the legendary Robin Hood."

"It *is* a quite fanciful story," she said with a smile, before growing serious again. "But I understand why the weavers are angry. Many are losing jobs passed down in their families for decades. They have no other way to provide for their wives and children."

Lucien nodded in agreement. "Your feelings for their plight do you credit, my lady, and I sympathize with them too, but are their actions getting them what they want? More than a dozen have been publicly hanged and unknown numbers shot or beheaded. They alienate themselves from their employers and add to the Crown's troubles at a time when it is already overwhelmed." He lifted a hand to concede a problem with no solution and laughed at himself. "To conclude my rather lengthy explanation, I daresay a foreign spy here and there and a bit of misbehavior by the Prince Regent's cabinet and cronies have slipped by Whitehall's notice amongst such other pressing issues. Thus, my free time and our extra days together." He gave her a rueful look. "You must not get used to it, my dear—it will rarely be so quiet for me. As we speak, half a dozen of those neglected matters may be simmering, ready to explode into a crisis the Crown cannot ignore. A summons from Rothe could arrive at any hour."

"Then let us hope Sherbourne does not linger indefinitely in the country and leave you to face those catastrophes alone. He has been gone quite a long time."

"A few weeks, but I cannot begrudge him." Lucien's lips twitched with humor. "He is a promised man now, nearly leg-shackled." After three years of pretending his interest in his childhood neighbor was friendship only, Sherry had betrothed himself to Emily Selkirk two months ago. "They have a future to discuss, and he is taking advantage of Whitehall's distraction while he can. He knows this idleness won't last."

"Shh," she said, putting a finger against her lips. "If you keep saying that, you know something will happen."

"It will happen regardless."

"Yes, I know." She leaned forward and placed a hand on his arm. "Yet, I cannot help but wish for more time together."

His lean fingers gripped her hand. "I share your wish, Lady Anne."

And he did. Nonetheless, he'd begun to feel that restlessness that nagged at him when it had been too long between assignments. It was a remnant of war, an edge of unease, a knot in the gut that called for action, and he supposed it would follow him always.

"Enough talk," he said, ending his moment of disquiet. "I would much prefer to kiss you."

"Since that is most improper," she said with laughing reserve, "perhaps you should take yourself off. There will be no more liberties allowed today."

He stood with a languid sigh. "A man can hope, can he not?"

"Away with you." Lady Anne lifted her chin, but her dimple was showing again. "I have better things to do, my lord."

"Do you now?"

"Well…maybe not better, but I have things to do if I am to be ready for the Collingwoods' dinner party tonight."

"Then I shall bid you adieu for now, my lady." He bowed and kissed her hand, his eyes meeting hers for a moment. "I look forward to this evening."

"As do I."

Resisting the desire to throw convention aside and kiss her again, he took his leave.

• • •

Andrew Sherbourne, the second-born son of the newly elevated Earl of Sherbourne, slouched in a cushioned wing-back chair before the hearth in Lucien's study. His feet were stretched out toward the warmth, his chin nearly resting on his chest. He was drinking a glass of his friend's excellent brandy and staring morosely into the flames.

Upon his arrival in London, he had come straight to Lucien's townhouse on Hays Mews, put General in the hands of a stable boy, and hurried inside to share his shocking news—only to find Lucien gone. Hughes, the butler, had shown him to the study, and he'd been there long enough to dry off, have a brandy, and think about the dreadful news his family had received less than twenty-four hours ago. After talking it over with his father, Sherry had hastened to London to request a favor from the only man he could trust to dig out the truth.

At the sound of booted footsteps on the stairs, Sherry sighed. Lucien was home. He didn't straighten in the chair, but he turned his head to glance toward the hall. His friend stood in the doorway, his tall, lean form—more compact than Sherry's lanky build—was immaculately attired in a blue coat, fawn breeches, and highly polished Hessians.

Lucien cocked his head of dark hair and cast him a speculative look. "Hughes said you were here. He neglected to say you were guzzling my best brandy."

"And I could use a refill." Sherry dropped his gaze. The emotional drain of the last day and night had left him numb and close to exhaustion now that he was here.

Lucien frowned and came forward to take Sherry's glass. "Allow me. I gather something is seriously amiss." He poured another glass for Sherry, handed it to him, then poured one for himself and took a seat. "Want to talk about it?"

Sherry glanced at Lucien before slowly shaking his head at the incredulity of it all. "The most damnable thing has occurred. My half-brother Graham, Lord Audley, is dead. A bloody carriage accident."

"Good lord." Lucien jerked his head up in surprise, nearly choked on his drink, and frowned. "What of the wife and infant child?"

"They were not with him, thank God, but I'm concerned for them all the same. Lady Phoebe is country-bred, shy, gentle, even fragile. Father immediately sent for her and baby Eliza to come to Sherbourne Manor, but I doubt she will agree. Her own family lives much closer, and they have a definite influence over her."

"How did the accident occur?"

"Well, that's the thing—they say Graham had been on an overnight trip to Maidenhead, and on the way home, his four-in-hand, closed carriage went off into a ravine, killing both Graham and his coachman. A witness reported the horses were running at breakneck speed."

Lucien cocked his head, his gray eyes fixed on Sherry. "It sounds like a runaway."

"It probably was, but Graham's driver didn't simply lose control."

"Unlikely, I own, but situations do—"

"Not this time. My brother was a careful man. His coach would have been in top condition, his horses steady and reliable—he didn't buy for show—and he wouldn't have tolerated a driver who handled them recklessly. Father and I were skeptical the moment we heard of the incident, and then a second message arrived late last night." Sherry straightened to take a note from his pocket and hand it to Lucien. "The neighbor—Squire Levington, who is also the local magistrate—thinks it was murder."

"Bloody hell, Sherry. Does he have proof?"

"Just read it. You'll see."

Lucien skimmed the brief message before lifting a brow. "The harness was sliced?"

"That's what he says. God knows, Graham and I were not close—being reared apart, we were little more than acquaintances—but I still have a responsibility to his wife and child to learn the truth." Sherry hesitated, feeling awkward about this next part. "His death puts me in the succession as heir, and it leaves urgent estate matters that Father and I must handle over the next few days."

"'Pon rep, my friend," Lucien interrupted, staring at him, "you are Viscount Sherbourne now. No, that would be Andrew Sherbourne, Viscount Audley—Lord Audley."

"Do not remind me. I find the thought overwhelming. It was never supposed to be this way. I know nothing about running an estate. I'm not prepared for this."

"Tell me about it," Lucien muttered. "You will learn."

Sherry drew in a sharp breath as he realized just how similar their situations were. They were spying on the Continent when Lucien received word his elder brother had died, making him Salcott's heir. At the time, Sherry had not comprehended just how hard the sudden change of circumstances had been for his friend. Now, he had a greater appreciation for those early, demanding days and the challenges that followed.

"Setting my situation aside," Sherry went on, "what I was getting at is Sherbourne and I are asking that you go to Audley to determine if Lady Phoebe has everything she needs and if there is any truth in the magistrate's allegation."

"Most certainly, I shall go. You cannot have doubted it."

Sherry gave a faint grin. Something about Lucien always lifted his spirits. "Well, no, I did not doubt it, but it is polite to ask. In other circumstances, I would wish for you to join the family at the funeral, but I feel a sense of urgency to support Lady Phoebe and get an investigation under way."

"You seem quite concerned about her. Is there something in particular that weighs on your mind?"

"Sherbourne is very concerned, and after talking with him, so am I. The situation at Audley is a bit delicate. If Graham was murdered, the constables may consider her to be the obvious suspect, and to quote Sherbourne, she is 'too sweet and helpless' to defend herself. She is just a small thing who couldn't have done this herself, but they may say she had someone do it for her."

"Why the devil would they think that?" Lucien asked sharply.

"I see what you're thinking," Sherry said, straightening in his chair. "And no, he didn't beat her or berate her, not Graham, but Sherbourne says he was neglectful, an inconsiderate husband, I suppose. Her family certainly thinks so…and perhaps others." Sherry heaved a sigh. "Graham was obsessed by his historical research and would not have married at all, if Sherbourne had not insisted he produce an heir. He chose Phoebe only because she wouldn't expect him to make changes in his life."

"That is common in many arranged marriages," Lucien said.

"True, but Sherbourne hoped they'd do well together. What I didn't know was that Graham has ignored Lady Phoebe since their little girl's birth. It wasn't that he blamed her for not producing an heir, he was simply too caught up in his own world of historical research and writing. He even moved her and the infant to the former Dower House because he found them *too distracting*." Sherry shook his head sadly. "What a damn fool he was."

When Lucien didn't comment, Sherry went on. "Given the estrangement, you know someone will point an accusing finger at her. And if there is no other suspect..." He looked at Lucien. "Regardless of his neglect, Sherbourne says she was fond of Graham. I don't know her all that well, Lucien, but I'm confident she is not a murderess."

"Won't her family step forward to protect her?"

"Lord, no. Even if so inclined, they have no influence in the community. To the contrary, her brother, Jasper, the head of the household since her father's death, is a bully, and even the sisters are greedy and manipulative. Graham provided a shield to keep them from constantly preying on her for funds or whatever else they wanted."

"Charming family," Lucien remarked. "She must be feeling rather lost without Graham to stand up for her."

"Father is concerned she'll just let Jasper have his way." Sherry leaned forward, speaking earnestly. "What I cannot fathom about this whole situation is how Graham made someone angry enough to kill him. I thought he was too immersed in his maps and history books to offend anyone."

"I hope to find the answer for you."

"I do not doubt you will, and I shall make haste to join you as soon as I can." He hesitated, then added, "One other thing, considering how fragile Lady Phoebe is, you might consider taking Lady Anne with you."

Lucien raised a considering brow. "It is true that no one understands a woman like another woman."

"Would Lord Chadley allow it?" Sherry responded. The earl would, of course, but would he expect Lucien to commit to marriage in return? Sherry wasn't certain either Lucien or Lady Anne was ready for that.

"He'd want a proper chaperone, at the very least. Let me discuss it with Lady Anne. I shall see her at a dinner party tonight…unless you are staying over?"

"I'm not." Sherry set down his empty glass and rose. "After picking up a few things from the London house, I shall return to Sherbourne Manor tonight. Graham's body will arrive this evening."

"If it can be arranged, I'll leave for Audley tomorrow, but no later than Wednesday morning. I must make a few preparations if I am to be gone several days or weeks. And it may take some talking to convince Lord Chadley, assuming Lady Anne is willing to go."

"She will be," Sherry predicted. "I haven't the slightest doubt."

Chapter Two

London, England, evening, Monday, 21 March 1814

The dinner party was large, a hundred guests, attired in the height of fashion and seated at two long, candle-lit tables. Lucien and Lady Anne were not seated at the same table throughout the lengthy seven-course meal of soup, fish, mutton, pigeon, and a variety of vegetables, pickles, custards, and puddings. And even if they had been, the lively conversations and quick laughter that filled the room would have precluded private discourse. After the last course was served, the ladies retired for a hour of gossip while the men enjoyed their port.

It was well into the evening, during the after-dinner music, when Lucien was finally able to approach Lady Anne.

"Would you care to go for a stroll, my lady? Perhaps a few moments in the garden."

She tilted her head to look up at him. "It is not precisely strolling weather. Is something on your mind?"

"It is, and I'd rather not discuss it in here." He retrieved her dark green pelisse from the front hall and held the door while she preceded him outside.

The well-tended gardens, though graced by only a few blooms of crocuses, were lit by dozens of lanterns, and regardless of the cool, damp March air, Lucien and Lady Anne weren't the only couple taking a turn on the paths for a bit of privacy. He held the cloak for her to slip her arms inside, and she immediately pulled it closed over her pale green gown.

"I shall try to keep this brief," he said, "but let me know if you get chilled enough you wish to go inside."

She nodded, studying his face. "What troubles you, Lucien?"

"When I reached home this afternoon, Sherry was waiting in the study."

Her face brightened with a smile. "Surely that is good news."

"Ordinarily, it would be, but his half-brother has been killed, and the local magistrate believes it was murder."

"Heaven forbid, my lord. He must be devastated."

"Definitely shaken. Graham was raised by the family of Lord Sherbourne's first wife, and the two boys rarely saw one another. His grief is not so much personal as that natural to loss of family. Part of Sherry's shock is what the future holds for him as Sherbourne's heir. With Graham only in his middle years, Sherry never thought he'd be in this position. In less than a year, he's gone from being the second son of a baron—before his father's unexpected elevation in rank—to becoming Viscount Sherbourne of Audley, the heir to an earldom. It is a lot to take in."

"Oh my, yes, it is, and you, of all people, can relate to his situation."

Lucien's eyes darkened. "Far too well, except I was very close to my brother and admired him greatly. I was devastated by his loss and would give up everything gladly to have him back."

"I am so sorry and do beg pardon," she said, her brows furrowing as she tightened her hold on his arm. "I did not intend to make light of your loss. It is only the abrupt changes of circumstance that are the same."

"I didn't take it amiss, my dear. You're getting cold," he said, as he placed a hand over her chilled fingers. "Let us start back, and I'll tell you the rest on the way. Tomorrow, I leave for Audley. At the request of the Sherbournes, I'm to look into the magistrate's suspicions and offer support to Lady Phoebe."

"Poor lady. She will need it. Raising a child alone will not be easy."

"She need not do it alone unless she chooses so. The Sherbournes will see to her every need, but there are changes and potential trouble ahead." He stopped on the path and turned to face her. "Sherry describes her as shy, rather fragile, and he expressed concern her own family will be less than supportive, and may, in fact, try to take advantage of her. What makes things even worse was Lord and Lady Audley were estranged, and if this was murder, she will become a suspect. The situation requires careful handling, the kind best provided by a woman."

She raised her brows in surprise. "Why, Lord Ware, are you inviting me to accompany you and assist with your inquiry?"

"Sherry suggested it," he said with a wry smile. "What do you think?"

"I hear hesitation in your voice."

"Only because it is a lot to ask. We could be gone a few days or several weeks. What might your father make of that?"

"Ah, yes." She gave a knowing nod, her eyes gleaming with intelligence. "I see what you mean. Father might assume more than we wish him to at present. Allow me to approach him. I shall explain the journey is at a request from the new Viscount Audley. And, then, I shall obtain a proper chaperone." Her eyes suddenly lit with glee. "I know—Margret. She is a married woman now, making her a very respectable chaperone."

Lucien laughed. "Not if your father knows her well. The two of you have an excessive love of adventure."

"Which is why she would be the perfect companion for another murder inquiry." Lady Anne grinned at him. "And Father does *not* know her well. I shall send a note to her yet tonight. If we are fortunate, the captain will be engaged in one of Lord Rothe's secret intrigues."

Mrs. Jack Wycliff, the former Miss Margret Barnett, was a close friend of Lady Anne's, and they were often found together whenever Margret and Captain Jack Wycliff were in town or visiting her parents' home on the outskirts of London. Prior to her marriage, she and the captain had been drawn into two of Lucien's inquires, to the extent that Wycliff had been recruited as a full-time, employed member of Lord Rothe's unit of spies. As his assignments often drew him away from home, Margret was left with extra time on her hands, and Lucien very much feared she would agree to go without hesitation. Not that he wouldn't enjoy her lively company, but Lady Anne's headstrong confidence and Mrs. Wycliff's impetuous nature might lead the ladies into trouble if he relaxed his vigilance for even a moment.

Lady Anne pressed his arm and looked up with excitement in her eyes. "I am certain Father will agree. How could he not?" She stopped and peered at him hesitantly. "Unless you want me to say no…otherwise, I know you're keen to leave, we could try to be ready by midday tomorrow. Would that suit your plans?"

"Very much so, but do not assume you will be investigating a murder. You and Margret are to provide companionship for Lady Phoebe while I conduct the inquiry."

"Naturally, we shall befriend her. Nonetheless, you implied I should gather information from Lady Phoebe, and surely that would include other household members."

He eyed her doubtfully. "Only if you promise to confine your questioning to Audley Manor—not the neighbors and not the village. I cannot run a proper inquiry if I'm worried about where you are and what dangerous individuals you might be pursuing."

"Naturally. Now, may we go inside? I am becoming a bit chilled," she said with a shiver.

They hurried to rejoin the other guests, but knowing Lady Anne as he did, Lucien suspected she'd chosen that particular moment to complain of the cold in order to avoid further restrictions on her actions at Audley. He frowned, wondering how much trouble he was getting himself into…for he had no doubt that Lady Anne would convince her father and Mrs. Wycliff to do whatever she wanted.

• • •

Arriving at Audley Manor, Buckinghamshire, Tuesday, 22 March 1814

As Lady Anne had promised, the ladies and their luggage were ready and waiting at noon the following day, and Lucien's coach was entering Buckinghamshire by late afternoon. It had been a long but lively trip. Lady Anne and Mrs. Wycliff hadn't seen each other for the last six weeks, and they had their heads together the first two hours, flaxen curls bent close to the light brown of her friend, blue eyes and hazel both dancing with amusement or mischief.

Lucien mostly lounged in a corner of the coach and watched, a half-smile on his face, speaking only when he was appealed to for a comment or opinion on some issue of dispute. They were a charming pair, and so far he had no cause to regret bringing them, but it was early hours.

Dusk had fallen when they pulled into the circular drive of Audley Manor and stopped at the front entrance of the three-story, white stone and red brick edifice. It wasn't as large as Sherbourne Manor but larger than the surrounding estates. From what Lucien could see, the grounds and gardens appeared well-tended, if not elaborate. A modest-sized stable and attached coach house stood north of the manor.

By the time he'd made this brief survey of the property, three servants had appeared to help with the trunks and numerous band boxes the ladies had brought. A few moments later they were shown into the drawing room to meet Lady Phoebe.

A petite woman with large green eyes, dark ginger curls, and a shy smile rose to greet them. She was appropriately attired in a black gown and a shawl of black-lace. "I was very pleased to get Lord Sherbourne's message that you would be coming, my lord and ladies."

Lucien bowed. "A honor to meet you, Lady Audley. May I present Lady Anne Ashburn and Mrs. Wycliff. I regret we come to you under such sad circumstances."

"You are all so very welcome. It is a difficult time but shall be easier to bear with others beside me." She smiled at Lady Anne and Mrs. Wycliff. "I have been without feminine companionship for a while and am eager to chat, but we shall have plenty of time for that. You must be tired and hungry after your journey. Dinner shall be ready in an hour, and I assume you would wish to get settled and freshen up before then."

"Oh, yes, please," Anne said gratefully. "I, for one, promise to be on time. I am famished."

"As am I," Margret agreed. "The food basket we brought in the carriage was empty ages ago."

Lady Phoebe offered a soft laugh. "I shall notify cook to serve right on time and expect to see you soon."

To Lucien surprise, the ladies were downstairs in time for a glass of wine or Madeira before dinner, and they were all seated in Audley Manor's cozy dining room within the hour. They kept the conversation light, mostly chatting about London gossip or the latest fashions. Tomorrow would be soon enough for serious business, and tonight was an excellent opportunity to get acquainted and for him to assess the household.

While the ladies were talking, he studied Lady Phoebe. He understood why Sherry and Lord Sherbourne were worried about an inexperienced country lass left on her own, but he wondered if they weren't underestimating her. Under Lady Anne's and Margret's skillful attempts to draw her out, the widow was exhibiting unexpected glimpses of astuteness and resilience. He certainly welcomed the thought he might not have a wilting flower on his hands, yet it raised the specter she might be a valid suspect after all.

• • •

Audley Manor and surrounding area, Wednesday, 23 March 1814

Over a country meal in the light and airy, white and yellow breakfast room the following morning, Lucien brought up the carriage accident. "I shall be out most of the day. I want to see what I can learn about the accident."

Lady Phoebe's face clouded over, not unexpected as her bereavement was so very recent. "I wish I could help you, my lord. I was not with him, nor have I been to the scene since it occurred. The squire inspected the carriage and suggested it was not an accident at all, but how can that be? Who would wish to harm my husband?" Her chin trembled for a moment, then she gathered herself and regarded him with an anxious frown. "I understand you investigate such matters, and that is why you are here—to discover what happened and why."

"I shall certainly try." He paused. "My lady, I have no wish to add to your distress, but I must ask a few questions of you."

She nodded in acquiescence. "Ask me anything. I want to help."

"Very good. Can you think of anyone who has argued with your husband recently? A neighbor, perhaps, a shopkeeper or someone he owes money?"

"I doubt you will find he had a lot of debts. He believed in prompt payment." She shook her head, her expression more reserved now. "As for the rest, my husband did not share much with me. I…I have been living at the Lower House and have little knowledge of who he saw or where he went." Her eyes fell to her lap, her cheeks flushed.

"Well, that does not matter now," Lady Anne said bracingly. "You should turn your attention to the future and trust Lord Ware to uncover what is necessary from the past."

"Perhaps you could show us the gardens," Margret added.

"Oh, yes, of course. They aren't very large, but I am particularly proud of the herb and vegetable garden. There is not much to see yet, but the bushes are finely trimmed, and a few spring flowers are showing their heads." Lady Phoebe popped to her feet, all too obvious to be quit of Lucien's questions. "Unless there is something else you need, my lord…" She looked at him uncertainly, her eyes nearly begging him to say no.

"Not at present. I intend to ride over and meet the squire this morning."

Lady Phoebe brightened. "Oh, good. I know he is keen to speak with you."

Lucien gave a nod. "Then I shall see you ladies later. I hope to be back for tea."

• • •

When Lucien arrived at the stables, Finn already had his stallion Aziz, a spirited gray Arabian, saddled and waiting. Since Lucien had needed the large, enclosed coach to accommodate the ladies and their luggage, he had brought his favorite riding horse to get around during his inquiry.

Aziz welcomed him with a whicker, and Lucien stopped to rub the stallion's nose. "Ready for a ride, lad? We have at least two stops today, but you'll have a chance to stretch those legs." He turned to Finn. "I don't know what the ladies have planned, but the coach and team are at their disposal. I'd rather rest the bays a day, but they should be fine for short trips in the area."

Finn jerked his head toward the stalls. "They be a'right to go, milord. I rubbed 'em down good."

"Splendid. I shall be off then." He swung into the saddle.

Aziz tossed his head, and they high-stepped out of the stable. Once clear of the cobblestone yard, Lucien loosened the reins, and the stallion broke into a canter. He allowed him go for a quarter mile before easing him into a trot. The squire was the closest neighbor, and it wasn't long before they were moving briskly along a long lane leading to Levington's square but stately brick home. Lucien dismounted at the front entrance, presented his card, and entered the front hallway while his stallion was led away by a stable lad.

The polished woodwork in the hall, the quality furnishings, and the very proper butler indicated the owner was not only a man of stature in the community but also a man of respectable wealth.

Thomas Levington did not keep him waiting, emerging from a side room and striding toward him with a friendly smile. "Lord Ware, I am honored to welcome you to my home."

"Thank you, sir." Lucien returned the smile while taking his measure of the man—medium height, dark brown hair, and dark blue eyes appraising him with a steady gaze. "The Sherbourne family has asked me to follow up on your concern regarding Lord Audley's untimely death."

"Yes, of course. I have been expecting someone." Levington gestured toward the back of the hall. "Please join me in my study. May I offer you tea or coffee?"

"No, thank you. I am quite fond of coffee, but I have just risen from the breakfast table."

"Many in the military acquired the taste, I believe," Levington said as they walked down the hall.

Lucien lifted a brow. "How did you know?"

"That you served? You have the look about you." He chuckled. "But I must confess I have heard a bit about you from Lord Audley. He was rather proud of his brother and had mentioned his associate was a Viscount Ware."

The squire stopped at the study door to allow Lucien to enter first. The room was tastefully done in typical bachelor style with wine-colored leather and mahogany furniture.

"I had not realized he was aware of our ventures during the war," Lucien said, wishing Audley had been more circumspect. "The brothers did not keep in close touch."

"I believe it was by way of correspondence with their father." Levington waved Lucien to one of a pair of chairs near the window before going to the desk, taking two pieces of horse harness from a drawer, and handing them to Lucien. "This is why I wrote to Lord Sherbourne. Take a look for yourself." He sat in the other chair and waited.

Lucien fingered the cut edges on the pieces of what had once been a belly strap. "I see what you mean, a clean cut with no sign of natural fraying. Was this the only strap cut?"

"No. Someone wasn't taking any chances. They sliced the harness on each of the four horses on the underbelly where it wouldn't readily be noticed. There is no doubt in my mind that this was a deliberate act of malice."

"Do you have the rest of the harness?"

"I left it with the carriage. To my knowledge, everything is still in the ravine. The bodies were removed, of course, and the dead horses buried. Otherwise, I ordered the rest to be left intact, as I assumed Lord Sherbourne would want to see it, or he'd send someone else who would."

"I appreciate that. Perhaps you could show me the wreck when we finish here."

Levington gave a nod. "Certainly. I anticipated your request and have rearranged my morning." At Lucien's look of surprise, he added, "Your arrival at Audley Manor last night did not go unnoticed in such a small community."

"Ah, yes, of course. Speaking of the community, is anyone else aware of your suspicions?"

Levington shrugged. "Everyone, I assume. The inquest was delayed, pending further inquiry, and gossip will have filled in the reason that was done. I have not discussed it with anyone local except the coroner."

"And Lady Audley."

"Well, yes, I felt the widow deserved to know."

"I agree," Lucien said, although he would have waited for family to give her the news. The squire was acting a trifle defensive. Did he too feel he might have overstepped, or was his unease the typical rural distrust of city folk? Regardless of the squire's discomfort, Lucien moved on. "Have you any suspects in mind?"

"I have thought about it quite a bit, but no one appears to have a strong enough motive. Audley kept to himself, his attention on his history books and his dissertations much of the time. He had strong opinions, if pressed, but since he rarely mingled with other folk, it is unlikely he raised such ire in a debate. He'd had a minor land dispute with a neighbor, but that is hardly grounds for murder. I haven't come up with even one likely suspect." He tapped his fingers on the chair arm. "He recently made two trips to Maidenhead, and was, in fact, returning from there when the accident occurred. That has to be where the evil mischief was done, and it may also be where you'll find both cause and culprit."

"Why did he make these trips?"

"The first was early in the month when he attended a three-day horse sale. Last Friday was just an overnight stay, and he was rather vague about it. I believe he told his wife he had business to conduct, but he'd mentioned to me that he wanted to select a birthday gift for Phoebe…Lady Audley. He felt guilty about their estrangement and had expressed his wish to buy her something special. A package with a beautiful silk shawl was found in what was left of the carriage, but I wonder if there was more to his trip than just shopping. Don't ask me why," he hastened to say, "because I don't know. It was just a feeling."

Lucien frowned. Even a feeling had to be based on something. "When he returned from the horse sale, did he mention anything in particular that had occurred?"

"He didn't talk about it much at all. Although… something was on his mind. He was more pensive than usual—I assumed it was some historical problem he was mulling over—but at one point he said he might need my advice on something."

"No hint as to what?"

"No," the squire chuckled, "but it sure wasn't history. I would be of little help with that. When I asked him about it, he said he wanted to think on it some more. Didn't bring it up again, but that was just last week, a day or two before his second trip."

"Is there anyone else he might have consulted with a problem?"

"I doubt it. He often confided in his father through their letters, but I assume that didn't happen on this occasion."

"No, Sherbourne knew nothing. Perhaps it will become clear to me when I discover his actions while he was in Maidenhead. But tell me, who is the neighbor with the land dispute?"

"Percy Slade." Levington shook his head. "I cannot believe he would do such a thing. He is a mild-mannered gentleman farmer. They would have worked it out."

"Nonetheless, I must consider every possibility in order to rule out those of no consequence."

"While you're at it, you might take a look at Lady Audley's family. Her father, Doc Wheatley, was a fourth or fifth son of a baronet, a good doctor, and an honorable man. However, when he died on a fox hunt a few years ago, his son Jasper became head of this branch of the family. You wouldn't believe how he and the other two sisters took on airs when Miss Phoebe married Sherbourne's heir. Jasper is quite encroaching. The day after Audley's accident, he suggested moving his family into Audley Manor and taking over management of the estate."

"Well, that won't happen," Lucien said with a dismissive huff. "The land and buildings belong to the Earl of Sherbourne, and Andrew Sherbourne, the new heir and viscount, will be taking possession. Naturally, generous provisions will be made for Lady Phoebe and her child, but none of that has anything to do with her brother."

"And he should know that, but don't be surprised if Jasper Wheatley refuses to accept it. He will bully Phoebe into complying with his wishes if he gets a chance."

Lucien lifted a brow. "He won't, at least not for the near future. Two very strong-willed ladies accompanied me to Audley Manor. He will be wasting his time annoying Lady Phoebe or demanding anything while they are here." He chuckled. "In fact, if his character is as you describe, I hope I am lucky enough to see him try."

"Just so." Levington smiled and rose. "Shall we make our way to the accident scene?"

• • •

"Good lord," Lucien murmured under his breath. He stood at the edge of a ravine, holding Aziz's reins in one hand and gazing at the scene below. The river that had once rushed through the gorge had long ago been tamed to a small stream at the very bottom. Halfway down the steep slope lay the broken carriage. The coach roof was partially intact, but the rest was a scattered pile of broken boards, shattered wheels, and tangled harness.

"Audley and his coachman, Gordon, were both dead when help arrived, and so were two of the four horses," Levington said. "The other two were so badly injured they had to be shot. The team must have been in a full run when the coach went over the edge." He nodded toward a stand of nearby trees. "Let's tie the horses over there and make our way down on foot. I'll show you the other harness and the condition of the brakes."

Levington continued to talk as they picked their way down the slope. "A witness saw the carriage go over the edge, you know. A passing mail coach driver. He stopped to give aid and alerted the nearest neighbor before continuing on his way."

"Have you talked with him?"

"I have not, but I can tell you what he said to the neighbor. Audley's coach passed the mail coach on a dead run with the driver hauling on the reins and calling to the horses. Audley's coachman had no visible control, and looking at the cut harness, I can see why. At the sharp turn, he saw them plunge off the road into the ravine."

Levington showed him the other cuts on the harness, and they inspected the wooden brakes that were nearly burned through in the coachman's desperate attempt to slow the rampaging horses.

Lucien looked up at the ravine edge above. It was easy to picture what must have happened. The team would have done fine with the top reins as long as they were at a walk or trot but once Graham's coachman put the horses into a gallop, the cut harness came loose, striking the sides and underbellies of the team. Confused by the unexpected freedom and the slap of the harness, they took the bit in their mouths and ran wildly once they hit the straight stretch of road. When they reached the curve, however, they would have been going too fast to make the turn, and the carriage toppled over the edge, dragging everyone to their death.

His jaw tightened as they finished examining the wreck and climbed back up the sharp incline. No question this was murder. Harness cut that badly would not have been over-looked, so it was sliced in Maidenhead after the coach was readied for departure… unless there was a stop on the way home. He'd have to explore that possibility, but it was for sure that a trip to Maidenhead was in his near future.

"Well, what do you think?" Levington asked when they returned to their horses.

"The deliberate, malicious intent is inescapable. Whoever did this cut just enough harness for the coachman to have no control and yet the horses were still hooked to the carriage. A terrible accident was inevitable."

"And anyone familiar with this sharp curve knew the chances were high they'd be killed," Levington added. "What will you do now, Ware?" he asked as he swung aboard his big, roan gelding.

"I came here to discover what happened and that includes who was responsible and why." Lucien patted Aziz on the neck and put a foot into the stirrup. Settling into the saddle, he added, "I believe Maidenhead is my next stop."

"You will keep me apprised?"

"Naturally. In your capacity as magistrate, I hope to turn the culprit over to you to measure out his punishment."

"I shall welcome the opportunity."

Chapter Three

Taplow and Maidenhead, Buckinghamshire, Thursday, 24 March 1814

On Thursday morning, Lucien left for Maidenhead, indicating to the ladies that he would be gone at least overnight and perhaps a few days. Lady Anne assured him they would take good care of Lady Phoebe in his absence.

"Well, old fellow, shall we shake off a bit of that energy?" he asked, as Aziz side-stepped his way across the cobblestone stable yard.

The Arabian was feeling frisky, raring for a gallop, and it was not long before Maidenhead was spread out before them on the horizon. According to Squire Levington, the village had grown into a thriving market town of nearly two thousand inhabitants since the opening of the seven-arched bridge over the Thames River. It had become a popular stopping place on the Bath Road between London and the seaside resort and saw as many as ninety coaches passing through in a single day from spring to autumn.

Due to its advantageous location, Maidenhead boasted numerous taverns and inns with a few large stables that could hold up to fifty horses per night. Coachmen were particularly eager to end their day there to avoid the highwaymen who hid in the nearby bushes of Maidenhead Thicket after dusk.

In spite of Levington's depiction, Lucien was surprised by the congestion and hectic bustle on the town's streets this early in the spring. His task here might be tougher than he thought. With so many visitors and people staying overnight, there were bound to be a large number of establishments where a visitor could find entertainment of all kinds—and trouble too.

As he rode down main street, the clip clop of Aziz's hooves was buried by the sounds of street vendors hawking their wares, children laughing at play, the rattle of harness and carriage wheels, all the sounds of a busy market town—and the smells, both good and bad.

Lucien looked up and down the street, considering where to start his inquiries. Perhaps the logical beginning was to locate the inn where Sherry's brother had stayed and at the same time arrange a bed for himself and stabling for his horse. His first stop was an inn on the east side of town, and then he moved westward. The Goose & Gander was his seventh stop. One of the larger Inns, it was among the cleanest and the oldest, built of heavy timber with small windows during the late 1600s or early 1700s. At one time, the Goose & Gander was likely the only inn before the town's recent growth spurt.

Lucien approached the innkeeper.

"Aye, Lord Audley was here. Yes, twice, I believe, in the past month or so. Said he liked our sheets." The publican grinned at that and then sobered. "I was sorry to hear of his death."

Lucien lifted a brow, but he should have anticipated the news of the carriage accident was known around town. The shire wouldn't have that many members of the aristocracy in residence, and the doings of the haute ton were always food for gossip.

"It was indeed a blow to his family and friends." Lucien decided to confide in the publican in hopes that he might prove helpful. "I'm in town at the widow's behest to discover what happened."

"I heard it was a runaway."

"Yes, that part is true, but the local magistrate is not satisfied it was a simple accident. He is concerned the coach or equipment was damaged by someone."

The publican's eyes widened. "Deliberate, you mean?"

"Perhaps. Did anything unusual occur while he was here? Anything that made him worried or upset?"

"It's a busy town, but I don't recall any trouble involving his lordship. I didn't know him well, but he was quiet, reserved. I do hope the magistrate is mistaken."

Lucien shrugged casually. "It is hard to say at this point, but you can understand the widow's desire to learn what she can. I promised her and the magistrate, Squire Levington, that I'd see what I could do. By the by, I'm Ware." He handed over his card.

"Giles. Sam Giles," the publican said. "Call me Sam. Most folks do."

Lucien gave a nod. "A pleasure, Sam. I could use a room for at least tonight, most likely longer." He waited until those arrangements were made before asking, "Did you see Audley with anyone to whom I might speak? Or can you recall his actions while he was in town?"

Sam scratched his head. "Well, the second stay was just the one night, and now that I think about it, he may have been even quieter than before, as though he had something on his mind. He mentioned he had to speak with someone, that he had a couple of appointments, but I have no idea who or what they were."

"Not even a hint of why?"

"Not really." Sam frowned, pursing his lips in thought. "Wanted to clear up a few things, as I recall. It was just a brief chat when he arrived."

"What about his first stay, the longer one?"

Sam flipped through his ledger. "I see he was here three days. Oh, yes, he came for the Spring Horse Sale, the third through fifth. It was an eventful few days. Always is with crowds that large. He was alone whenever I saw him, but he may have done a bit of gambling because he was talking about the big fracas afterwards. But then, everyone was."

"What fracas?"

"Card cheating. It led to a duel, but no one was killed, thank the lord." He glanced over at two men waiting to order. "If you could wait just a moment, my lord. I should take their orders."

"Go right ahead. I need to settle in my room. We can chat another time." Lucien picked up his overnight bag and climbed the stairs, thinking about what Sam had said.

Audley would have been acting sorely out of character to get involved in such sordid affairs as card cheating or an unlawful duel. If he was present, it's possible he saw something he shouldn't, but the tampering to the harness took place two weeks later. Why the delay?

Lucien decided he'd have more success keeping to his original plan to concentrate on Audley's last day—where he went, who he saw, which of his neighbors and acquaintances from Audley village were in town that day, and if anyone was seen hanging around his coach and horses.

Once he'd dropped off his bag, Lucien headed for the Goose & Gander's stable and coach house where he assumed Audley's team and carriage had been kept. In contrast to the pile of odorous manure outside the back door, the inside smelled pleasantly of horses and fresh hay. He approached the boy of about sixteen who was brushing Aziz. After they chatted about the stallion a few minutes, Lucien asked if he had known Lord Audley. Receiving a negative shake of the head, he tried again. "Perhaps you recall his coachman, Gordon, and a team of four Cleveland Bays."

The young man face brightened with recognition. "Oh, aye, sir, I knew Gordon. And them horses be sweet goers."

"Did you care for the bays last Saturday?"

"No, sir. Andy did. Gordon always used 'im. He be in the last stall carin' fer a mare that just come in."

"Thank you."

Lucien found a straw-haired lad in his twenties talking softly as he rubbed down a chestnut mare who looked like she'd been nearly run off her legs.

"Are you Andy?"

The lad looked up, his brown eyes assessing Lucien with one glance. "Yessir, that's me. Are ya bringin' in a horse? I'll be right with ya."

"My horse is being attended, thank you. I wanted to talk a bit. Perhaps we can do that while you work. The mare looks as though she needs prompt attention."

"Yessir. She was ridden a mite hard."

Considering the mare's sweaty neck and drooping head, Lucien thought Andy's assessment was a gross understatement. But then, the lad might not keep his job long if he was heard criticizing the horse's owner.

Andy threw him a questioning glance. "What was it ya wanted to know?"

Lucien asked him about Lord Audley and last Saturday.

"'Course I knowd 'im and Gordon. Terrible accident. Always took care of them bays. And, yeh, I helped Gordon hitch 'em up for the trip home that day."

"And everything looked fine?"

"Yep. Can't figure how it happened. Gordon was a careful driver, and that team was steady as can be."

"A witness said it was a runaway."

Andy screwed up a doubtful face, shaking his head. "Nah, gotta be wrong."

"When we looked at the carriage harness, it had been cut," Lucien said quietly, eyeing the lad.

"What?" Andy sprang to his feet. "Are ya sayin' I done somethin' wrong? I dint. I swear I dint."

"No, not at all. I'm telling you this because I need your help. Think back to Saturday and everything you can recall about that day…particularly if anyone came near the team once they were harnessed."

Andy nearly sagged with relief. "Yessir, I can do that. Which traces were cut?"

"The belly straps."

"Zounds," the lad muttered. "All of 'em?"

"Yes." Lucien leaned against the stable wall. "What time was Gordon told to have the coach ready to leave?"

"Three o'clock," Andy said promptly, squatting again to resume rubbing the mare's legs. "I reckon it was another hour before his lordship arrived."

"Where was the coach and team during that hour?"

"Out front, but Gordon was with 'em."

"Are you sure he didn't step away for a few minutes, perhaps to get a drink or use the privy?"

Andy shrugged. "Wouldn't know about that. Once they're outside, we don't watch 'em no more."

"Let's say he needed to step away. Would he have tied them to a post or found a lad to watch them?"

"Gordon wouldn't leave 'em alone. No, sir." Andy shook his head. "A street boy most likely. You should ask out front."

"I'll do that when I leave. Did you notice anyone hanging around the stable that afternoon? A stranger or someone else with no reason to be there?"

"Nah, I don't 'member anybody, but I could think on it. And ask 'round ifn you want."

"Excellent. I'm staying at the inn. If you learn anything, just ask for me or give Sam Giles a message. And you might also ask the lads if anyone else has been asking questions about Lord Audley or his horses either before or after that day."

Andy paused his work with a troubled look. "I think somebody did, sir, but don't know who. Maybe one of the other lads will know."

"I'd appreciate anything you learn. By the by, Andy, for now, don't mention the cut harness to anyone else. Just say we're concerned the coach was damaged in some way." When Andy assured him he'd be mum on that point, Lucien slipped him a couple of coins and left the stable.

On the street, he looked around for likely young boys and called one over, a lad of ten or so with thin shoulders showing through a shirt inadequate for the weather. Intelligent eyes regarded him from a dirty face and a mop of fair hair that would benefit from a cut and a good wash.

"What's your name, lad?"

"Joey, sir."

"See this shilling, Joey? I want you to ask around for anyone who held Lord Audley's bay horses for his coachman Gordon last Saturday afternoon." He cocked his head and eyed the lad. "Now, you could keep the coin and do nothing, but if you find the boy and bring him to me, there will be another shilling for you and one for him. What do you say? Think you can find him?"

"Yes sir! I rightly can, sir."

Lucien smiled at the boy's eagerness. "I'm Lord Ware, and I'm staying at the Goose & Gander."

"Got it, sir."

When the boy ran off on his task, Lucien hesitated and then went back inside the inn to speak with Sam again. "I forgot to ask if anyone from Audley village or near there was in town on the eighteen or nineteenth. I assume you have a record of anyone who stayed overnight or kept their horses in your stable."

Sam frowned, his look rather hesitant. "Yeh, I write it all down, but I don't know as I should tell you. Folks like their privacy."

"Fair enough, but Audley's coach was damaged, possibly by someone he knew, and anyone from that general area who was in town that day is a potential suspect."

"I'd guess you're pretty sure it was murder. Say no more." Sam shook his head. "Damn shame. He never caused no bother, not like some." Pulling out his ledger, he ran his fingers down the columns. "Only one name I recognize from around that area on those days was the squire himself."

"Levington?"

"Yep."

Well, now. Why hadn't Levington told him? Could he have done this for some reason yet unknown? Lucien had thought he was the gentleman everyone assumed him to be. Just proved it was too soon to be eliminating anyone.

"How long was he here?"

"Just the one night. The eighteenth. But surely, being a magistrate, you don't suspect him."

"It's just a coincidence, I'm sure," Lucien said, not wanting to get rumors started. "Thanks, Sam. I better get on my way if I want to question most of the lads at the inns and stables today."

Sam frowned. "Just occurred to me, milord, that Audley village is close enough most folks don't stay overnight at the inns. The stables are your best bet for locals and others nearby, but some of the smaller ones may not even keep owners' names on horses stabled by the hour."

"I shall keep that in mind. All I can do is ask."

• • •

Lucien thought about what Sam had said and realized he might need to extend his inquiries to commercial shops, taverns, and coffee shops where customers might be known by face and name.

Over the next few hours, he made the rounds of likely looking places inquiring if anyone had seen Lord Audley on his latest visit to town or noticed anyone else from around the village of Audley in town on that date—and he subtly mentioned Jasper Wheatley and Percy Slade when he could do so without it being awkward. He explained his questions by saying he was attempting to trace Audley's movements that day—which was true—and Audley might have run into someone he knew from home—which, in fact, was possible. Lucien tried to keep it casual, yet at a few places he had to reveal the accident was under investigation before anyone would talk with him.

He gathered the names of a few villagers, including Levington, and wrote them down, but most of them were unfamiliar to him. No one mentioned Wheatley, but Slade was a different matter. The gentleman farmer had kept his horse at a stable on the edge of town on the night of the nineteenth, having arrived around noon, placing him in Maidenhead during the time the harness was damaged, between the hours of three and four.

Lucien was tempted to ride back to Audley immediately to confront both Levington and Slade and to make inquiries of the other names he'd collected, but over a second glass of ale at the Goose & Gander, better sense prevailed. He still had other places to visit, and he needed to wait to hear what Andy and Joey discovered. There was much he didn't yet know. Before he confronted anyone he'd need better evidence than their mere presence in Maidenhead.

• • •

He broke off his search at dark, returned to the inn to clean up, and visited the public common room for a meal. As he lingered over a tankard of ale, he got to thinking about the duel that had occurred during the Spring Horse Sale, and he finally called the barmaid over.

"Do you know anyone who was present during the card cheating incident about three weeks ago? I've heard just enough to make me more than a bit curious."

"The one with the duel?" When he nodded, she straightened and looked around the room. "Oh, yes, that's Siegfried Hazelton." She pointed to a ruddy-faced, round-bellied gentleman drinking with four other men in a darkened back corner. "He was there and can tell you all about it."

Lucien thanked her and approached the table a few minutes later. "Pardon me, gentlemen. Would one of you be Mr. Hazelton?"

"That would be me. And you are?"

"Lord Ware. I wonder if I might have a private word."

"Regarding?"

"The card cheat and duel."

Hazelton cocked his head. "Well, I don't see why not, as long as you buy me a pint of porter."

"It would be my pleasure."

Standing with an indulgent smile, Hazelton nodded to his companions, "I'll return shortly." He looked at Lucien as they crossed the room to his original table. "Are you having a pint?"

"Absolutely." The bitter drink wasn't his favorite, but in a sense of comradeship he was prepared to have a pint or two.

Hazelton raised two fingers to the barmaid as they seated themselves. She brought the tankards immediately, and Lucien gave her the proper coins.

The big man took a long swallow before setting it down. "Now, just what do you want from me, Lord Ware?"

"Answers, I hope. I've heard you were present at the game."

Hazelton gave him an assessing look. "I was. What's your interest?"

"Perhaps nothing but curiosity. I won't know until I hear more about the incident. I'm a friend of Lord Audley's family and making inquiries regarding his death. Did you know him?"

"Slightly, but I know nothing of his accident."

Lucien nodded. "I gathered as much, but his death may not have been an accident. An incident may have occurred while he was in Maidenhead that caused someone to wish him harm."

"Egad, sir, I had not heard the death was suspicious." Hazelton frowned in doubt. "And you think that event was the card game? I don't see how, but it's true that Audley was there that night. Never seen him at the tables before. He played a game or two, lost a small amount, and then withdrew to watch."

"Was he still there when the cheating occurred? Was he involved in any way?"

"He was there when the *accusation* was made," Hazelton said slowly. "But as far as I could see, he wasn't involved. As for the cheating…to be honest, my lord, I'm not certain any occurred, not by Raven, the man accused. If you repeat that, however, I'll have to deny it. I don't fancy being challenged to a duel."

"I doubt there is much danger of that. I've heard the participants left town, but rest assured, I won't mention your name. What did you see?"

Hazelton took a long swig of porter. "At the time of the incident, five of us were playing hazard at Galloway's Pub: myself, two regular horse dealers from London, and these two strangers in town for the sale, although I doubt either wanted to buy a horse— George Ponsonby and Charles Raven."

"Why do you think they were in town?"

"For Raven, the gambling. Ponsonby, I'm not certain."

Lucien gave a thoughtful nod. "What can you tell me about them?"

"Never seen either man before…or since, for that matter. Raven was rather reserved. Very much a gentleman, I thought, but Ponsonby eyed him with dislike all evening. It was bloody odd.

They introduced themselves as though they'd never met before, yet Ponsonby goaded him on nearly every hand—chortling at his losses or what he claimed were misplayed cards. Raven shrugged it off until Ponsonby accused him of cheating, saying he'd played a hidden Ace."

"Was there an extra Ace?"

"There was, but I'd almost swear it was Ponsonby himself who played it. I can't prove it, mind you, or I would have spoken up. Nonetheless, I believe Ponsonby made the scurrilous accusation as an excuse for challenging Raven to a duel."

"To what end? Are you saying he was looking to kill Raven?"

Hazelton gave him a sharp look. "You said it, Ware. I did not."

"A rather serious affair." Lucien frowned, considering the various possibilities of how Audley might have gotten involved. "Could Lord Audley have seen Ponsonby slip in the extra card?"

"I suppose he could have, but no one else did. Wouldn't he have spoken up in Raven's defense?"

"I'm sure he would, unless, like you, he was uncertain." And, Lucien added to himself, he may have returned to town two weeks later to pursue his concern. Is that what happened and got him killed?

"I wonder if you're right. It might explain why Audley showed up at the duel. I hadn't thought him to be the type to attend, and yet he did."

"Did he?" Lucien said, immediately alert. "I did not know that. It *is* curious. Did he have any part in the duel?"

"Not to my knowledge."

"Back to the night before, why did Raven agree to the duel?"

"After Ponsonby threw down the cheating accusation and Raven denied it, Ponsonby said that his denial implied that he—Ponsonby—was a liar, and he demanded satisfaction. The rest of us tried to brush it off as a simple misunderstanding, but Ponsonby wouldn't let it go. He left Raven no choice as a gentleman but to meet him for pistols at dawn."

"Extraordinary. Apparently, you also attend the duel."

"I'm sorry to say, I did. That's how I know Audley was there." Hazelton shook his head with a disgusted twist to his lips. "It was a disgrace. Ponsonby fired his pistol before the agreed count was finished, wounded Raven in the left arm, and then Raven deloped, deliberately shooting into the air. Ponsonby was all for demanding another round, but his second hustled him away, agreeing the duel was over. That was the end of it as far as I know."

"Where were these two men from?"

"Raven mentioned London, and I assumed Ponsonby was from there too." Hazelton drained his tankard.

"One other thing, how did Audley happen to join your card game?"

"A fellow brought him over from another table because they were full. Said he'd sold him a horse that day, and they'd been celebrating. Now, there's a connection I'd look into."

"Oh, why?"

"I didn't know the horse man myself, but someone said he had a reputation for making crooked deals. Maybe he swindled Audley."

"Thanks for the tip. You've been most helpful, sir, and I shall not keep you longer from your friends." Lucien rose to his feet.

"The cheating call was bad business," Hazelton said, rising with him, "And, disregarding what I said about the horse seller, if anyone from that night was involved in Audley's death, my wager would be on Ponsonby."

Lucien understood Hazelton's comment. Ponsonby sounded like the worse kind of scoundrel, but he'd heard nothing that involved Audley with him in any significant way. It was a curious affair, but the crooked horse seller was more promising in that a bad horse sale would likely have resulted in an argument when Audley discovered the deceit. If nothing more pressing turned up by morning, Lucien would visit the sale barn and get the name of this dishonest horse dealer.

Chapter Four

Audley Manor and estate, Buckinghamshire, Thursday, 24 March 1814

"My goodness, I believe we have guests already," Lady Phoebe exclaimed, looking expectantly toward the drawing room door upon hearing a carriage at the front entrance.

"Are you ready for this?" Lady Anne asked. The widow had shown a reluctance to face the community and expressed a concern that she didn't know what to say to all the sympathy. Lady Anne had suggested a simple "Thank you" was enough.

Lady Phoebe patted her hair in place and smoothed the front of her black gown. "I guess I'd better be ready."

Whether word had spread the ladies were alone or the community was merely keen to meet the newcomers and see how Lady Phoebe was coping with widowhood, the first visitors arrived no more than two hours after Lucien left for Maidenhead. Vicar Pope and his wife were quickly followed by the sisters Hargrove, a spinster pair in their seventies, friendly but a little two nosey to suit Lady Anne. They kept bringing up questions about the carriage accident and Lady Phoebe's future plans, appearing oblivious to the widow's discomfort. They finally left when three church ladies arrived with a lovely basket of fruit.

Then came Squire Levington. Anne noted the blush Phoebe tried to hide when he was announced and wondered if there was something between the two. Was it so unthinkable that a neglected wife might have her head turned by a handsome man with charming manners, or that he would be drawn to a sweet and pretty young woman? If such an attraction existed, it could provide both of them with a motive for wishing Audley dead. And yet, Phoebe was such a dear…it was unlikely she would even think of being party to a murder. And the squire, a magistrate and officer of the law, would he kill to have her?

"I shall not overstay my welcome," he said as he rose after only a few minutes. "Since Lord Ware is away, I wanted you to know you can rely on me if you are in need of anything."

The ladies murmured their thanks.

"We shall not hesitate to call upon your services," Anne said. She couldn't tell from his manner whether he returned Phoebe's affections or not. Maybe it was just a blooming thing and neither was fully aware. She'd watch their future conduct toward one another before forming an opinion.

Their next visitor was announced almost immediately, as though he had been waiting for the squire to leave.

"Jasper Wheatley." The butler had barely spoken the words before a dapper young man breezed past him.

"Phoebe dearest, how are you? I heard you had visitors from London."

While he was bending over his sister's hand and being introduced to Anne and Margret, Anne looked him over. By town standards his attire would label him a dandy—high shirt points, padded shoulders, a pinched waist consistent with the cut of his dark blue coat and embroidered waistcoat. He carried a fancy cane and wore several large rings on his fingers. In Anne's opinion, at least some of them were paste. Fortunately, he was young enough in his mid-twenties and slender enough to carry off the foppish style without looking utterly ridiculous. That didn't mean it was flattering.

"So very honored to meet you, Lady Anne," he gushed. He held her hand a little too long, and the suggestive look in his eyes was far too easy to read.

She formed an immediate dislike for him but nevertheless greeted him quite civilly. "As am I of you, sir. Lady Phoebe's description did not do you justice."

He straightened, preening himself. "That is a sister for you, never giving the credit due to a sibling. I endeavor to keep myself up on all the latest fashions."

"Do sit down, brother, and join us for tea," Lady Phoebe said. "I have just sent for a new pot."

"Don't mind if I do." He spread his tails and perched on the edge of an upholstered wing back chair before turning to Anne again. "I did not know my sister was acquainted with you, Lady Anne. How long will you be staying?"

She ignored his hint for information regarding her relationship with Lady Phoebe and answered his direct question, albeit, vaguely. "I am unsure regarding the length of my stay—a fortnight or more, perhaps. Lady Phoebe has been kind enough to give us carte blanche."

"Oh, my. I see," he said appearing to be taken aback by her response. "If you are concerned she will be lonely otherwise, I assure you that will not be the truth of it. My family knows our duty. In fact, we are quite ready to join her here at the manor for the foreseeable future."

"Lady Phoebe told us of your generous offer, but I am confident it will not be necessary," Anne said. "As soon as the estate is settled, the new Viscount will arrive to claim his property and see to her well-being."

"You cannot mean he would eject a widow from her home!" He spoke with overblown indignation. "What manner of man is he?"

"Jasper," Phoebe protested. "You have no call to talk that way. You know the estate and manor are not mine."

"It is not right, and I accept no such thing. My solicitor is looking into the matter."

"Oh, Jasper, no. You ought not. I told you it was beyond the pale," she said, distress written across her face. She twisted a lace handkerchief in her lap.

"Certain things you must leave to me, Phoebe." Jasper rose and wandered around the room, his hands and gaze sliding over furniture, vases, even the Persian carpet as though he was assessing the value. For what purpose, Anne wondered. Dreaming it could be his or calculating how much he could sell it for before Sherry arrived?

He stopped abruptly and said, "Phoebe, dear, may I have a private moment?"

"Not if you want to talk about the solicitor again."

Surprised, Anne silently applauded Phoebe's forthright response.

"No, it is not that."

"Well, I …" She peeked at Anne and drew in a breath. "If you're in dun territory again, I cannot help you with that either. Jasper, you *have* to take responsibility for your debts."

He turned to look at her with disapprobation. "Honestly, Phoebe, must you refer to such personal family matters in front of strangers? I only came to console you. But now that you have brought up the issue, your sisters and I could use a bit of blunt, just enough to get us through a week or two. Perhaps you have another bauble you never use that I could pawn."

Anne was appalled he would even suggest such a thing in front of her and Margret. He must be desperate, or regardless of his stated reservations, he was so used to imposing on his sister that he saw nothing untoward about it.

"Just like last month?" Lady Phoebe said. "No, brother dear, I must be careful with my funds now. I have to think of myself and Eliza."

"But, Phoebe, how can you be so selfish?" he said pettishly. "Your sisters—

Lady Phoebe rose to face him. "Are not my responsibility. You overstep, Jasper, and are embarrassing both of us in front of my guests. I must ask you to leave and not come back until you can talk about something other than this foolishness about the estate or your debts."

"Well, I never—" Wheatley's eyes widened, and he stared at her open-mouthed.

"You would do well to heed your sister's words," Lady Anne said mildly. "Perhaps visiting another day would be better."

Phoebe pulled the bell for the butler. When he appeared promptly in the drawing room doorway, she asked him to get Wheatley's hat and show him to the door. "My brother has remembered a pressing engagement and cannot stay after all."

"Very good, madam. After you, sir."

For a moment, Anne thought Wheatley was going to refuse to leave, then he drew himself up and walked out in the small, mincing steps favored by the more extreme London dandies.

Phoebe sank onto the sofa. "I must apologize for our behavior."

"Oh, no," Anne said crossing the room to sit beside her. "You must never apologize for disputes with family. We all have relatives we wish we could change."

"Or disown," Margret added. "Or transport to Australia."

"Surely not that," Phoebe said with a reluctant smile. "But Jasper is so aggravating."

"Tell us about him," Anne encouraged. "Has he always been… this way?"

"If you mean vain and self-absorbed, then yes, but he did not display such domineering ways until Father died and Jasper became the head of the household. He grew very puffed up in his consequence when I married Lord Audley—as though the title was his."

"And the dandy style?" Margret asked.

Phoebe smiled. "He went to London for a week three years ago to gain a bit of town bronze and came home dressed like a peacock." She shrugged. "If only that was the worst of his behaviors."

"Pardon me for mentioning it, but I take it you've been paying his debts. Did he not inherit sufficient funds from your father?" Margret asked.

"A country doctor?" Phoebe laughed ruefully. "No, but the land is good, and we lived comfortably when Father was alive. It's just that Jasper has such expensive taste in clothes and horses and well…other things."

Anne lifted a brow. Other things? And what would those be? Something significant, guessing from Lady Phoebe's reaction. Gambling or women, perhaps.

"The day is slipping away, and I have much to do," Lady Phoebe said. "I shall leave you now while I get a start on gathering things for packing. I fear I have acquired a lot of belongings since my marriage. Lord Audley was very generous."

"Surely there is no hurry to pack," Margret said.

"I agree," Anne said. "In due time, Lord Sherbourne and the new viscount will see you comfortably situated in a place of your own, but not in such a rush."

"I wish to be prepared. After all, I have two households to pack—here and at the Lower House. An infant requires so many things."

Anne did not understand Lady Phoebe's rush. Did she have plans to move away from Audley and not live on the estate? Was it too painful to remain in the community? Perhaps she wanted to live in a bigger town, such as Maidenhead or even London. Questions best asked another day when they were better acquainted. For now, Anne thought a change of topic was called for.

"Speaking of Eliza," she asked, "where is she? I have not seen or heard her since we arrived."

"She and Nanny stayed at the Lower House. I only moved up here temporarily to greet you and see you comfortable. I did not wish to upset Eliza's daily routine for such a short stay."

"When may we see her?" Margret asked.

"Now, if you wish," Lady Phoebe said, her face emitting a warm glow. "I fear the packing takes a distant second to seeing and talking about my daughter. I, of course, will visit her daily during your stay, but an extra visit is an added pleasure."

As soon as the ladies gathered warm shawls to ward off the March chill and parasols to protect their complexions from the direct sun, they walked down the hill to the Lower House.

Anne studied the square home ahead of them, made of yellow stone and trimmed in white. A sturdy-looking house, well-maintained. "I assume it took its name from being down the hill from the manor," she said. "But was this originally the Dower House?"

"Yes. Since there has not been a proper dowager in several decades, I guess the name just evolved," Phoebe said.

"But aren't you a dowager?" Margret asked.

"Not truly. As I understand it, Graham's title was only a courtesy bestowed by the earl. The title and land are still Lord Sherbourne's."

"While that is true," Anne temporized, "you are still a widow viscountess and may use the title of dowager if you wish, and the Lower House can easily revert its name to Dower House. In fact, I am convinced we should call it that from now on. You must know that you and Eliza will be provided for according to the marriage agreement. There is no need for you to worry about your future."

Phoebe looked surprised. "I am not worried. Oh, you mean what I said to Jasper. That was just an excuse to stop him from asking for more money. I know our prospects are secure. The Sherbournes are an honorable family."

As they had reached the newly renamed Dower House, the conversation ended. A maid met them at the door, and Lady Phoebe sent for the nanny to bring Eliza. By the time they were seated in the parlor, a plump woman with a round smiling face arrived with a squirming one-year-old in her arms. Like her mother, baby Eliza had a sweet face, green eyes, and ginger curls.

"Mumumu," Eliza squealed upon sighting Lady Phoebe. The nanny set her down and the child toddled across the room as fast as her baby legs would take her. Lady Phoebe scooped her up in her arms.

"Hello, darling. Did you miss me?" She kissed the child on both cheeks. "Mummy missed you."

Anne smiled at this affectionate exchange. Clearly there was no lack of love in this household. Eliza would have all the love she needed…as long as Lady Phoebe had no part in her husband's death, she reminded herself. She sighed, realizing it was a struggle for her to keep an open mind about the widow.

Chapter Five

Maidenhead, England, Friday, 25 March 1814

"No, sir. Sorry. No one that I recall."

Lucien sighed and turned away. He had been getting the same response all morning as he'd visited the stables and inns he had missed the prior day. He'd hoped to collect a name or two for his list of Audley villagers and neighbors who'd been in town the previous Saturday, or perhaps some promising information about the names he already had, but no luck. Nor had he heard from the street boy Joey or from Andy, the stable lad.

He looked up and down the street. Perhaps this was the time to visit the horse barns and find out who sold the horses to Audley. One of them knew how he ended up at the card game. While there was no big sale in progress, there were a few horses for auction or private sale almost every day—and the auctioneer and regular staff should be there.

The sale arena stood at the edge of town, and Lucien took Aziz to get the frisky stallion out of his stall for a while. The show barn was nothing like Tattersall's in London. No fancy subscription club where gentlemen could drink or play cards while contemplating their purchases—although Lucien spotted a nearby tavern—and the horses he saw were not quite so handsome as one might expect on the London market. The current stock had been bred more for endurance—farming, hunting, and pulling heavy coaches through inclement country weather—than for speed or parading through Hyde Park. Nonetheless, Lucien noticed a pretty chestnut mare being exercised in a paddock that he wouldn't mind having if his stable at home was not already full.

He dismounted and was prmptly approached by a sharp-eyed gentleman wearing typical country attire, a brown clawhammer jacket, buckskin breeches, and serviceable jackboots.

"I say, sir, what a fine-looking animal," the man said running his eyes over the gray Arabian. "Are you wishing to sell him?"

"Assuredly, not. I could not part with Aziz." Lucien patted the stallion's neck. "Actually, I'm looking for information. Are you the sale owner?"

"I am, and auctioneer. Name's Ralph Coleman."

Lucien introduced himself and handed over his card, watching the man's eyes grow speculative at the title.

"How can I help you, Lord Ware?"

"Were you acquainted with Lord Audley?"

"I know who he was. Bought a couple of carriage horses at this month's spring sale. As I recall, he wasn't much of a talker."

Lucien smiled. "So I'm told. Was he with anyone?"

Coleman frowned in thought. "No, I don't— Oh, now that I think about it, he went off one evening with a man who'd just sold him a horse, I believe."

"Do you recall the seller's name?"

"I don't, but it should be in the sale books. Check with Mr. Thadeus in the stable office."

"I shall do that. Thank you." After arranging for a young lad to care for Aziz, Lucien walked through the stable area to the auction office at the far end. Mr. Thadeus, a middle-aged man with thinning brown hair, was busy recording the sale of a pair of chestnut carriage horses. As soon as the buyer left, Lucien asked about Lord Audley's purchases and learned the two horses had come from different horse dealers, John Donnelly and Eli Fleming. Armed with those names, Lucien returned to Coleman but the auctioneer could not tell him which man Audley had been with.

"I just don't recall." Coleman shrugged. "But it was right after he paid for his purchases. I vaguely recall the seller clapping your friend on the back and saying, 'You won't be sorry you bought from me. Let's have a drink on it.' Or something like that."

"So, they went to the tavern nearby?"

Coleman shrugged again. "I suppose so. Didn't really see where they went."

Lucien thanked him and walked away. It was clear the auctioneer had paid little mind to the incident. At least Lucien had the two names to pursue. He entered the tavern just across the road—small and dark, probably built before Maidenhead became a stop on the Bath Road. At this early hour, it had only a handful of patrons, and Lucien was able to put his questions to the publican without interruption.

"Sorry, I didn't know Audley—well, not to put the name with a face. Naturally, I heard about the accident."

"Perhaps if I described his lordship. Tall, very thin, dark hair, and heavy side whiskers. A learned man."

"Sir, there are hundreds of gentlemen in here on sale days. I just don't recall."

"Are you acquainted with John Donnelly and Eli Fleming? One of them may have been with Audley."

The publican shook his head. "I only bought this place a year ago. Fleming sounds kind of familiar, but I don't know either man. Sorry."

"It was a long shot." Lucien thanked him and turned away.

Stepping outside into the sunlight, he looked around. The shops on Maidenhead's main street were busy, mostly with ladies. So where were the gentlemen at midday? Only a few had been at the auction yard. Perhaps greater numbers could be found at the larger pubs in the inns or the coffee houses.

He returned Aziz to the Goose & Gander's stable and then ambled down the main street, looking in shop windows, bowing to the ladies he met. He stopped at two more taverns with no better luck and finally asked an innkeeper where he could find a card game or gentlemen's gathering at this time of day.

"Try the Sleeping Pig. Large inn at the far end of the street. They always have a game going."

The Sleeping Pig was more modern than the other inns he'd visited in town—newer timber, smaller beams, more windows—

in other words, Georgian style. Lucien assumed it had been built since the bridge was constructed across the Thames. Two barmaids hustled about, and he soon discovered much of the business was due to the back rooms where not one but four card games were already in progress. They even had a betting book on a table, similar to the clubs in London, to record bets that were outside the scope of table games. He took a quick glance at the book and smiled to discover Londoners weren't the only ones who bet on trivial matters—the latest recorded wager was on how many piglets a certain sow would farrow.

Lucien joined those who were watching the four game tables and looked over the various players, frowning when he spotted a red-whiskered gamester at table three. He recognized him from London, where the man had been barred from both White's and Boodle's. Lucien wondered if the "house" knew who—or what—he was. Two of the other tables had house dealers. As Lucien watched the dealers for any sleight of hand, he decided they were honest fellows. So why was the innkeeper allowing Simpson to play?

He ambled over to the bar and ordered a pint. When the tavern keeper set a tankard in front of him, Lucien asked about the red-whiskered player.

"Has he been around long?"

"Stops in every once in a while. Hadn't seen him for several weeks this time. Why? Do you know him?"

"I know *of* him from London. If I were you, I'd suggest he move on."

"A Captain Sharp? Like that, is it? I wondered. I've noticed he wins more than his share of the time, and he never plays at the dealer tables."

"Doesn't surprise me."

"Thanks for dropping a word, sir."

Lucien nodded and took a swallow of ale. "Perhaps you can help me in return. Were you acquainted with Lord Audley?"

"He was in here once recently. Nice enough gentleman. Heard about the accident. Too bad. He had a small child, did he not?"

"Yes, an infant girl. Do you recall what day you saw him?"

"T'was during the big horse sale. He stopped in one night and watched the Faro table for a while." The innkeeper chuckled. "He stuck in my mind 'cause he was the only one drinking tea. Why the interest in him?"

"I'm a friend of the family. Just making a few inquiries on Lady Audley's behalf."

"It's a hard thing to accept, I s'pose. Gone so quickly. I hope she is doing well."

"Under the circumstances, she is. I'm trying to piece together what he was doing on his last couple of trips to Maidenhead—once for the sale, and two weeks later when the accident occurred."

"I can't help you other than what I've already said. A lot of folk were in town for the horse sale."

"I heard he might have been making the rounds with one of the gentlemen he purchased a horse from. Are you acquainted with John Donnelly or Eli Fleming?"

"Fleming has a farm about five miles north of town and rarely comes to stay overnight, maybe once a year to sell any extra yearling foals he's got. Donnelly…" He wrinkled his brow in thought. "He might be the new stable master for Josiah Terrell." His brows deepened into a frown. "I've heard the new fellow of Terrell's likes to gamble. You could ask the dealers what the recall. If Audley was with Terrell's fellow, well, anyone who works there…"

"Is that a problem?" Lucien prodded.

The tavern keeper shook his head. "Naw, I talk too much."

Lucien got directions for Fleming's place and how to find Josiah Terrell's stable, thanked the innkeeper, and laid a coin on the counter. To his surprise, the man pushed it back.

"No need, sir. If somethin' happened to my father or brother, my mum would want to know why. I'll ask around if anyone knows what the young lord was doing in town, and if so, I'll send them your way."

"I'd be much obliged," Lucien said. "I'm staying at the Goose & Gander, and a message to Audley Manor will always reach me."

"Very good, sir. And god speed. I hope you find the answers the widow needs."

Chapter Six

Maidenhead, Friday, 25 March 1814

As Lucien exited the tavern, he noted the sun was close to the horizon. The day was too far gone to visit the horse dealers today. Instead, he strolled down main street, wishing he was at Audley Manor where he could spend the evening with Lady Anne and their friends. He missed her. If he came to a final conclusion that his way of life was too dangerous for her, would he be able to walk away? Or could he turn his back on Whitehall for her?

He stopped abruptly and turned as he realized someone was calling his name. Joey was scampering down the middle of the road, his hair flapping around his thin face.

"I found 'im, sir."

Lucien grinned and waited, feeling a keen edge of excitement.

"I done found 'im," Joey repeated, returning the grin and brimming with satisfaction as he came to a halt. He took several gulps of air before going on. "Eddie got a job to do first, but I kin bring 'im later. He knows Gordon and watched them horses for him one day not long ago. I hope it be the right day."

"Well done, lad. I'm having dinner at the Blue Bottle, and then I'll return here." He pointed to the Goose & Gander. "When Eddie is free, you can locate me one place or the other."

"Right, sir. We'll find ya." And Joey was off again.

• • •

Lucien had just finished a fine meal of roasted goose and set down an empty tankard of ale when he heard a commotion near the door of the Blue Bottle's public room.

"Milord! Over here, milord!"

He narrowed his gaze on Joey and another lad arguing with the innkeeper. The man was attempting to shove them out the door until he saw Lucien rise and move hastily toward them.

"Sorry, my lord. I didn't realize you knew them," the publican said anxiously.

"We shall be on our way," Lucien said, "as soon as you bring us a loaf of bread and a hunk of cheese. "I am sure the lads are a bit hungry."

"Yes, my lord. I can do that," the man said. He disappeared into the back, appearing quickly with two small loaves of bread and a large chunk of cheese. Lucien paid him and then hustled the boys outside. It was dark, but the lamplighter had already been around, and they found an empty bench in the public green.

"Now, Eddie," Lucien said once they were seated, properly introduced, and the boys had consumed half of the food, "I understand you knew Lord Audley's coachman, Gordon. Is that right?"

"Yes, sir. He pay me a couple of times to watch them bays. But not as much as the shilling Joey says ya promised."

"And you shall have it as soon as we finish talking."

"That be mighty fine."

Lucien smiled. "I'm interested in the last time Gordon was here. It was last Saturday. They had been here overnight and were getting ready to go home."

The boy nodded eagerly. "Tea time at the inns. Gordon been waitin' but still plenty time to get home 'fore dark."

"Where did you see him?"

"Right down there. Outside the Goose stable. His lordship were late, and Gordon was getting' fidgety 'cause he had to, uh, do his bus'ness."

"Business?" Lucien asked, just to be clear.

"The privy, sir."

"Yes, of course, and did he ask you to watch the coach and horses?"

The lad nodded, "He did, and I watched 'em good."

"I'm sure you did. Did he tell you anything to watch for, such as someone who'd been hanging around?"

"No, same as ever. Just stay with 'em 'til he got back."

"Did anyone approach you or the horses, maybe someone who stopped to admire them?"

"No, sir. I woulda tol' 'em to move along."

Lucien suppressed a smile. He could just see this lad doing that. Eddie clearly took his jobs seriously, but no one just stood and stared at a team, not unless you expected trouble—which Eddie didn't. Had he been distracted, talked to a friend, or just been looking the wrong direction? Who could say? Unfortunately, he hadn't seen anything that would narrow Lucien's hunt for the killer. "Thanks for talking to me, Eddie, and you too, Joey, for bringing him." He took the coins from his pocket and handed one to each lad.

"Is that all ye want to know?" Joey asked with a worried frown. "Don't seem worth two more shillings."

"It is to me," Lucien assured him. "Sometimes it is just as important to know what didn't happen as what did."

The boys looked perplexed by that, no doubt thinking the Quality said some odd things, when Eddie suddenly brightened.

"There be somethin' *did* happen, sir: After Gordon come back, he be digging for a coin, and we seen this fella rubbin' one of the horses' legs, like he was thinkin' of buyin'. Gordon yelled at 'im, and he run off."

Bloody hell. It could have been the killer. "Did you know him? What did he look like?"

"I dint get a good look, but I'm sure he be a stranger."

"Young? Old? Large or small?" Lucien persisted.

Eddie pushed out his lower lip in thought. "Kinda small, I reckon, and he run off real quick. He had on a old cap pulled down and a large brown jacket, so's I couldna see much." He shrugged. "Sorry, sir."

"Did he say anything?"

"Naw."

"How about Gordon? Did he seem to know the man?"

Eddie shook his head again. "He just yelled at 'im 'nd that was all. I guess I should have ran after 'im. Sorry."

"No need to be sorry, lad. You've done a fine job and earned your coin. Thank you. You may run along now."

"Yessir! Thank you, sir."

The boys disappeared down the street, and Lucien returned to the Goose and Gander. Deciding against another drink, he climbed the stairs to his lodgings, running the conversation with Eddie over in his head. It was highly suspicious that the stranger had taken the one moment of relaxed vigilance to approach the horses, but he'd hardly had time to cut through four sets of harness while Gordon looked for a coin, one or two at best. Nonetheless, they'd found four slashed at the carriage wreck.

It didn't fit—not unless the stranger had been around longer than Eddie thought and had made more than one attempt at the harness. In that event, someone else might have noticed him "admiring" the horses. Would they recollect the incident? Even if so, it was likely someone just passing by. No, his only hope of locating a witness was to question nearby shop owners or clerks. Someone might have looked outside at just the right moment, but since the shops were already closed for tonight, he'd have to be patient until morning.

Chapter Seven

Audley Manor, Friday and Saturday, 25-26 March 1814

The first footman stood straight for Lady Anne's inspection.

"Very nice, William." He actually looked quite fashionable in a black mourning armband and black gloves. "Go along with you now."

Anne sighed as the servants were now properly attired, and she could join the others for Saturday afternoon tea.

Although Phoebe had been eager to start packing, the ladies had been kept too busy on Friday and the early part of Saturday by visitors with condolences and by ensuring the house was appropriately draped in black and the household and staff attired as they should be.

When Lady Anne, Mrs. Wycliff, and Lucien had originally arrived on Wednesday, they had found the mourning wreath was above the door, and the drapes were closed, as they should be. Lady Phoebe was wearing the sole black dress she owned, but much was still to be done as befitted the mourning household of a deceased aristocrat. While women were considered too delicate to attend funerals, they were expected to follow certain mourning traditions.

Consequently, Lady Anne and Margret helped the new widow take apart two old gowns and dye them black. As she would be in deep mourning for six months and half-mourning until a full year had passed, she would soon need additional gowns in black and gray, hats, shawls, parasols, and undergarments of a better quality obtained from a dressmaker in Maidenhead or London.

On Friday, Anne and Margret visited the village and purchased a black cap for Lady Phoebe, black ribbons for the female servants to tie on their caps, black bands for the male servants to wear on their sleeves, and black gloves for the footmen. The butler had his own black gloves, which wasn't surprising as many people kept mourning clothes packed away. This was often not the case for younger people, particularly of the servant class.

"The final mourning task is complete," Lady Anne announced as she entered the drawing room on Saturday afternoon. "I am quite ready for tea."

"Oh, bless you, Lady Anne. Both of you have been so very helpful."

"It was my pleasure to be of assistance," Anne said, taking a cup of tea from Lady Phoebe. Due to her mother's recent death, Anne was all too familiar with what was expected in the situation, many niceties the daughter of a country doctor would not know or not recall.

"We've been chatting while we waited for you," Margret said. "Lady Phoebe has reminded me that she wishes to pack as soon as possible."

"Not on Sunday, of course," Phoebe amended, "but I am determined to begin early Monday morning."

"And we shall assist," Anne said.

Lady Phoebe hesitated. "Are you sure? You have done so much already."

Both Anne and Margret protested they had done very little, and regardless, they had come to Audley hoping to be helpful.

"If you truly mean that," Lady Phoebe said, "there is one task we might do tonight, something I have dreaded and avoided."

"What is it?" Margret asked. "I'd be happy to lend a hand."

"A box in the boot room contains my husband's things returned by the undertaker. I haven't had the heart to sort through it."

"Very understandable. We should do it right now." Anne turned toward the door where she had seen Godwin hovering in the hall and asked that the box of his master's things be brought to them.

"Right away, my lady. I shall take care of it myself."

While he was gone, the ladies cleared off the drawing room's tea table and pulled their chairs closer. When Godwin returned with what resembled a square bandbox, he set it on the table.

"If that will be all, my lady…"

Lady Phoebe smiled. "Yes, of course, Godwin. Thank you."

With a sympathetic look toward his mistress, he softly closed the door behind him.

"Are you ready to do this?" Anne asked. "I know it is not easy."

"What better time than when I have both of you to support me?" Lady Phoebe reached out and lifted the lid, revealing a blood-stained shirt on top. She drew in a sharp breath and shoved the box away. "Oh, I did not realize—"

Anne swiftly put an arm around her. "You should step out of the room while Margret and I sort things and lay out the items you might want to keep."

Lady Phoebe finally tore her gaze away from the box. "I hate to be such a ninny…"

"You are doing wonderfully," Margret asserted. "Some things are just harder than others." She got up, and together Anne and Margret urged Lady Phoebe toward the drawing room door.

"Give us a quarter hour," Anne said. "We shall go through everything and dispose of the clothes."

Lady Phoebe let out an sigh of relief. "Thank you. I shall attend to a question the cook had about tonight's menu."

The moment Lady Phoebe's footsteps could no longer be heard in the hallway, Margret turned to Anne indignantly. "Why in heavens would the undertaker send back his blood-stained clothes?"

"They return everything so there is no question of thievery. Other family members often perform this task so the widow or widower is not obliged. I went through my mother's things by choice, but father could not have done it."

Margret picked up the shirt with two fingers and set it aside. Anne examined every piece of clothing for pockets, lapels, or cuffs that might contain jewelry or other items of interest. The undertaker had been thorough, and she found nothing. Once that task was complete, she rang for a maid and had the clothing and boots removed.

"Do with it what you will," she said. "Give it away or sell it. Some of it will wash and can be useful, but I trust that her ladyship will not set eyes on these things again."

"Yes, my lady. I will see to it."

The bottom of the box held the other items found on his person, and they carefully spread them out on the table top. Anne had just set the empty box on the floor when the drawing room door open and Lady Phoebe returned. Margret explained what they'd done with the clothing, and Lady Phoebe nodded, her gaze already on the tea table.

"He had all of these on him?"

"Well, gentlemen do have more pockets," Margret said. "And then there are cuff links, stick pins, and so on."

"This is a lovely snuffbox," Anne said picking up a small silver box engraved with vines and small rubies to represent berries. She opened it and sniffed. Remnants of a brandy-scented tobacco lingered inside.

Margret reached out to run a finger over the top. "Exquisite workmanship."

Anne handed it to Lady Phoebe.

"It was a gift from Lady Sherbourne," Lady Phoebe said fondly. "I shall save it for Eliza."

They inspected each piece one at a time. While Phoebe waxed sentimental over the personal items, and Margret listened sympathetically, Anne looked over the other objects for hints to what Audley had been doing in Maidenhead that last day. In addition to the typical gentleman's jewelry, she examined three calling cards, coins, a pocket watch, bank notes, two folded papers (one containing the name of an inn, the other from a horse sale), and various other items one would expect to find upon a gentleman's person.

Anne glanced over them one last time. "I wonder…" she began. "Perhaps we should save all of this as it is for Lord Ware to go through. One of the items might mean something to him in regard to his inquiry."

"It does not look at all helpful to me," Lady Phoebe said doubtfully, "but if that is what Lord Ware would wish, then let us return everything to the box and put it away in the master bedchamber."

Truthfully, nothing appeared significant to Anne either, but one never knew when the smallest thing might be just what one wanted. In any event, she was certain Lord Ware would prefer to look for himself.

Chapter Eight

Maidenhead and thereabouts, Buckinghamshire, Saturday 26 March 1814

"Certainly, I recall Audley." Fleming leaned against a fence pole, keeping an eye on his latest foal as the newborn filly was still a bit unsteady on her legs. "But we didn't spend any time together. You have the wrong man. I don't make a habit of drinking with strangers, and Audley wasn't especially talkative or friendly."

Lucien sighed. So far today he might as well have stayed abed. Although he'd had no trouble tracking down Eli Fleming, a gentleman farmer who occasionally sold a few extra horses and had sold one to Audley, he'd had a late start that morning, and then he'd spent more than an hour talking with the stable boys at the Goose and Gander and their friends from nearby stables, hoping someone would recognize the "small man" described by Eddie. A couple of the regular lads were away, including Andy, and he didn't have any success with the others. Nonetheless, it all took time, and it was mid-afternoon before he had reached Fleming's farm.

The farmer continued, "It was a simple horse sale, nothing more. He bought one of my best two-year olds, said he planned to use it as a coach horse, then paid me, and that was that."

"Did you see him again? With someone else or at the gaming tables?"

Fleming lifted his brows. "Was he a gambler? Didn't strike me as the type, but no I didn't lay eyes on him again." He shrugged. "I'm afraid you had a ride out here for nothing."

Lucien smiled with a casual lift of his shoulder. "I wouldn't say that. Pretty day, clear skies, fresh country air." He nodded toward the horses in the field. "And it's been a while since I've had the pleasure of seeing a foal born." As they turned and walked toward the house where Lucien's horse was waiting, he added, "Do you know the other seller he purchased from, a John Donnelly?"

The farmer's face clouded. "I do, indeed. He manages the stables for Josiah Terrell, and if Audley bought from him, I'd be checking that horse over mighty good."

"Why do you say that?"

Fleming started down a long list of local people who had been cheated by Terrell and sold horses that were sick, had flaws in their conformation or gait, or were poorly trained. Lucien finally stopped him. "I believe I have the idea, sir. I'm surprised he stays in business."

"Needless to say, it's rare that Terrell sells to folk around here. Mostly he hits the big sales that bring in strangers or takes his horses to auctions out of the area. I'm not saying he doesn't have some good horses, but much of his stock is inferior. You can't trust him. I assume Donnelly is no better, or he wouldn't be working there."

"Where would I find Terrell Stables?"

"Can't miss it. The turn off is on your way back to Maidenhead." He gave more precise directions, and Lucien set off to visit the disreputable horse breeder.

• • •

The Terrell stables were on a well-traveled lane about a mile from the main road to Maidenhead. Fleming might be skeptical of the owner's ethics, but it was a large and busy horse farm. There were two sizable stables, that would each hold no less than two dozen horses, and at least that many more were grazing in the large pastures on both sides of the lane. Four men were training young horses in two fenced yards, and a blacksmith was shoeing a restive stallion just outside the first stable. Other workers were carrying hay and feed or buckets of water, and two were sitting outside cleaning harness.

Lucien dismounted and led Aziz toward a man in a drab jacket and long pants who appeared to be in charge. "Good day, sir. Can you direct me to John Donnelly?"

"You found him. I'm Donnelly." His eyes immediately went to the stallion. "Prime horse you got there. I don't suppose you're looking to sell him?"

Lucien gave Aziz a fond pat on the neck. This was the second offer in two days. "Not on your life. Bought him as a yearling, and he has turned out to be the best purchase I've ever made."

"He is a beauty. If you're not selling, are you buying?"

"Only looking for answers." He pulled one of his cards from his waistcoat and handed it to Donnelly. "I'm Ware. I'm making inquiries on behalf of the widow Viscountess Audley. If I'm not mistaken, you sold her husband a horse about three weeks ago, and after the sale, you and he went for drinks together. Do you recall the incident?"

Donnelly's rather wary look morphed into a smile. "Sure. He bought a carriage horse late that afternoon. Nice bay gelding, and I bought him a pint at Galloway's."

"Did both of you end up playing cards?"

"Well, yeh, but not together. I ran into some mates playing Hazard, but they only had room for one at the table. So, I introduced him to a table playing Commerce. I don't know what he did after that."

"You didn't see him leave, or with someone else?"

"Didn't see him again at all." Donnelly shrugged.

"Did he mention anyone he'd seen or anything else he'd done while in town?"

"Not that I recollect. Didn't have much to say."

"Well, thanks for your time. I should get on my way if I hope to reach town before dark."

"You bet, sir. I'd hurry. It's clouding up a bit. Going to be a foggy night." Donnelly tipped his cap and walked away disappearing into the nearest of the stables.

Lucien mounted Aziz, glanced at the sun setting just above the trees, and urged his mount down the lane toward the main road and Maidenhead.

• • •

Lucien had lingered too long in the countryside. When he was over four miles from Maidenhead, dusk fell. and with it, fog settled in. Another forty minutes. If there had been an alternate path, he would have taken it, but the road led through Maidenhead Thicket, notorious for its highwaymen who preyed on those unfortunate enough to be caught there after dark. The area was bog land, the fog denser there, and Lucien was forced to keep Aziz at a slow trot.

Lucien stayed to the middle of the road, keeping an eye on the dark shadows along the edges and listening for any sounds of movement. Twenty tense minutes passed in this fashion, the fog grew a bit lighter, and he allowed Aziz to quicken his pace.

As they crested a hill, Lucien took a deep breath thinking the worst was over, then a rifle shot echoed through the fog as a bullet whizzed past Aziz's head. The stallion startled, nearly unseating Lucien.

How the devil had someone come that close under these conditions?

Not waiting to be surrounded by a band of ruffians, he slapped the reins and Aziz leapt into a run. As they sped along the path, Lucien pulled the pistol from his right pocket and fired behind him. He could see nothing, but even a wild shot would serve as a warning that he was armed and willing to use it. He had one more shot in this pistol and two in its twin in his left pocket. He never left home without them in his carriage or on his person. He also had a knife in his right boot, but he hoped it wouldn't come to that.

From the fog, someone returned his shot. The bullet went wide this time, not even close enough for him to hear a buzz in the air. Nonetheless, he heard the pound of pursuing hoofbeats. Almost convinced it was a single rider, he began to look for a spot where he might pull off and surprise his pursuer. Regrettably, it was too dark and foggy to make much out of the shadows, leaving him no option but to run for it until they were out of the bog area. Once clear, Lucien would have a greater chance of confronting the shooter.

"Come on, lad," he whispered, leaning over Aziz's neck. "There is no horse alive that can catch you."

As though he understood every word, the stallion stretched out his legs, gradually leaving the sound of pursuit behind.

When Lucien saw the lights of Maidenhead on the horizon, he reined his horse to a trot, then a walk. He listened for sounds coming up from the rear, but whoever had been chasing them had broken off the attack. There would be no opportunity for Lucien to confront him tonight.

Aziz's neck was lathered with sweat, and Lucien spoke quietly to calm the nervous stallion. By the time they reached the Goose & Gander's stable ten minutes later, Aziz was breathing normally again, but Lucien looked him over to be sure there were no injuries and paid a stable boy to give Aziz a thorough rubdown and extra oats. Afterward, he headed into the inn to see to his own needs.

Taking the back stairs, he washed up quickly and descended to the public rooms seeking a pint of ale and a hearty meal.

"Lord Ware." Sam Giles waved a letter at him from the bar. "I didn't see you come in. This message was left for you."

"Thank you." The note had nothing but his name on the outside, written in an unfamiliar hand. "Who brought it?"

"Couldn't say, milord. I found it on the bar counter a few minutes ago, but it could have been put there earlier. It's been a busy day."

Lucien nodded his understanding, gave the publican his meal order, then took a seat at a table and unfolded the message.

"Ye willna lern nothin here. Go home."

Well, well. Someone had taken an interest in his inquiry. The writing was crude, the spelling poor, suggesting it was written by an uneducated person, perhaps a laborer or lower-class servant. But both could be deliberately done to mislead him. The writer wanted him out of Maidenhead, but why? Was he too close to the answers? Or was someone hinting the answers were elsewhere? Had this been left by his recent assailant? The timing felt off, but Lucien *had* lingered in the stable and then washed up and changed clothes. His pursuer might have had just enough time to slip into the inn and leave the warning.

He took a swift look around the inn's public room wondering if the man could still be there, watching and waiting to see what Lucien would do. Then he sighed, shaking off the thought. He mustn't let the eerie menace of the fog get inside his head.

The barmaid set down the pint he'd requested, and he took a long drink. The attack in Maidenhead Thicket puzzled him. It *might* have been a highwayman—due to the locality—but it was a rather clumsy attempt for a thief. Little chance had existed of catching him to steal his blunt or his horse in that fog. The incident must have been another warning to leave town, although he doubted the assailant would have minded killing him with a lucky shot.

Lucien frowned. In the last two days or perhaps just a few hours, he had stirred up Audley's killer with his questions, making him angry or fearful. It was disconcerting that the killer knew who he was, while Lucien had no idea of the other man's identity or where their paths might have crossed. Lucien had been all over town, out to Fleming's and to the horse breeder's. He'd spoken with dozens of people—and that didn't include those living near Audley Manor who could have followed him to Maidenhead. The killer could be any of them.

He smiled grimly and took another sip of ale. He'd ruffled feathers, for sure. While a worried killer was inherently more dangerous, he was also more likely to make mistakes.

And yet, what if the shots and the note were not from Audley's killer or even an accomplice? What the devil would that mean?

Chapter Nine

Audley Manor, Buckinghamshire, Sunday, 27 March 1814

On Sunday, the ladies went to church in the village. The 17th century structure of stone and heavy beams was showing its age, but it was built to last, and the sturdy benches would be around another two hundred years or more. Nor did the ladies need to worry about snagging their clothes on seats worn smooth by hundreds of past church goers.

The service was well-attended, and from what Lady Anne observed, the widow Audley in her black veil and her London guests were part of the attraction. Heads turned the moment they walked in, and the locals were still lingering and watching when Lady Phoebe stopped on the way out to speak with the vicar and introduce her guests. As Anne's prior experience had led her to conclude the local clergy was an excellent source of information, she had urged Lady Phoebe to invite him for afternoon tea on Monday.

Vicar Reeves was flattered by the invitation and readily accepted.

"Shall we say four?" Lady Phoebe smiled sweetly.

"My wife and I shall look forward to it with great anticipation, my lady." He bowed, and the ladies proceeded to their carriage.

"Well, I did as you asked," Lady Phoebe said once they were seated inside the coach, "but I must warn you he is not a particularly erudite or stimulating guest."

Lady Anne smiled. "Are you saying the poor man is dull?"

Lady Phoebe looked taken aback and then laughed. "I envy how direct you are."

"Not everyone would agree it is an asset," Anne said.

"I do," Margret said, laughing, "but I am rather outspoken myself."

"Rather?" Anne said in amusement. "You can put me to the blush, my dear."

"Name once I have done so," Margret demanded.

"Oh, how shall I choose among the many. What about the time when you congratulated Lady Sarah for increasing when she had merely indulged herself in too many sweets over Christmastide." Anne choked off her laughter.

Margret giggled. "That was just an unfortunate mistake."

"Oh, yes? And when you rushed over to meet Lord Hanby's daughter?"

"Another simple mistake." When Lady Phoebe gave her an inquiring look, Margret confessed, "The very young lady with him turned out to be his latest mistress. How was I to know?"

They were all laughing by the time the coach stopped at the front door of Audley Manor.

"You two are so good to have around. I am already dreading the day you must leave," Lady Phoebe said as she stepped out of the carriage.

"It is much too soon to worry about that," Anne assured her.

Lord Audley's favorite hound, Elsie, bounded up from the stables to greet them. As they crowded into the front hall, laughing, and taking off pelisses and gloves to hand to Godwin, the hound ran past them and up the stairs.

"Tea will be ready and served shortly in the drawing room, my lady."

"Thank you, Godwin. That will be delightful," Lady Phoebe said.

"I shall join you in a trice," Margret called, already climbing the stairs. "I need to change to my slippers. I think I've bruised my foot." When Elsie began to bark, Margret added, "Don't worry about that. I'll find out what's bothering her."

Anne and Phoebe had almost reached the drawing room doors when a scream from upstairs brought them to an abrupt stop. Anne turned to gaze up the stairs. "Margret, is something amiss?"

Another scream, then Anne heard Margret shout, "Stop thief! Come back here with that."

Grabbing the pistol from her pocket, Anne lifted her skirts and ran for the stairs. The footman William was right beside her clutching a pistol of his own.

Good Heavens. Why on earth was a footman carrying a pistol?

As they reached the staircase, Margret appeared on the balcony above. "Outside, quickly, William," she shouted. "He is getting away."

"Come on, Elsie," William shouted.

While Anne rapidly climbed the stairs to see if Margret had been injured, Elsie nearly flew past her and followed William as he ran out the front door, brandishing the pistol.

"Margret, good heavens, are you all right? What happened?" Anne demanded.

"I was a bit startled, but I nearly caught a thief." Margret gripped Anne's arm, tugged her into the master bedchamber, and pointed toward an open window. The curtains were flapping in the cool breeze. "Elsie was barking at the door so I opened it, and there he was…a strange man, climbing out the window. He had the undertaker's box under his arm."

"Whatever would he want with that box?"

As they thrust the curtains out of the way, they saw a fleeing horseman. "That's him," Margret exclaimed. "Oh, Anne, he's taking Lord Audley's things."

The rider wore a greatcoat and hat pulled down, making it impossible to determine his stature or features from this distance, and he was already beyond the tended grounds of the house. William was valiantly running after him shouting "Stop thief." Elsie was ahead of William, barking wildly, but the horse and rider had too much of a lead. William fired a pistol shot at the fleeing man, and even when the thief disappeared behind a dense stand of trees, the undaunted footman continued to pursue him.

Anne sighed and put her own pistol back in her pocket.

"Can you believe it?" Margret asked, both indignation and awe in her voice. "His horse was waiting below the window, and he jumped into the saddle. I've seen young boys do that, but still…"

"A rather remarkable escape," Anne agreed. She considered the distance to the ground. The fellow must have practiced that jump in order to have confidence in making it. How long had he been planning this housebreaking? What did he want?

"Why would he take that box?" Margret said, still frowning out the window as she mirrored Anne's thoughts. "It held mostly trinkets from Audley's pockets and his everyday jewelry."

"Nothing of much worth, except the snuff box—and that wasn't worth taking this kind of risk. Of course, they have great sentimental value for Phoebe and Eliza."

"We might recover one or two if we look around the ground below. I believe the box tipped, and he lost part of its contents," Margret said.

They hurried down the stairs and exited the front door to find Lady Phoebe and half the servant staff standing on the front lawn.

"What happened?" Godwin asked as spokesman for the group. "Is everyone all right? Who was that rider?"

"No one was harmed," Lady Anne assured him. "It was a thief. William fired at him, but he got away."

"William has a gun?" Phoebe asked.

"It is fortunate he did," Lady Anne said staunchly, not wanting the enterprising young man to get into trouble. "Elsie and Margret nearly caught the thief, but he escaped out a window."

"Good heavens." Lady Phoebe turned to Margret. "You should not have tried to stop him. That criminal might have hurt you."

"Actually, I didn't try," Margret said, "but I did walk in on him… and I shouted at him." She explained the details of the encounter in the master bedchamber.

"I cannot believe he took Lord Audley's personal things," Phoebe said in dismay.

Margret shook her head. "Not all of them, at least I don't think so. It appeared as though some of it spilled."

"Oh, I hope so."

Everyone spread out and searched the ground below the window. They recovered the pocket watch, one of the cuff links, and a ring.

"It's better than losing it all," Phoebe said, clearly trying to look at the positive side after they had combed the area for a second time.

"I saw William returning to the house and sent him back to search along the path the thief took," Anne said. "We may find more. The box was an awkward size to carry on horseback. He may take whatever he wanted and discard the rest."

Lady Phoebe sighed. "I cannot imagine what he came for, but I hope he got it, so we will not see him again." She rubbed her arms at a chill gust of wind. "Shall we go inside? I am confident we could all use that tea tray by now."

• • •

While Lady Phoebe and Margret proceeded directly to the drawing room, Lady Anne hurried upstairs and took a quick look around the master bedchamber. As she suspected, there was no sign of disturbance such as a search might have left. She nodded to herself. The thief had known exactly what he was after.

She walked out, closing the door behind her, and joined the other ladies as Margret was repeating the story of how the thief had leapt out the window onto his horse. Lady Anne was barely settled before a tap on the door announced the arrival of the maid and butler with two trays laden with tea and coffee along with small sandwiches and biscuits.

For a few minutes talk was desultory, but Lady Anne set down her second cup of tea and said, "I am so puzzled by the thief. What did he want?"

"He may have just grabbed what he could when he heard Elsie," Margret said.

"But the room hadn't been searched," Anne protested. "He wanted that box or rather something in it."

"I don't recall everything in it," Lady Phoebe said.

"You needn't worry about that." Margret gave a nod toward Anne. "She has the most extraordinary memory. So, tell her, Anne, rattle off everything that was in it."

"Perhaps I should write it down if Phoebe would not mind ringing for pen and paper."

"Of course." Phoebe reached for the bell pull. "Can you really do this?"

"I believe so."

In fact, it didn't take Anne long to complete the list. When you have the gift of total recall, there isn't much thought that had to go into the process.

Lady Phoebe and Margret looked over the list in Anne's neat handwriting. "I had forgotten the other rings," Lady Phoebe said. "And the folded papers. I wonder what they were."

"The name of the Goose & Gander Inn was written on one," Anne said."And the other was the sale sheet for the purchase of a horse."

"Margret was right. You are wonderful at this," Lady Phoebe said in obvious admiration.

Anne shrugged it off. "I was just born with a good memory."

"It's much better than good," Margret declared. "A few years ago the symbols on a tiny part of a war code she had seen allowed Whitehall's code breakers to read enemy dispatches written by the French."

"Truly?" Phoebe looked at Anne her eyes shining. "What a marvelous talent."

Anne blushed. "It does come in handy. I wonder if I should note all the details for Lord Ware. Unless he finds the answers in Maidenhead, he shall be interested in the contents of the box."

"Include everything," Margret suggested. "If William finds other items, and we can determine what is missing, Lord Ware would definitely want to know what the thief took away."

A knock on the drawing room door interrupted. "Beg pardon, Lady Phoebe," Godwin said. "William has returned and wishes to see you."

"Tell him to come in."

The young footman entered, carrying the stolen box.

"You found it," Lady Phoebe said in surprised.

"Yes, ma'am. The box was empty. I guess he gave it a toss from horseback, but I looked around real good and picked up several things."

"That is wonderful, William." She brought her hands together in a single clap. "Thank you."

He tipped his head to Lady Phoebe with a grin and set the box on a footstool next to her. Anne and Margret scooted their chairs and leaned over to look, comparing its contents and the few pieces they'd already found with Anne's list.

"Most everything is there," Margret said in surprise.

"Excellent job, William." Lady Anne slipped him a quid and whispered, "For the extra effort."

"Thank *you*, my lady. I just wanted to help her ladyship."

"You have, William." Lady Phoebe looked up and beamed at him. "I am so pleased to have these things for Eliza." She picked up the snuffbox. "It would have been a shame to lose this beautiful thing. Thank you, again. I'm sorry we've kept you from your tea."

"No trouble, my lady." The lad left with a broad grin on his freckled face.

"This was no ordinary thief," Anne said, not being able to shake the belief the thievery had been carefully planned with a particular goal in mind. "Everything of value is here, except the other cufflink, which I suppose got dropped somewhere along the way. Otherwise, the only items missing are the two papers and the calling cards."

"Easy to stuff into his pockets," Margret said. "Although, I suppose, the wind might have blown them away."

"Except, we know he came for something," Anne said. "It has to be one of those five items."

"How do we determine which one?" Margret asked.

"Well, can we eliminate any?" Lady Anne turned to Lady Phoebe. "Is the Goose and Gander in Maidenhead?"

"Yes, I believe that was where he always stayed. I don't know why he wrote it down, but it doesn't appear important."

Anne agreed. "I am curious why he had the sale sheet from Terrell Stable. Didn't you stay he bought the horses three weeks ago?" When Lady Phoebe nodded, she added, "Rather odd he'd be carrying it around that long, but maybe he forgot he had it."

Phoebe pointed to the three calling cards on the list. "Do you recall the names on these?"

"Edward Marchant, Charles Raven, and Joseph Galvin. Do you know them?"

"Two of them. Mr. Marchant is our solicitor, and Mr. Galvin is a local merchant. I don't believe I've heard of Mr. Raven before, but Lord Audley exchanged calling cards wherever he went. Usually it had something to do with his historical research." She sat back in her chair. "I suppose he had Galvin's card because he planned to place an order and kept it so he wouldn't forget. He was rather absent-minded, you know." She fell silent and smiled rather wistfully at this reminder of her husband's forgetfulness in practical matters.

Anne brought up another possibility. "What if the intruder did not get what he came for because Margret interrupted him?" She shifted her gaze to Lady Phoebe. "Could it have been Jasper, looking for information on the estate and inheritance provisions?"

Instead of defending her elder brother, Lady Phoebe sighed. "Considering his obsession with holding onto the estate, it could have been him but, seriously, Lady Anne, I cannot imagine him making that jump to the horse."

"Not even if he was desperate enough?" Margret frowned, puzzling over what Jasper might do. "I suppose not. He is not exactly the athletic type. I must admit I don't understand him. Surely he realizes there are no legal grounds for him to have the estate."

"He has been told often enough—by everyone," Lady Phoebe said. "He just won't listen."

"There are other suspects," Anne said. "Did Lord Ware not say there was a land dispute? Someone might have sought those documents."

"But nothing of that sort is here. The solicitor took everything."

"Perhaps the thief didn't know that."

"While we're speculating, what about something more sinister," Margret said. "What if the murderer thinks Lord Audley had something that could incriminate him, and he came here looking for it?"

"Oh, my heavens." Lady Phoebe's eyes rounded. "Is it possible? Could we all be in danger?"

Anne sucked in her breath wondering if Margret could be right, then hastened to reassure Lady Phoebe. "You needn't worry, my lady. We are surrounded by servants who will protect us. Moreover, the thief didn't appear to be violent. He went to great effort to enter the house when everyone was at church, he had no obvious weapon, nor did he offer to harm Margret. Nonetheless, we should inform Lord Ware, and I shall dispatch a note immediately."

"We should also inform the squire," Lady Phoebe said.

"Why?" Margret asked.

"Phoebe is right," Anne said. "He is the magistrate after all, and I am sure we would all feel safer if someone nearby was looking after us." At least Lady Phoebe would feel safer, and Anne saw nothing wrong with that. She herself was wishing Lucien would walk through the door, and doubtless Margret wouldn't mind a reassuring hug from Capt. Jack.

"Speaking of someone looking after us," Lady Phoebe said, "I meant to ask William why he has a gun."

"Why don't I talk with him for you," Anne suggested. "I'm sure he felt it was necessary with no gentlemen residing at the manor."

"Yes, I'm sure you are correct. I just wish he had told me."

"I shall convey that," Anne promised.

Phoebe sighed. "It is kind of you to offer, Anne. Thank you."

• • •

The ladies had just finished with the laden tea trays when they heard a carriage arrive. It was barely one o'clock, too early for proper Sunday visitors.

"Do not disturb yourselves, ladies," Phoebe said. "Have another cup of tea. I shall ask Godwin what all the commotion is about." She rose and left the room.

Anne heard women's voices from the front of the house. Surely it wasn't more neighbors. Hadn't they already spoken with everyone at church? "I think I shall see what is happening."

"Me too." Margret followed Anne to the front hall.

They found Phoebe talking with two young women. The front doors stood open, and a coachman was unloading several trunks and bandboxes from an old but large carriage.

"Lady Ware, Mrs. Wycliff," Phoebe said, turning as they approached and using formal address, "I would like you to meet my younger sisters, Charlotte and Dora."

"A pleasure," Anne and Margret responded, nearly in unison.

The girls curtseyed. "How delightful you could be here to support Phoebe in her time of sorrow," Charlotte said.

Anne heard the flatness of insincerity in her words. According to Phoebe's earlier discussion about her family, Charlotte, a square-jawed, ordinary-looking young woman of nineteen, had her father's looks—dark hair and brown eyes—but not his pleasing temperament.

Those brown eyes now turned on her older sister. "I am sorry we could not be here sooner, but packing and all took some time."

"Yes, I can imagine," Lady Phoebe said, gazing at the number of trunks and boxes that were accumulating on the front drive. "What I don't understand is why you have arrived with what appears to be everything you own. Has some tragedy occurred of which I am unaware? A fire perhaps?"

"We have come to stay as long as you need us," Dora said.

"But I told Jasper—"

"Nonsense," Charlotte interrupted. "There is no need to be brave and pretend with us, sister dear. Where else would we be but here comforting you?" She looked expectantly down the hall. "Are you not going to offer us tea? We were up very early this morning getting ready."

"Yes, of course. We were just finishing a light meal. Perhaps you would like to join us."

"Splendid," Dora said. She definitely shared Lady Phoebe's coloring, the auburn hair and green eyes, but there the likeness ended. Where Phoebe was delicate, slender and petite, Dora was pleasantly plump with a childish naïveté—rather fetching in a young lady of six and ten but would be less pleasing as she grew older. She also had a good appetite which became obvious a few minutes later as both sisters tucked into the food on the sideboard.

When Dora reached over to refill her plate, Charlotte gave a sharp scold. "Your new gowns will not fit if you keep eating like that. Besides, it is time we located our rooms and arranged to have our trunks unpacked." She turned expectantly to Phoebe. "I assume you have servants available to do this. We could not deprive Jasper of any from our household."

"I fear you do not understand the situation," Lady Phoebe said. "I cannot invite you to stay overnight, much less for days or weeks. I am no longer mistress here, nor is the Lower House my property."

Anne noted Phoebe had deliberately not called it the Dower House, and she was laying it on a bit thick, but perhaps that was what it took with her family.

"Shall you have to leave?" Dora asked wide-eyed. "Where will you go?"

"I suppose I shall have to return home to stay with you," Phoebe said with a loud, exaggerated sigh. "Hopefully, for just a short time, but I am not certain what the future holds."

"But I have your bed at home now," Dora said. "I don't want to move back to the nursery."

"We shall worry about that when we have to," Lady Phoebe said, soothingly. "Meanwhile, I shall have your trunks put back in the carriage."

Charlotte's frown deepened. "Where are we to stay tonight?"

"There is a small inn at the edge of Audley village. You'd have to put the room to Jasper's account, I'm afraid, as I cannot place any burden upon the Audley estate."

"This cannot be," Dora said. "Jasper told us we should come…"

"I am sorry. I did try to explain the situation to him," Phoebe said oozing sympathy.

"Since you are here, we could use your assistance," Anne interjected, hoping to hurry them on their way. "We were about to organize your sister's and niece's belongings so we can get an early start on packing in the morning. Having just arranged your own trunks, your experience would be most welcome." She nearly laughed at their sour expressions.

Charlotte set down her tea cup and rose. "I wish we could stay to help, but Jasper would not like for us to add a stay at the inn to his debts. If we are to reach home and unpack before bedtime, we should start now. Come, Dora."

The younger girl looked uncertain. "If you think it best, Charlotte." She rose. "Phoebe dear, I hope your husband's family will do right by you and Eliza. At the very least, they should find you a home."

Anything to ensure Phoebe didn't return to Wheatley House to reclaim her old bed, Anne thought cynically.

"I am confident it will work out," Lady Phoebe murmured.

Charlotte started toward the door but turned back, a suspicious look on her face. "If you cannot invite anyone to stay, then why are they here?" she asked, jerking her chin toward Anne and Margret.

"I can answer that," Anne said smoothly. "We were sent by the new Viscount Audley to stay with Lady Phoebe until Lord Ware completes his inquiry."

"What inquiry?" Charlotte demanded.

"Lord Sherbourne wants to know exactly what happened to his son," Lady Phoebe said. "He has a right to know."

Dora shivered. "Who would want to hear all the ghastly details?"

Charlotte was not so easily diverted. "Was there something suspicious about the accident?"

Dora looked round-eyed at Charlotte. "What are you suggesting?"

"Think about it, Dorie. A sudden, unexplained accident, then a gentleman from London comes around asking questions, and these two ladies are here keeping an eye on Phoebe." Charlotte stared at her elder sister. "Just what have you done, Phoebe dear?"

Stunned silence filled the room for several seconds, then Lady Phoebe and Charlotte exchanged a few sharp words, Dora got into it, and Lady Phoebe finally burst into tears. At that point, Margret comforted the widow while Anne ushered Charlotte and Dora to their carriage. She stood in the doorway so the girls didn't attempt to re-enter. Within minutes, the trunks and bags were packed on top and the carriage was on its way.

"Where's Lady Phoebe?" Anne asked when she saw the young woman was missing.

"She ran upstairs," Margret said. "I thought it best to let her be for a while."

• • •

A half hour passed before Lady Phoebe came down, her eyes red and puffy. Anne and Margret had been out walking in the garden. As they returned to the house, Lady Phoebe met them at the door. She waited until they were inside, then asked, "Is that what you think? And Lord Ware thinks? That I had something to do with that horrible accident?"

"Of course not," Margret said.

But Lady Phoebe was looking at Anne.

"No matter how unlikely," Anne said carefully, "in any investigation, one has to consider all the possibilities. The accident *did* free you from a loveless marriage."

"For Goodness Sake, Lady Anne." Lady Phoebe sounded shocked. "He was Eliza's father, and I respected him. He was a good man and kind to me in many ways. It was not his fault that he did not love me."

"Or his child," Margret reminded her.

Shock turned to anger now. "You are so very wrong about that. He loved Eliza, doted on her. He came down at least once a week to play with her for hours. If you could have seen them together, you would not doubt his affection for her. Yes, he was a difficult husband, but I would never have wished him ill. I miss him, and Eliza will be without her father her whole life. Do you honestly believe I would do such a thing?"

"No, I do not," Anne said. "But someone could have arranged it for you."

"Who?" Phoebe's face showed a mixture of anger and bewilderment. "Who would do such a terrible thing? And why/"

"Oh, my lady, I beg pardon," Anne said suddenly contrite that she had pressed her so hard. She was doing the very opposite of what Lord Ware had asked of her. She was supposed to be getting close enough to form an accurate assessment of the widow, not antagonize her. And she genuinely liked Phoebe. "I can get caught up in the bare facts and forget they involve real people—in this matter, people I care about. The question had to be asked, Lady Phoebe, but it does not mean I believe it. I am truly sorry it sounded that way. I had hoped we were on our way to being friends."

Phoebe stared at her a moment, then sighed. "We *are* friends, my lady."

Anne let out a silent sigh. "Then please call me Anne."

Margret hurried to agree. "Yes, let us do be friends and speak informally among ourselves. I am Margret."

Phoebe relaxed with a smile. "And I am Phoebe. I fear I have been too sensitive. My siblings have a way of setting me off. Let us forget we had this conversation, but I *do* understand the spouse must be questioned in a suspicious death."

"Most are quickly cleared," Anne assured her. "In all truth, Phoebe, I cannot see you wishing harm to your husband…or anyone else."

Phoebe's smile broadened. "Now, may we talk about something else? I thought we'd start packing in the morning by sorting the winter linens…or should it be the winter clothing? And then there is Lord Audley's bedchamber and his other belongings…"

An hour later they had their last visitor of the day. Squire Levington arrived in response to Lady Phoebe's note regarding the morning intruder. He expressed his deep concern over the house breaking and insisted on checking all the ground floor doors and the windows throughout the house to ensure they were secure. Afterward he spoke with Godwin, suggesting increased safety procedures, and then Anne saw him talk with William. It reminded her she had offered to speak to the footman regarding his pistol. She assumed the squire was exploring the same subject. She hoped Levington was encouraging him to continue his vigilance, which is what Anne intended to do.

Before the squire departed, he stopped in the drawing room doorway. "I shall return tomorrow, if I may. Rest assured someone will be keeping an eye on the manor in my absence." He smiled and was on his way.

Anne saw no indication he had a tendre for Phoebe, unless it was in his assumption of personal responsibility for their well-being, and certainly nothing improper or hinting at a murderous intent.

After such an exhausting day and with a busy one planned for tomorrow, the ladies had a light dinner that evening and retired early. Lady Anne checked her windows and hallway door for herself, not eager to meet their housebreaker if he decided to return during the night.

Chapter Ten

Maidenhead, Buckinghamshire, Sunday 27 March 1814

Knowing the town would be quiet on a Sunday morning, Lucien made a late breakfast of it and didn't leave the Goose & Gander until after midday. He found two shops open near the spot where Graham's coach had stood, but neither shopkeeper recalled a nondescript, small, and agile man from eight days ago. They didn't even remember the coach.

"It is such a common sight to have coaches standing outside that I pay little mind to them," the man at the tailor shop said.

After that, Lucien reviewed his strategy. He should have realized the commercial shops weren't likely to remember customers unless they were regulars, and Eddie had said plainly the man was a stranger. And who would recognize both strangers and locals better than the boys who haunted the streets hoping to earn a coin now and then?

Unless Eddie had lied to him. And why would he do that? If he had seen someone he knew, maybe,…say another street boy, would he have lied? Perhaps. Lucien's shilling would hardly be reason enough for one lad to peach on another—not and survive on the streets. And yet, Joey trusted Eddie, and somehow Lucien felt Joey wouldn't have brought Eddie to him if he knew he was going to lie.

Lucien frowned. Last night as he lay awake in bed, he'd thought about what kind of person would reach under the belly of not one but four horses to cut the harness. It had to be someone very comfortable around them. So why was he visiting shops and inns? Wasn't it most likely he was looking for a stable boy or groom who'd been dismissed from their job? Or a horse handler down on his luck and not particular how he earned his blunt? Perhaps a homeless man who hung round the stables or even a farmer who worked with horses every day.

So, he'd go back to the stables, this time asking about a *small, agile stranger* but also exploring the possibilities of anyone they knew who was very familiar with horses and wouldn't shirk from committing a criminal act.

Fortunately, all the stables would be open on a Sunday afternoon.

• • •

As usual the stable boys were busy feeding, grooming, and exercising horses, mucking bedding, mending harness and polishing carriages. Nonetheless, they could talk as they worked and had no lack of suggestions for who the unknown man might be, including former workers who'd been dismissed for various reasons, a couple of town drunkards who often stopped to chat or sleep a while in bad weather, strangers coming through town looking for work, and young local lads waiting for opportunities to exercise or water the horses for a few pence. Most were known only by first names, or no names, and a handful were known by everyone.

Lucien eliminated the chronic drunkards; the culprit had been agile, swift, and stealthy. As Lucien moved from stable to stable, he continued to ply the lads with questions about other names he had gathered and struck off several as either too tall, too heavy, or too old. Nonetheless, by the time he returned to the Goose and Gander stables, he still had a list of seven possible culprits.

Upon locating Andy, he explained what he'd been doing and ran the seven names past him.

"Were any of them here that last Saturday when you cared for Gordon's team?"

Andy swiftly knocked off the names of two stable boys who'd been dismissed for neglect of a horse. "They'd be run off if they came around, but all the rest, I reckon they're around most days."

"Did any of them assist you and Gordon with the team? Help with the harness or leading the horses out?"

Andy set the empty water bucket down. "Not on your life, m'lord. Only our regular lads are allowed."

"But it was Saturday," Lucien persisted. "Was it busy enough you might not have noticed someone near the bays?"

"It woulda been busy, all right. Saturday always is. But not noticing a fella 'round our horses?" He shook his head slowly. "Nope, wouldna happen."

"So, if we assume this incident occurred outside the stables, would any of these five do something like snip the harness?"

"Who can say, sir?" Andy shrugged. "I s'pose it depends on how much they was paid, but Danny or Richy are looking for regular jobs. Doubt if they'd chance getting caught. Who were the other three?"

"Charlie, Bobo, and Nappy."

"Oh, yeh. Well, Nappy, he's a mean one, a'right. He could of, but don't tell 'im I said so."

"I won't tell any of them I talked to you. That's a promise. What about the others?"

Andy cleared his throat. "I don't like peachin' on other lads."

"I understand, but whoever did this killed two good men and four prime Cleveland Bays." Lucien mentioned the horses knowing their loss would be equally important to a stable lad.

Andy leaned forward and lowered his voice. "We talked among ourselves 'round here… and it coulda been Charlie and Bobo, brothers who sneak around. They snitch things, and we heard they done some nasty stuff."

"Such as?"

"Horse thievin', robbery, maybe worse."

Hanging offenses, but still a long way from murder, unless the "maybe worse" was a lot worse. And yet, cutting harness took less resolve than shooting or stabbing someone. There was a distance from the deed, and damaging harness might not feel like murder… not unless you knew the road from Maidenhead to Audley with its sharp curves and rocky creek beds.

Lucien spent the rest of the day looking for Nappy, Charlie, and Bobo without success. Their ordinary appearances that allowed them to go unnoticed while *snitching* things also made them hard to find. As best Lucien could discern, Nappy was a lad of fifteen, the brothers in their early-twenties. All three had brown hair and were thin, standing between five foot and five foot three inches tall. Charlie and Bobo were viewed with genuine fear, while Nappy was just another street bully.

By all accounts, none of them had friends or frequent companions, which could work in Lucien's favor. There was no one to warn them he was searching for them.

• • •

Lucien returned to the inn for a pint and to take stock of what he'd learned so far before planning his evening. Sam looked up when Lucien walked in the door and gestured to him. "A message for you, my lord." He reached behind the bar and handed him a sealed note.

It was Lady Anne's handwriting. He smiled, ripping it open, and read rapidly. "An intruder? Good lord," he exclaimed. She assured him they were fine, and he shouldn't come rushing back.

They might be all right for now, but what if the intruder came back? What if this wasn't a common thief but the killer looking for something? Wouldn't anyone who got in his way be at risk?

"Bad news?" Sam asked, wiping the bar counter.

"Bad enough to change my plans. Could I trouble you for a light meal? I may have to ride out tonight."

"No trouble at all. Let me see what the missus has ready."

While Sam disappeared into the back, Lucien chose a table and went over the brief contents of Anne's message again. Why would anyone break into Audley Manor? What was he looking for? Did this mean Audley's murderer was local to the village and his death had nothing to do with any of the strange happenings in Maidenhead?

He pulled out his pocket watch. Audley Manor was no more than an hour and a half away. He could be there by nine-thirty or ten if he left soon.

When the barmaid brought out his meal and another pint of ale, he dug into the slices of cold beef, cheese, bread, and a dish of baked apples. He hadn't realized how hungry he was. He was almost finished when Sam came over.

"I been thinking about that last day Audley stayed with us. I don't know if it matters, but he did mention seeing his solicitor."

"Did he? Well, that's good to know. You've reminded me that I already had a few questions for the fellow."

Lucien thanked him, finished off his ale, and went upstairs to pack a few things for the trip to Audley Manor. A conversation with the solicitor would be a priority when he returned in a day or two. He turned at a tap on the door.

The barmaid from downstairs handed him another note. "It was a rider from Squire Levington, the magistrate down by Audley."

"Thank you." Hoping this wasn't more bad news, Lucien opened it and began to read.

"I just heard of the incident at the Manor. I am going over there now and shall keep a close eye on the ladies until you complete your business in Maidenhead."

Well, the squire certainly was taking an avid interest in the ladies…or was it one particular lady? But could he be trusted?

Did his apparent fondness for Lady Phoebe and his presence in Maidenhead on the nineteenth make him a serious suspect in Audley's death? While she would be in no danger from him, what about Anne and Margret if Levington thought they might learn the truth? But bloody hell, if that man had been lying, he was the finest actor Lucien had met. Surely he would not expect Lady Phoebe to cover for him if he harmed her guests. The thought was too incredible. And while it was worrisome that Levington hadn't mentioned his trip to Maidenhead, he most likely had a reasonable explanation that did not include concealing his guilt for a murder.

Lucien sighed and sat on the edge on the bed. Call it instinct, experience, or common sense, but he did *not* believe Levington was a killer. So, why was he still planning to tear out for Audley tonight? Levington had offered to guard the ladies. And hadn't

Lady Anne proven she was capable of handling most situations? Moreover, she had clearly told him not to rush back.

Confound it. This was one of his worst fears regarding his relationship with her—that he'd become so worried about her safety he could not focus on his inquiries.

The situation in Audley appeared to be under control—more so than here in Maidenhead. How could he ignore last night's attack in the fog and the ominous note? Didn't those indicate the killer was in Maidenhead?

He shook his head with a wry smile. He missed having Sherry's help. Perhaps it was time to call on the resources he had by writing to Mr. Sloane, Lord Rothe's secretary at Whitehall for background information on several names: Slade, Levington, Donnelly, Terrell, and the duelers, Raven and Ponsonby. He could also inquire if Jack Wycliff could follow-up as needed. While awaiting their replies, he'd stay at least another day or two to find out why Audley went to see his solicitor and to continue his search for the street bully, the two notorious brothers, and a witness to identify the mysterious small man.

Having made his decision, Lucien wrote and posted his letters, and then went out for a walk. It was too early for bed, and with his mind running in circles over this investigation, he needed a break—something to clear his head. Earlier in the day he'd heard about a hazard game at the Blue Bottle Inn. He walked into the establishment's back room a short time later and joined the table.

• • •

Close to midnight, Lucien climbed the stairs to his lodgings, finally tired enough to sleep. His hand on the door latch, he glanced upward, paused, and carefully drew his hand back. The thread he habitually left on the top of his door was missing. Someone had been inside his room…or was still there.

He drew the knife from his boot, crouched low, and entered his room in a rush, slamming the door behind him. He froze with his back against the wall, listening for movement or breathing, and waited until his eyes adjusted to the dim light. The window curtains had been open when he left. Now they were shutting out all but a small glow from the street lanterns.

He swept the room with his gaze, stopping to study the dark corners. Seeing nothing, he flung the wardrobe open, brushing his hands inside to ensure no one was hiding there. Only then did he light a candle. After looking under the bed, he inspected the rest of the room to see what had been disturbed or was missing.

Small things—the bed blanket slightly rumpled, a used cravat out of place in the top of the wardrobe, his bag set on the wrong side of the bed—were the only evidence of a search. Nothing was missing. But then, after his years on the Continent, he knew better than to leave anything to be found. The real question was what had the thief been after? Money, jewelry, information? Or was this the same intruder who'd been at Audley Manor?

Chapter Eleven

Audley Manor, Monday, 28 March 1814

Following breakfast the morning after such an eventful Sunday, the ladies at Audley Manor put those things behind them, at least for the moment. The housekeeping staff set to work packing the winter linens in large trunks while the ladies took on the task of sorting the master bedchamber.

"Not only will we be getting a difficult task done," Anne said, "but Phoebe can keep watch for anything else the thief might have taken. The things we know about just don't look important enough." And yet there were those calling cards. Who was Charles Raven, and why did Audley meet with his solicitor? And then, why was he still carrying a sale's sheet from the horse sale?

"I keep wondering if the wretched thief dropped the one thing he was after," Margret said.

"Like what?" Phoebe asked.

Margret shrugged. "The snuffbox? Oh, I don't know. Maybe Anne's right, and he took something you don't yet know is missing."

"You could also have frightened him away before he found what he wanted," Anne said.

"I cannot think what he would have wanted, but yes, of course, we shall look for anything that should be there but isn't or an item valuable enough to tempt a housebreaker." Phoebe stood in the middle of the room, looking around, her eyes landing on several of her husband's belongings. "This will be harder than I imagined. No matter the state of our marriage, I was very fond of my husband."

"I did not have the pleasure of meeting him," Anne said gently, "but Lord Ware described him as a fine gentleman…and he was Eliza's father."

Phoebe sighed. "It is a pity she will not know him."

"Shall we start with the wardrobe?" Margret asked brightly in an obvious attempt to lighten the mood. "I assume your servants will be given some of his clothing."

"I would like that. We must set aside the everyday clothing they could use. The rest will go to the church or the rag bag for housekeeping to use or for the servants to sell at the market."

They worked steadily, holding up things for Phoebe to scrutinize before adding to one of the three piles she had suggested or to a fourth pile of things that required further attention. The formal wear, fancy hats, dancing shoes, and such went to the church—the servants would have little practical use for those—but other jackets, shirts, and long pants would be offered to them, along with the everyday hats, scarves, boots, and nightshirts. Of his personal items—pipes, snuff boxes, cuff links, cravat pins, rings, and other jewelry—Lady Phoebe kept those of value or sentiment to pass on to Eliza when she got older—the rest were discarded or added to one of the other piles.

Near midday, Anne noticed Phoebe holding one of her husband's pipes and wiping away tears. She suggested they take a break. "I could use a cup of tea. Anyone else?"

"Oh, yes," Margret agreed. "I am quite parched."

Clearly relieved at the interruption, Phoebe set the pipe down and rang the bell. "Shall we retire to the drawing room?" She ordered tea when the maid appeared, and they went downstairs.

"I think we'll be finished in the master bedchamber in another hour," Anne said. "Then perhaps we should do the study next."

Phoebe nodded. "I shall ask Godwin to go through the front hall closet. That will leave only odds and ends of my husband's scattered around the house. Perhaps Godwin could collect those."

"A good plan. We'll get back to work once we've had a bracing cup of tea."

Over the next half hour, Anne kept the conversation away from any mention of Lord Audley's death or the disposal of his belongings. Phoebe needed time to regain her composure.

When the tea break was over and they were in better spirits, the ladies were keen to get on with their work while they still had the light of day. On their way upstairs they met the butler in the hall.

"A moment please, Godwin," Phoebe said. "I depend on you to dispose of his lordship's coats and other things from the hall closets and boot room, except for the canes. Please set those in his bedchamber."

"Very good, my lady. I shall see it is done yet today."

As they continued up the stairs, Phoebe said, "I know Jasper does not deserve it, but I thought I would offer him one or two of the fancier canes."

"Very fitting," Anne said. Although she felt Jasper didn't merit the least consideration, Phoebe was of a forgiving nature and the gesture appeared to provide her some comfort.

Less than an hour later, the master bedchamber was completed. Phoebe sighed with relief and nodded at Anne and Margret in satisfaction. "Thank you."

"The hardest part should be over now," Margret said, giving Phoebe a bracing look.

"I do hope so," Phoebe murmured.

A few minutes later, Squire Levington was announced, and Phoebe's solemn face lightened in a welcoming smile. At the very least, his friendship offered Phoebe a distraction from the sadness and uncertainty in her life.

• • •

At four that afternoon, Vicar Pope and his wife arrived promptly for tea, and the squire excused himself and left, having made a long visit. It wasn't long before Anne discovered the cause of his hasty departure. While the Popes were pleasant and well-meaning, they offered little in conversation beyond church matters. In fact, Mrs. Pope said only a few words, content to merely beam at her husband as he discussed the current state of the church coffers, his favorite hymns, and his struggle to choose among several possible themes for next week's service. As he began describing the care of the church cemetery, Anne struggled to suppress a yawn.

When the vicar finally paused to accept a second cup of tea, Anne attempted to steer the conversation toward villagers or neighbors who might have had disputes with Lord Audley and thus be potential suspects.

His eyes widened in dismay. "Oh, my lady, banish such thoughts from your mind. No one would bear such uncharitable feelings. We are all most grateful for the living the viscounty provides its tenants and indeed the entire community. And its support for the church. Just last year, his lordship had the roof repaired, and before that…" And Vicar Pope was off again, relating the many ways the Audley estate had provided for the church over the years, most of which had nothing to do with Phoebe's husband, often occurring years or decades before he was in residence.

When the Popes finally left, Anne gave a sigh of relief.

"I tried to tell you," Phoebe said.

Margret laughed. "Oh, dear, I shouldn't laugh, but it was a tedious forty minutes."

"I guess not all clergymen are attuned to the community outside the church. Or at least they don't gossip about their parishioners," Anne added with a smile. Whatever the cause, the Popes would not be contributing to the hunt for murder suspects.

• • •

Needing to get out of the house and stretch her legs, Lady Anne visited the stables in the early evening and wandered along the stalls and boxes.

Finn popped up from polishing harness and asked if he could do anything for her. "Mayhap I could ready a horse or hitch up the team?"

"Not today. Perhaps we'll go riding tomorrow." She smiled at him. "You must be bored with his lordship gone."

"It be a mite quiet," he admitted. "But I n'er be bored among horses."

"I suppose not. Do you know which horses Lord Audley bought earlier this month?"

"Them two," he said, pointing to a pair of nice bay geldings.

Anne saw nothing wrong with them, but she hadn't seen how they moved or behaved. "Is there a problem with them, particularly their markings?" she asked, recalling the circled description on the sale sheet, "all black, no stockings."

Finn chuckled. "Both fine animals, m'lady, but his lordship was tricked."

"Why do you laugh?"

"Seller dyed its white stocking black."

"Oh, I see, so the horse appeared to be all black."

"Sell better." Finn nodded. "'His lordship wanted 'em to match, I'm told."

Had Audley confronted the horse seller about the deception? Was the issue worth killing over? Gentlemen certainly took their horses seriously. So, maybe.

"Have y' heard from him?" Finn asked suddenly.

"Lord Ware? No. I assume we shall before too long. He'll be curious about the housebreaking." Was that not part of the reason she'd written to him, hoping he'd write back? Naturally, he was busy, and men were generally poor correspondents, at best, but yes, she had hoped. It wasn't her only reason. He needed to know about the thief in case it affected his inquiry, and she *had* told him not to rush home, although the odd intrusion into the house had shaken her as much as the others. It was just so inexplicable.

And now she had something else to tell him. Perhaps she would write again and suggest he take a long look at Terrell Stables.

Chapter Twelve

Maidenhead, Buckinghamshire, Monday, 28 March 1814

Lucien's night was restless, not only worrying about the investigation but plagued by concern for Lady Anne and what was happening at Audley Manor. He couldn't get it out of his head that the intruder might return. He finally gave up on further sleep and rose early. The sooner he finished his work here, the sooner he could return to Audley Manor. By nine he was out of the inn and on his way to speak with the lawyers. While it wasn't unusual for a man to consult his solicitor, the timing of Audley's visit so close to his death was interesting and worth exploring.

Upon entering the law offices of The Marchant Brothers, he discovered they were just that, three brothers working together, a solicitor, a barrister, and an accountant. After explaining to the secretary that he wished to speak with whoever was handling Lord Audley's legal affairs, Lucien was introduced to the firm's solicitor, Edward Marchant, a neatly dressed, rather diminutive man, with a mustache and slanted brows that gave him a perpetually somber look.

"My lord Ware," he said, glancing at the card the secretary had handed him. "I understand you are inquiring of the Audley account."

"I am, sir, on behalf of the Sherbourne family and Audley's widow. Questions have arisen regarding the manner of his death, and I hope to piece together his movements and concerns in his final days. I understand he visited your firm on the nineteenth."

Marchant looked at Lucien's card again before showing him into his private office. "In truth, I met with him twice this month."

"I had not realized." Lucien took one of two chairs with leather seats arranged in front of a rather large desk, while the solicitor seated himself and selected a file from a bottom drawer.

Marchant opened the folder to glance inside, then closed it again and lay it on the desk between them. "He visited with me on the fourth and the nineteenth. On the first visit he authorized me to draw up specific documents for him, and he returned to sign them on the nineteenth."

"The day he died," Lucien said.

"Yes, I'm afraid it was."

"Can you tell me the nature of these documents?"

"Ordinarily, I would not, but under the circumstances… Lord Audley asked me to draw up legal documents setting forth his verbal agreement with Lady Audley, providing her with the sole use of the Lower House, a quarterly allowance during his life time, and a generous settlement upon his death. These were in addition to the marriage settlement." He paused, then went on. "Over a year ago, upon the birth of his daughter, he signed another document setting aside funds for the child's dowry." Marchant looked up, frowning. "I am telling you this because his lordship, at the first of our most recent meetings, expressed his desire to legally prevent any of these funds from falling into the hands of his brother-in-law, Jasper Wheatley."

Lucien lifted a brow. "Did he say why?"

"He considered Mr. Wheatley to be a spendthrift. Since the marriage, Lord Audley had provided him with a quarterly allowance for his support and the support of the two sisters remaining at home. The account was regularly over-run. Audley made repeated attempts to curtail his brother-in-law's extravagance, including several signed agreements between them, but every attempt failed."

"Did something particular prompt Audley's most recent action?"

Marchant nodded slowly. "Wheatley's excessive influence over Lady Audley. He had just learned that Wheatley had importuned her to pay more of his debts, leaving her short of funds for her own needs."

"I cannot say I'm surprised. It fits with Wheatley's dubious reputation."

"Indeed, my lord." Marchant leaned forward. "I might add that there were no drafts or notes regarding these documents or his intentions when we collected his lordship's private papers from Audley Manor. He had extensive notes and proposed details that I would have expected to find in his study."

"Did you ask her ladyship about them?"

"She was not aware of the new documents."

Lucien lifted his brows. "Good lord, sir. Are you saying the documents are missing? The provisions unenforceable?"

"Not at all. We have the originals, and copies were sent to his father. Not exactly standard practice, but it was at his request. He suspected Wheatley had recently searched his desk." Marchant leaned back again and steepled his fingers. "In light of Audley's suspicious death, I feel compelled to add that Wheatley came to see me on Monday morning, the twenty-first, immediately after the accident. He claimed to represent Lady Audley and asked to see the Audley file, including the will and any documents regarding the assets of the Sherbourne estate or affecting his sister's future settlements."

"A brash and impudent young man," Lucien said, taken aback in spite of his knowledge of Wheatley's character.

"Just so. As you would expect, I advised him I could not allow him to see the file or anything from it without the expressed or written approval of her ladyship and Lord Sherbourne or the new heir. He was not pleased with my response and informed me of his extreme displeasure before leaving." Marchant stroked his mustache. "Perhaps I should not say this, and I have no proof of a connection, but I found it an odd coincidence that someone broke into our office that very night."

"They didn't—"

"Take the Audley documents? No. To my knowledge, nothing was taken. We keep all signed legal documents in the vault. Of course, the thief could just as easily have been after money or something else."

"Nonetheless, the suspicion is there."

Marchant sighed. "As you say."

"One last thing. Can you tell me what time you saw Audley on the nineteenth?"

"Our appointment was for two, and as I recall my three o'clock was waiting when we finished."

Which didn't explain why Audley was late in meeting his coachman, but perhaps it was nothing more than he'd stopped for a drink before his travel.

"You have given me much to think upon, sir. Thank you for being so candid." Lucien stood and Marchant rose to walk with him to the front of the office.

"My pleasure, Lord Ware." The solicitor hesitated a long moment, then said, "Lord Audley was a responsible caretaker of his estate and family. I was sorry to lose such a valued client." He bowed and wished Lucien a good day.

As Lucien stepped out on the dusty road, he stood for a moment gazing into the distance. He was tempted to go back and ask Marchant what he had nearly said before he stopped himself and offered his condolences instead. Was his hesitation meaningful? Perhaps he felt he had said enough and was simply reluctant to repeat more disparaging gossip about Wheatley. There was certainly enough of that.

Lucien shook his head in disgust. By all accounts, Phoebe's brother was a n'er-do-well, a scoundrel with few scruples, but would he go so far as to kill his sister's husband? And for what? The Sherbournes would provide well for Phoebe and her child but not for her brother. Surely even Jasper wouldn't kill for the small amount he might squeeze from his sister's allowance.

• • •

Lucien spent the rest of the morning searching for Nappy and the two brothers, Charlie and Bobo, but came up empty. After a stop for a tankard of ale, he finally located Nappy, shortly after midday, bullying one of the younger street lads, a boy of seven or eight.

Nappy was smacking him around the head and face, attempting to steal his apple.

"Me apple," the boy pleaded with him. "Fer me mum."

Nappy raised a fist to hit him again. "Give it t' me or ye'll be sorry."

Lucien arrived in time to grab Nappy's arm from behind. He held on when the older boy tried to yank away and gave a nod to the small victim. "Take off, lad. He'll be staying here a bit."

The youngster didn't need further encouragement. He was off at a dead run, his apple clutched tight in one fist.

Nappy struggled to break free and took a swing with his free hand, but Lucien easily caught and held it too. "Now, now. You don't want to do that."

"Let go a me. Be no bus'ness of yers."

"No, none at all," Lucien agreed amiably. "But it doesn't sit well to see a bully pick on a lad no more than a child. Moreover, I have other business with you."

"Oh yeh, wot ya want wit' me?"

Lucien released him, and Nappy jerked his arms away, jutting out his jaw.

Deciding not to mince words, Lucien said, "I want to know who paid you to cut the harness on Lord Audley's coach."

Nappy gave a loud, startled snort. "Y' be daff? Tweren't me. Who's this Audley nob?"

Refusing to accept the young scoundrel's angry denials, Lucien continued to question him for several minutes. Eventually, Nappy admitted he knew who Gordon was, but he grew increasingly defiant under Lucien's pointed accusations. He even refused Lucien's offer of payment in return for the truth.

"What if I was to say I had a witness?" Lucien didn't of course, but he wanted to see Nappy's reaction.

"Bollocks! N'er slit no traces nor kilt bloody nobody. Y'ain't fittin' me up fer no gallows."

In the end, Lucien let him go. He hadn't expected Nappy to admit the criminal act, but after he'd talked to him a while, Lucien knew the young bully hadn't the wit to avoid slipping up under questioning. He wasn't even an average liar. While Nappy might have done the deed if asked—and if paid enough—Lucien felt sure the job hadn't been offered. No one would hire such a cawker to commit a murder that was bound to be investigated, such as the death of an heir to an earldom.

Encouraged by locating Nappy, Lucien stepped up his pace, searching for Charlie and Bobo with renewed hope. According to the brothers' reputation, they wouldn't shy away from any wrong doing, not if paid enough coinage. Most people he spoke with believed the pair would have been hanged long ago, except they just hadn't been caught.

"Yeh, should have hung for sure," one pub owner said. "But they've only got hauled to gaol for fighting on the streets or in pub brawls."

Any arrest of the pair was news to Lucien, and he went straight to the local gaol to see what the constables could tell him.

"Oh, we know Charlie and Bobo Smith all right," the hefty jailor said. "A mean pair. I reckoned they'd rob and kill their own mother if it suited them."

"Smith? I hadn't heard their surname. Is the family around?"

The constable shrugged. "Who knows? Smith isn't their real name. They were dumped on the street when no older than five or six. Wild as foxes, and they grew up mean. I reckon they've done at least two killings, stabbed one fellow and beat another to death, but we can't prove it. No one will talk, too afeared." He shook his head and sighed. "But, we pick them up now and then. They're mean as snakes when they've been drinking."

The Smith brothers were sounding more and more like the men he was looking for, either of which could easily be the small, agile man that Eddie had seen near Audley's carriage. And, dangerous as they were reported to be, Eddie would never have peached on them.

"Yep. Locked them up just a couple weeks ago," the jailor went on. "Knocking a woman around. Should have kept them more than a week, but we only got one gaol cell."

Oh, no. Lucien had a bad feeling… "What was the date of their release?"

The constable pulled a ledger from a cabinet. "Arrested on the 12th of March, released just before midnight on the 19th because of a big tavern brawl. Cell was so full we couldn't squeeze no more in it."

Bloody hell. Lucien heaved a sigh. "I thought we had something going with these two, but you've given them an alibi for Saturday afternoon. And that acquits them of guilt in Audley's death."

Chapter Thirteen

Audley Manor, Buckinghamshire, Tuesday 29 March 1814

Lucien tossed and turned for a second night, unsettled by the housebreaking at Audley Manor. With his search for the mysterious small man at a standstill, he could no longer put off his desire to see for himself that Lady Anne was all right. He couldn't get it out of his head that the prowler might want a second look through the house with perchance disastrous results this time.

Immediately after breakfast, he set out for Audley Manor. With the day bright and clear, a gentle breeze, and Aziz keen to work off some energy, the journey was short, pleasant, and without incident. Although Lucien kept picturing calamities along the way, he arrived to find the ladies peacefully sorting clothes.

"What is all this?" he asked, smiling broadly as he stopped in the doorway of the spare bedchamber they were using as the upper floor center for their packing operation.

"Lucien! You catch us at our housekeeping duties." Anne hurried toward him with a smile, and he met her halfway, taking her hands and placing a kiss upon them. She blushed prettily. "I was not sure when we would see you again. I hope you did not hurry back due to my note."

"Even though I had your reassurances and Levington's, I could not stay away for long with a prowler in the area."

"It has been quiet since Sunday, but it is very pleasing to see you."

"What she means is she missed you and has watched the road several times a day," Margret said with a grin.

"If I had known, I would have come sooner," he said, meeting Lady Anne's eyes with a meaningful look. Good lord, how good it was to see her.

Lady Phoebe smiled. "It is a pleasure to have you with us, my lord." Her face turned serious. "Were you able to learn anything new in town?"

"Only enough to leave me more perplexed than ever. I shall have to go back, but I wished to see for myself that you ladies were safe, and I have at least two local inquiries I need to make. Those can wait, however, until I have heard all your news."

"Perhaps over tea?" Lady Phoebe suggested. "You must be parched after your ride."

"Oh, let us do so," Margret said. "A break from sorting and packing would be nice. I'm always ready for tea."

Lucien smiled. "It would be most welcome."

Lady Phoebe rang the bell, ordered a tea tray for the drawing room, and Lucien offered her his arm. Once they were settled in the drawing room—Lucien next to Lady Anne—and tea was poured, he asked about the housebreaking.

"It all happened very quickly," Anne said. "We had just arrived from attending church when Elsie started baying at the master bedchamber door." She turned to Margret. "Tell him what you saw."

"I opened the door to see what was upsetting the hound, and there he was…a strange man was climbing out the window. He had the box from the undertaker under one arm. When Elsie bounded forward, the fellow jumped right out the window onto his horse below. I recall being astonished, and I guess I screamed because everyone came running. Then I shouted for William to chase him."

"William is one of the footmen," Anne clarified. "And he had a pistol."

"The thief was armed?" Lucien asked, rather startled.

"No, the footman. William and Elsie gave chase, but the rider got away."

The rest of the story came out with Lucien asking questions now and then but mostly just allowing them to talk.

"Just to clarify," he said, when they'd finished, "after you gathered up the contents of the box, the only items missing were the five Lady Anne mentioned in her letter—the calling cards and two folded papers." He looked at Anne, and she nodded.

"I wrote down everything, but you can see the remaining items for yourself. We put them back in the box."

He grinned at her. "Your idea, doubtless."

"I knew you would want to examine them."

"And I do." His eyes twinkled. "Thank you, my lady."

"Let me ring for Godwin and have him bring it down," Lady Phoebe said, pulling the bell. When the butler appeared at the door, she sent him on the errand.

"While we're waiting," Lucien said, raising a brow at Anne, "tell me about the two folded papers. What was on them? Anything special?"

She gave him a wry look. "At the time I wrote to you, I did not believe so, but as it turned out, I was wrong about one of them. The first was just the name of the Goose & Gander Inn. The second was a sale sheet from the horse barn in Maidenhead. I did a bit of investigating on my own regarding that paper. All very safe," she added.

Godwin's return with the box interrupted her, and he handed the box to Lucien.

He set it down, still looking at Lady Anne. "Before we deal with the box, please go on, my lady."

"Oh, no," she said blithely. "I am happy to wait until you have looked at everything."

"My lady?"

"Lord Ware." She gave him an innocent look but her eyes danced. "I may not even tell you what I discovered. You will find out quickly enough for yourself." And she looked away, a smile playing on her lips.

What was she up to now? Clearly it was nothing too serious for her to be so playful about it. He could afford to bide his time.

"Very well." He set the box on a table and looked through the contents. "Lady Phoebe, I assume you've seen these items. Did they all belong to your husband?"

"I'm fairly certain they did," she said. "I'd seen them all before."

He picked up the list Lady Anne had made, and read her notes on each of the paper items. His gaze shifted to the calling cards, and his hand froze. Good lord, Charles Raven.

He paused, all the while trying to work out in his head why Lord Audley would have Raven's card. "I know Edward Marchant is your solicitor," he finally said. "Do you know the other two men, Lady Phoebe? Joseph Galvin and Charles Raven?"

"Galvin is a local shopkeeper, leather goods," Lady Phoebe said. "I doubt his card is significant, but Charles Raven…I know nothing of him, possibly another historian."

"Perhaps," Lucien said vaguely. "I shall see if I can locate him." Lady Anne was looking at him as though she knew he was keeping something back, but he had no wish to distress Lady Phoebe with the story of the card cheating and duel until he knew what part, if any, Audley had played in the affair. He had assumed her husband was an innocent bystander, but now he wasn't so sure.

Before Anne could ask about Raven, Lucien turned his attention to the missing papers. "The inn written on the paper is where he stayed on both recent trips and apparently in the past. The sale's sheet is on one of the geldings he bought from Terrell stables three weeks ago." He read the notes she'd made about the circled phrase "all black, no stockings" and began to smile. He looked at Anne. "I'm afraid I have the advantage of you in knowing the reputation of this seller. Am I correct in assuming the horse advertised as all black actually has white stockings?"

"Oh, botheration," she said laughingly indignant. "You are no fun at all, my lord."

"So, I'm right?" he teased.

"Yes, it has one white stocking," she said.

"How is this possible?" Lady Phoebe asked. "I know Lord Audley would not have inspected the horse as he should, but even he would notice a white stocking."

"He might not if it was dyed," Anne explained. "I spoke with Finn, Lord Ware's groom, and he'd heard the tale from your stable lads. Your coachman discovered the deception the day after the sale when they were arranging to bring the new horses home. Your husband went back to the horse auction to complain, but the seller had already left town, and Audley was impatient to get home."

"So, he was swindled," Lady Phoebe said.

"Well, yes and no," Anne said. "Finn says the gelding is worth every bit of the price Lord Audley paid. He just isn't all black."

"I shall examine him more closely if you like," Lucien said. "But I'm confident Finn has the right of it."

"Oh, would you?" Lady Phoebe said. "Just to be certain."

"My pleasure." He set the box back on the table. "I see nothing else of importance in here. Are you sure the thief took nothing aside from the box?"

"We've inspected the house for things easily portable—small paintings, silver, jewelry, and the like. It all appears to be there," Margret said. "Lady Phoebe even looked through the papers in Audley's writing desk."

"I'm not sure I'd know if papers had been stolen," Lady Phoebe amended. "Mr. Marchant removed most of them, anything he felt was important, so I really could not truly judge." She sighed. "I fail to understand what any of this is about."

"I don't know either…yet," Lucien said, "but I believe I shall in time. Getting to the truth may take a while. I have several lines of inquiry to follow."

"Several?" Lady Phoebe repeated faintly, her eyes widening. "Are there that many people who wanted to kill my husband?"

"By no means, my lady. With so little to start with, everything he did during his last few days and weeks must be examined, including minor disputes or even potential areas of disagreement. I'm looking both in Maidenhead and around Audley, so it could be a lengthy process. So far, I've spoken with a number of people, and I'm looking for a stranger who was seen near the coach that last afternoon in Maidenhead. It doesn't mean he had anything to do with the accident, but I have to keep following every possibility."

"A rather daunting task," Lady Phoebe said.

"More time-consuming than anything," he assured her. "I hope to have some answers for you before this is over."

"Does anything you've learned explain our intruder?" Anne asked.

Lucien lifted a shoulder. "Not right off, but then maybe there is no connection. Your intruder may have been a common thief taking advantage of a household with no master in residence." He set down his empty tea cup. "Now, if you will excuse me, I wish to speak with Godwin and William and look around a bit. Afterward, I'm going to see Squire Levington." He deliberately did not bring up his concern about the squire. If the man's intentions were honorable, there was no reason for Lady Phoebe to know Lucien ever had any doubts.

He turned to Anne with a smile. "I shall return in time for a stroll in the garden, my lady."

"A pleasure I shall await. In the meantime, we have plenty of work to keep us busy."

"Give the squire our regards," Lady Phoebe said.

"Oh, yes, do." Margret chuckled.

Anne met Lucien's gaze with a knowing smile. Yes, there definitely was a certain friendship, perhaps fondness, between Lady Phoebe and Squire Levington, and it appeared to be the worst kept secret in the manor.

While the ladies returned to their task, Lucien went in search of the butler. Godwin was happy to walk him through the details of Sunday's burglary, but when they finished, Lucien knew no more than he'd gotten from the ladies.

"Did you determine how he got in?"

"No, my lord, but we were all at church. A few of us leave early to get home before Lady Audley, but he could have entered anytime in the previous hour."

"And you heard nothing when you arrived, and no one saw the horse standing under the window?"

"I'm afraid not." Godwin shook his head. "It is hard to explain, I know, but that is the truth. I am thankful Elsie chased him off. I hate to think what would have happened if Mrs. Wycliff had come upon him without warning."

Lucien nodded but, in truth, he wondered if Margret had really been at risk. From the story he'd heard, the thief might have been more frightened than she was. Nonetheless, even frightened people can be dangerous.

He found William and the other footman Harry in the upstairs hall moving the trunks that had already been filled with winter clothing and extra bedding. The packed trunks were being stored in a downstairs room near the kitchen until they could be moved to the Dower House. The two young men were tugging on a particularly heavy trunk.

"If you can wait a moment, my lord," William said looking up. "I'd like to get this one down the hall and out of the way of the ladies."

"No hurry," Lucien said, watching as they attempted to navigate it through the bedchamber door. When it got stuck, Lucien went over to give them a hand.

William immediately stood up, shock written across his face. "My lord, this is not a task for you."

"Nonsense. When you've been in the war you learn to do many things you might not have considered before. I certainly know how to move a trunk. Now, shall we get this done." He took hold of one end and among them they had the trunk into the hall, and the lads moved it from there.

Two minutes later, William was back, while Harry ran down to the kitchen for a cup of tea. "I beg pardon for keeping you waiting, my lord. Did you have a task for me?"

"Only to answer a few questions. Shall we go downstairs to the study?"

When they arrived, Lucien took a chair by the window, and William, although invited to sit, chose to stand. "Tell me about the intruder, William. Did you see his face?"

"No, my lord. He had an cap pulled low. I couldn't even see his hair. And he wore an old greatcoat, too big for him, kind of a dirty brown. He looked sort of like a laborer, but I don't think he was. His boots were shiny, and the horse was a prime one."

"You are very observant."

William grinned. "Thank you, my lord. I knew somebody would want to know."

"Any idea whether he was young or old?" Lucien was already sure the intruder had been young judging by his exit, but he wanted to hear William's opinion.

"By the way he sat a horse, I'd say he was near my age, uh, nineteen, and my height too."

"Would you describe him as a small man?"

William shook his head. "I wouldn't say so."

"I understand you fired a pistol at him."

"Not exactly at him. I didn't want to hurt anybody, but I didn't want him to come back either."

Lucien lifted a brow. "I find it unusual that a footman would be carrying a pistol. Did Lady Audley know?"

William looked uneasy. "No, my lord."

"And the butler?"

"It was my idea, sir."

"That is not what I asked. Did Godwin know you were carrying a pistol? I could ask him myself, I suppose, but no one is in trouble, lad."

William sighed. "We all talked it over after the master died. It didn't seem safe for Lady Audley to be all alone with no one to protect her, particularly with that brother of hers sneaking around."

"Wheatley?" Lucian interrupted. "I knew he had been to visit. Are you saying he's been here when Lady Audley was not aware?"

William nodded. "At least twice. Godwin caught him coming in the back door when the mistress was resting one afternoon. Another time, a stable boy seen him looking in the window of this room. He took off running when he knew he'd been seen."

"Interesting," Lucien said thoughtfully. "Has he continued this behavior since Lady Anne and Mrs. Wycliff have been here?"

"No, sir. I'd guess he was afraid they'd catch him."

"And well he might be. If you see him sneaking around again, tell Lady Anne. Now, go on about the pistol."

"Well, after we agreed someone should have a pistol, I offered. I'm a good shot, and my father had this pistol from the war. After the intruder was here, Mr. Levington asked that I continue to watch over the ladies."

"He knew you were armed?"

"Yes, my lord, but now that you're here…"

"I shall be leaving again," Lucien said. "I daresay you have acted in Lady Audley's best interests. I would not ordinarily encourage such behavior, but under the circumstances, are you willing to carry on for a few more days?"

William stood a bit straighter. "Yes, my lord, of course. I'd be proud."

"Then it's settled. Thank you, William. I think it is best not to worry Lady Audley with this, but I shall inform Lady Anne. She also has a pistol, and knows how to use it if you should need assistance." William's eyes grew bigger. "Perhaps you should keep that knowledge to yourself."

The lad grinned. "Yes, my lord. I can surely do that."

"Mind you, William. I am hopeful you will not shoot anyone."

"Yes, sir." His grin broadened. "Me, too."

Lucien dismissed him and rose to gaze thoughtfully out the window. While he had been hesitant for the lad to shoulder such responsibility, there were younger lads on the Continent fighting against Napoleon. Indeed, Lucien hadn't been much older when he first reported to Wellington. William had acted swiftly and with good judgment on Sunday, and Lucien concluded he would sleep easier knowing William was guarding the household while he was away.

Chapter Fourteen

Audley Manor and thereabouts, Tuesday, 29 March 1814

Good lord. Lucien whistled to himself, gazing at the drop below. After talking with William, he'd climbed the staircase, entered the master bedchamber, and gone straight to the window to view for himself the distance to the ground. Quite a hard landing for the thief and requiring a well-trained horse.

Descending to the main floor again, he walked outside for a closer look. The flower bed along the side of the house bore the prints left by hooves and by the servants searching for the box's spilled contents. None of it told him a thing other than the thief had been athletic.

The rest he had to surmise: the intruder had either been inside the house before or had it under surveillance a few days to determined the layout of the rooms. Then he had left his horse under the window of the master bedchamber for a swift escape and likely slipped in the back door while the household was at church.

But none of that provided a hint of why the thief had taken such a risk or if he'd found what he came for.

• • •

On his way to see Squire Levington, Lucien spotted him just turning onto the road to the village. "Squire," he called. "A word, sir." Lucien nudged his horse into a brisk trot and reined to a halt beside the other man.

"I have a court hearing today," Levington said. "Ride with me. We can talk on the way, and I shall buy you a pint at the tavern."

"An offer I gladly accept. I am interested in your thoughts on Sunday's housebreaking."

Levington nodded, and they set off for the village.

After a moment, Lucien added, "But before we get into that, I have something I must ask you."

Levington frowned. "You sound serious."

"I'm…concerned over something I learned in town in regards to you." Lucien paused to give the squire a chance to bring it up himself.

"Me?" Levington turned in his saddle to stare at him. "I cannot imagine what."

"You stabled your horse in Maidenhead overnight on the eighteenth, placing you in town the day Audley's harness was cut. Why didn't you tell me?"

Levington brows shot up. He appeared genuinely surprised. "Confound it, Ware. Surely you are not accusing me of murdering him? What possible motive could I have? Audley and I were friends. I was the one who told his family about the harness."

"That is all well and good, sir, but it is strange you didn't mention it. And you still haven't answered my question."

With his face set in lines of annoyance, the squire turned his gaze to the road ahead. "It didn't seem relevant. I didn't see Audley in town—didn't even know when he was going for certain." Levington sighed. "Yes, I made a quick trip on that Friday to visit my tailor, but I was home by mid-morning on Saturday, long before the damage was done."

Lucien held his response while they dismounted in front of the village tavern. "Is there someone who can verify that?"

Levington's jaw tightened. "I am trying not to be put off by your questions, Ware, but yes, there are several in my household who could. If you'll follow me, however, I believe I can put your mind at ease."

"I would welcome that, sir."

They left the horses in the care of a village lad and walked down the street. "As I was returning home that morning," Levington said, "one of my carriage horses threw a shoe, and I stopped at the blacksmith's to have it replaced."

The smithy was working with a nervous mare, and they had to wait a few minutes until the last hoof was done and the owner led her away. As soon as he saw who was waiting, he smiled at Levington. "Don't tell me your horse has thrown another shoe?"

"No, everything is fine. I'm trying to recall exactly when I was here."

The farrier scratched his ear, looking a bit perplexed but answered readily enough. "A week ago last Saturday."

"Do you recollect what time of day?" Levington asked. "It's important."

"Well, sure. It was before me missus brought my midday meal."

The squire grinned. "Thank you for jogging my memory."

The big man shrugged. "Any time, squire." If he continued to wonder why it was so important, he didn't say so, but picked up a damaged wheel and set to work.

On the way back to the tavern, Lucien attempted to regain the squire's good humor. "I meant no offense, sir. This is not the first inquiry I have conducted, and I've learned to ask the hard questions early on before misunderstandings arise."

Levington's stiff back appeared to relax a bit. "I have noticed you are comfortable asking direct and rather personal questions. I suppose I should have expected it. I must admit Audley had talked rather more than I had previously indicated about the secret work you and his brother did in the war and have continued in some manner for Whitehall."

Ah, Graham, you should not have shared that. "An indiscretion I hope you will not repeat to others, sir."

The squire gave him a wry look. "Certainly not, if you wish it so."

"It would be appreciated. Sir, if I have not offended you beyond pardon, perhaps we could talk about the prowler at Audley Manor."

Levington laughed, shaking off his tension. "I cannot hold it against you for doing what I would have done in your situation. As for the thief, I assumed he had been watching the house long before he went in. Thus, I've had one of my men riding the perimeter four times a day to prevent it from happening again."

"An excellent precaution," Lucien said, somewhat surprised the squire had taken such a defensive measure. "It could also be someone who has been in the house before, but most locals wouldn't be familiar with the layout of the bedchambers."

"I would not disregard family members," Levington said. "Jasper Wheatley has been seen lurking around the village. I cannot say he'd break into the house, for he has been more direct in the past by wheedling whatever he wanted out of Lady Phoebe."

"The servants have caught him twice trying to get in or peeking in windows prior to Lady Anne and Mrs. Wycliff's arrival."

"Well, there you go. I guess I'm not that surprised, but I can't see him jumping from the window. He'd kill himself or break a leg if he tried."

Lucien chuckled. "I have to agree."

"I've asked around about strangers. A few have been noted, but it isn't uncommon with the village sitting on the road to Maidenhead. No one reported being asked questions regarding Audley Manor."

"I'm relieved to hear that. You have done a fair amount of investigation and protecting the manor while I've been gone," Lucien said. "I appreciate it."

"No more than I should as Magistrate. I felt a personal responsibility for the ladies in your absence."

"I daresay they felt much safer due to your visits, and I understand you recruited William."

Levington laughed. "I believe he recruited himself. In any event, he is a level-headed lad. I assume you've talked with him."

"I have and asked him to carry on when I leave. I'm hoping the thief won't be back, but it's hard to make a good assessment when I don't know what he was after."

Levington shrugged. "It had to be something small if he expected to carry if off on horseback, and he must have thought it was in Audley's possession at the time he died. Otherwise, why would he have taken the undertaker's box?"

"I thought it might be a document," Lucien said. "But the only papers in that box had the name of the Goose & Gander Inn on one, and the other was from the Spring Horse Sale." He related the deceit regarding the gelding purchased from Terrell Stable. "I hardly think it was worth killing for or stealing the sale sheet. As for other papers in the house, Lady Phoebe says the solicitor removed anything important. The thief should have known that would happen. The only other items of possible interest were three calling cards."

"Did any of the names on them mean anything to you?"

"Perhaps," Lucien said, "but that's a longer story I'll reserve for the pub, and so far I don't see its importance. Which leaves me at a loss over the intruder's objective."

"Likewise, which is why I asked William to keep particular watch on the study and library," Levington said as they reached the tavern door. "If the thief is looking for papers or something else Audley might have hidden, those rooms are the most likely he'd search next."

"Yes, I'd say so, and the prospect worries me. William would do his best to frighten a prowler away, but I wonder if he could shoot someone if necessary. Perhaps we should set a trap while I'm here, provide the thief with an opportunity to return and hope he gives in to temptation so we can catch him."

"While you think on how we might do it, allow me to buy you the pint. I still have time before my hearing to discuss everything else that's happened."

• • •

It took more than one pint of ale, but the tavern was warm and comfortable, and the gentlemen chatted for almost an hour before Levington was fully apprised of Lucien's recent activities in town.

The squire slowly shook his head. "Egad, Ware. Your trip raised so many questions it is difficult to know what to pursue. Have you a sense of which path holds the answers?"

Lucien sighed heavily. "Honestly, I hoped you could help me sort it out."

The squire laughed and pulled out his pocket watch. "Tell you what, I have a bit of magistrate business I need to take care of in a few minutes, but I should be done by two thirty—it's a dispute over water rights to a pond, and I already know how I'm going to rule. They both need the water, and I'm going to order them to set up a schedule for watering their herds. Afterward, I have a very good brandy back at the house. I am thinking it might assist us in solving our problems. What do you say?"

Lucien grinned. "I'm willing to try." The case might not be sorted that easily, but a chat over brandy could go a long way to soothing the last of Levington's annoyance. "While you conduct your hearing, I should have time to stop by Percy Slade's place. Isn't he the farmer who had a land dispute with Audley?"

"I told you, it isn't anything that would lead to murder."

"But I need to question him, do I not?"

"I suppose you do. Then you'd best come to court with me. I understand Slade is a witness in the water dispute."

"Truly?" Lucien was surprised by the coincidence.

"It's a small community, Ware."

And informal too. The magistrate hearings were held in a backroom of the tavern. Once Slade, a short, pudgy man with receding dark brown hair, gave his testimony, Lucien found the landowner sitting in the front room of the tavern having a drink with a man he introduced as his friend Jed Harris.

"I guess you two want to talk," Harris said abruptly, scowling as he set down his empty tankard with a decisive clunk and rose. "Got things I need to be doing."

"See you later, Jed."

The man didn't reply as he tromped out.

"Sorry, for interrupting." Lucien took the bench Harris had just vacated. "Your friend seemed upset." Or downright angry might be a better characterization.

Slade frowned as he watched his friend go out the door, closing it loudly behind him. "Yeh, I guess. He's had more than his share of bad luck this last year. Lost his tenant farm, and then his wife run off." He shook his head. "It left him bitter. A pity. But you didn't seek me out to talk about Harris. What can I do for you?"

When Lucien explained his interest in the land dispute between him and Audley, Slade became defensive. "Wait just a minute, your lordship." Slade eyed him. "I heard you been asking questions because you think he was murdered, but don't look at me. Sure we had our differences—that piece of land is mine—but it's not worth killing over."

"I'm not accusing anyone, just asking questions. Help me to understand your problem."

Slade huffed skeptically but went on. "A large berry patch grows at the northwest corner where our lands meet. We'd always shared it until Sherbourne's estate manager fenced it off five years ago."

"Before Lord Audley took over the property?"

"Yep. I told Gibson, the former estate man, he shouldn't have fenced it, that it was Slade property, but he wouldn't listen. When Audley and his wife arrived, I tried to talk to him too, but he acted as though it was a settled matter. He said he'd talk with his father, and that's where we left it." He shrugged. "So, you see, there was no big quarrel, just a gentlemen's disagreement. Guess I'll need to speak with the new lord now."

"I'll pass on your concern to the family."

"All I want is for them to take the bloody fence down. My missus makes jam every year off the gooseberries in that patch, and that hedge fence has made her feel like she's taken what ain't ours. That's just not right. Besides, Audley hasn't done the early spring pruning those bushes need."

"I'm sure you can work out something with the new viscount or his father." Lucien rose hiding a smile and sought his own table while waiting for Levington. As the squire had said, Slade was an unlikely suspect. Lucien had not yet heard of murder being committed over a few jars of jam.

• • •

Late that afternoon, after sharing a very find brandy and a lengthy discussion with the squire, Lucien returned to Audley Manor in time for the promised walk in the garden with Lady Anne. He explained to her why he had been gone so long.

"Did you and Levington solve anything?" she asked.

"Not truly, but I believe I've been forgiven for doubting him." He smiled down at her, thoroughly enjoying the closeness of her arm linked with his. "Have you had a pleasant day?"

"Oh, no, you don't get to change the subject," she said. "I want to hear all the things you've learned that you didn't tell Lady Phoebe. I know you were holding back."

"Only to spare her the facts she didn't need to hear."

"I understand your reasons," she said, her eyes filled with approval, "but you need not spare me."

"Nor did I intend to do so."

As the temperature was rather mild, they indulged in a long walk while he shared the details previously omitted, except for the ambush in Maidenhead thicket. Since he hadn't been harmed, he saw no reason to worry her needlessly. He did, however, provide all the particulars of Jasper Wheatley's contemptible behavior.

"He broke into the law office?" she asked, sounding shocked.

"I cannot say for sure, nor could the solicitor, but it is suspicious. I'll leave it to you if you want to share this with Mrs. Wycliff."

"I certainly shall and perhaps some of it with Lady Phoebe too. She knows what her brother is like and has stood up to him with us there to support her, but I'm worried about when we are gone. Knowing the entire truth might keep her from falling for his lies and half-truths again."

"It is your decision. It is pleasing to hear she is getting stronger. I thought she acted more confident than just a few days ago." He smiled down at her. "You and Mrs. Wycliff have been a good influence."

"Are you sure you want to encourage me, my lord?"

"Always." He saw the surprise on her upturned face and gently squeezed her arm. "Your independent spirit is one of your very admirable qualities."

"Thank you. Although, I'm sure, not one of the easiest to accept at times." He laughed, and she leaned her head against his shoulder. "When are you returning to Maidenhead?"

"In the morning."

She turned head to stare at him. "So soon? I had hoped we had another day or two. I'm sorry, I should not complain. You're here now." She put her head back on his shoulder. "Tell me what you will do when you're there."

"Continue the search for the unknown small man, and I feel I need to speak with the solicitor again. I cannot shake the feeling he withheld something that could be important. And I hope to find a letter waiting from London regarding the backgrounds of several people."

"What will you do about Raven's calling card?"

"That is certainly a puzzle. I was already curious about him, but the card appears to tie Audley to the notorious card cheating affair, which was, in truth, a disguised but blundered attempt to murder Charles Raven. Perhaps the same man killed Audley."

"Oh, Lucien, do be careful," she said, stopping and grasping his arm with both of her hands. "If Ponsonby was willing to kill Raven and killed Lord Audley, he would surely try to kill anyone who might expose him."

And may have already made the attempt in the fog of Maidenhead Thicket, Lucien thought. The fear he saw on her face was why he hadn't told her, and he didn't tell her now.

"I shall be careful, my dear. This wouldn't be my first brush with a killer." He kissed her on the forehead.

"I know, but…" She seemed to catch herself. "I have to get used to this, do I not? The constant risks you take?"

"No more than I do," he said, laughing. "While I was in Maidenhead, I imagined you were in all kinds of danger, and it nearly brought me galloping here Sunday night as soon as I heard about the intruder. I had to give myself a severe scold."

"I never intend to worry you, my lord, but truly this incident was not of my doing."

"I *do* know that." He pulled her close for just a moment before moving them on down the path. What he didn't say was how devastating the thought was of losing her. The constant risks to her kept him from asking for her hand in marriage. She wouldn't be in these situations but for his inquiries, and he often thought she would be better off if he ended their informal engagement and walked away. But that too felt unbearable.

Chapter Fifteen

Maidenhead, Wednesday, 30 March 1814

Shortly after breakfast on Wednesday, Lucien and Lady Anne ducked behind the staircase and shared a kiss in private before he left for Maidenhead. On his way to the stables, he asked the butler if Charles Raven had ever visited Lord Audley at the manor and was told no, just as he'd anticipated.

Since the Goose & Gander was holding his room and thus his mail, Lucien was keen to know if he had responses from London regarding the names he'd sent, particularly Ponsonby and Raven. Knowing that Raven's card had been among Audley's belongings and among the stolen items had raised that line of inquiry to the top of his list.

Where and when had Audley gotten the card? Had the two men had some kind of conversation on the night of the notorious card game or in the morning at the duel? If so, what had they discussed? Did Audley learn something that his murderer was afraid he'd reveal? Raven might be the only person who could answer that.

When Lucien arrived at the Goose & Gander near mid-morning, the innkeeper gestured for him to come to the bar counter. "Thought you should know a gentleman was looking for you last night. He hung around for a while but eventually just disappeared. He didn't give me a name. In fact, he was rather evasive."

Lucien lifted a brow. "Can you describe him?"

"About your height and age, reddish brown hair, brown eyes. As I said, a gentleman."

Lucien nodded, his lips twitching as he suspected who it might be. He thanked the publican and took the stairs two at a time. When he reached his door, the tell-tale thread was missing, but the door was locked. He used the key and stepped inside. The gentleman in question was sprawled across the bed fully dressed.

"Picked the lock, I see. Did you spend the night?"

"Naturally. Why pay for a room when this one wasn't being used?" Sherry grinned at him. "I fell asleep while waiting. I thought you'd return during the night."

"I was at Audley Manor. They had an intruder, and I wanted to be certain Anne was all right."

Sherry sat up, sitting on the edge of the bed. "I trust she was. And Phoebe and Margret?"

"Yes, of course. They were all well. It was foolish of me to worry."

"Do you know who the intruder was? Any connection with Graham's death?"

"Hard to say. It might have been a local thief hoping to take advantage of the ladies, except he didn't take much. He was frightened off by a hound and Mrs. Wycliff—possibly before he completed his task—yet he took a mortuary box. And a calling card in it may tie the thievery to events in Maidenhead." He sighed and ran a hand through his hair. "I have three or four angles I'm pursuing, but I cannot see how or which ones might fit together. Before I try to explain what I've just said, tell me why you're here."

"I told you I would come when I could."

"True, but I didn't expect you this soon or in my lodging in Maidenhead. How did you know to come here?"

"I'm a spy. I discover things." Sherry grinned. "In this case, I was in London on estate business, stopped at Whitehall, and Mr. Sloane and Wycliff told me you'd requested information on several men. Since the estate work was nearly done, I left Father to finish up the final papers and assisted Wycliff in running down the information you wanted. I thought the results were worth bringing to you directly." He picked up two papers from the table. "Sloane wrote down what he found on Slade and Levington, but I can sum it up for you. Slade is slightly behind on his taxes, but that is all Sloane found on him. Squire Levington was better known—a wealthy country gentleman with an excellent reputation, a solid citizen. Then Wycliff and I made inquiries on Terrell and Donnelly, and Tattersall's had plenty to say about them. The horse auctioneer was disgusted to learn they were working together. Both have been barred from Tattersall's for trickery."

"Not at all surprising," Lucien said. "They ran a minor swindle on your brother, but the horse is sound. Donnelly lost his job and is no longer around. I may drop that line of inquiry. What about Ponsonby and Raven? I notice you haven't mentioned either one."

"There is nothing to tell. We couldn't find a trace of them."

"Are you serious?"

"I'm rather certain that neither man exists, not by those names."

Lucien sat on the room's only chair. "Devil it, Sherry. I had doubts about Ponsonby, but it had not occurred to me that Charles Raven was a trickster too. Now, I wonder if the crooked card game and duel were all part of an elaborate scheme set up by the two of them."

Sherry's brows lifted. "A duel! What card game? Are you telling me my bookish half-brother got involved in something disreputable?"

"Honestly, I don't know." Lucien stood and gestured toward the door. "Would you care to partake in a pint of ale from the pub? I shall tell you everything I know, but it will take quite a while."

"I shall need a meal too," Sherry said, grabbing his hat from the table and following Lucien out the door.

• • •

An hour later, Sherry finished his ale, pushed it and his empty plate aside, and shook his head. "I cannot believe how many tangled lines of inquiry you have uncovered—the squire and Phoebe's apparent *tendre* for one another, giving them both a plausible motive; a land dispute with a neighbor; and a spendthrift brother-in-law that covets the estate. And then there is this horse swindler who Graham may have been about to expose, not to mention the card cheating and the duel, involving two men who have mysteriously disappeared. Egad, Lucien, where do we start?"

"That depends on whether you are here to stay."

"I am. Father can handle the estate work from there, and he was most anxious for me to come to Audley."

"That is good news, my friend. Is Wycliff still pursuing the London end of the inquiry on Ponsonby and Raven?"

"He is. So is Mr. Stone. If they learn anything, they will let us know."

Lucian rubbed his chin thoughtfully. "At least one of us should remain in Maidenhead for now. Although a few people around Audley village were annoyed with your brother or even wished him to perdition, the damage to the harness occurred here in town, and he might have been involved with the duel, also occurring in town. I'm tempted to suggest you return to London and assist Wycliff in tracking down Ponsonby or Raven. Their disappearance bothers me, particularly as they could be the key to everything else."

"What about the housebreaking at the manor? Are the ladies in any danger?"

"I don't believe so, or I would not have left them. If the intruder got what he wanted, he won't be back…but I confess I cannot rest easy. What if I'm wrong? Lady Anne is courageous and resourceful. and she is armed—as is William, the young footman—but she is no match for a man's physical strength, and I'm not sure William could kill a man if it was necessary."

Sherry shrugged. "Why don't I go to Audley while you continue your pursuits here? I could hang around a few days, explore a bit. If everything stays quiet, and Wycliff still hasn't found any trace of Ponsonby or Raven, I'll go back to London and double our efforts."

"I might even return to Audley by then." Lucien frowned in thought. "If you decide to leave before I get there, will you talk with Anne and ascertain if she is feeling comfortable? If not, take her and Margret to London with you. And Lady Phoebe, if she'll go. Otherwise, I'm certain the squire will look after her."

"Without question, I would consult with Lady Anne, but you know what she'd say. You forgot to mention how confident she is—and fearless. She would keep to herself any reservations she might have."

"This time could be different. She is responsible for Margret and Lady Phoebe…and you might mention that by way of reminder." He gave a wry smile. "For you are correct, she and Margret can be a bit impulsive."

Sherry laughed. "You are a master of understatement, my friend."

Chapter Sixteen

"Who's there?" a sharp voice called in the dark.

Sherry reined General to a halt outside the Audley Manor stable. It was nearly ten in the evening. "Andrew Sherbourne. Pardon my late arrival."

He heard muffled voices inside the stable, then a small figure ran outside, followed by a slightly larger man. "Lord Sherry?"

"Finn? Is that you?" Sherry dismounted. "Ware didn't tell me he'd left you here."

"He took Aziz. I'm lookin' after the bays."

"Oh, of course. He brought the coach for the ladies."

"Beg pardon, milord," the other man said. "I'm Joseph, the Audley head groom. Allow me to take your horse."

"This is General." Sherry handed the reins over. "Be good to him."

"Yes, sir. Sorry for the challenge, milord. I didn't realize it was you."

"How could you?" Sherry said amiably. "I did not have time to notify anyone of my arrival. Are the ladies still awake?"

"Lights are on. Last I heard, they were playing cards."

"Thank you. I should get up to the house before it gets any later."

Sherry glanced into the stable. The building was small but clean and well-maintained. It spoke well for the condition of the rest of the estate. While Graham might have taken little interest in the running of Audley, someone obviously had. Sherry turned and walked toward the manor. He'd been to the estate when he was a boy, but it was strange to realize the viscounty was now his to use as he wished until such time as he succeeded to the earldom and became the actual owner of this estate and much, much more.

Reaching the front entrance, he found the butler already waiting for him. The stable lads would have sent someone running to alert the household to the new viscount's arrival.

"Your lordship," the man said with a low bow. "Welcome to Audley. I am your butler Godwin, and I have sent word of your presence to Lady Audley. She and the other ladies are in the drawing room."

"Thank you, Godwin." Sherry handed him his hat. "I shall find them."

The ladies were talking among themselves, their cards abandoned on the table, when he walked in. They rose and hurried forward.

"My lord," Lady Phoebe said with a small curtsey, "Welcome to your home."

He stepped forward and took both her hands. "I am sorry such sad tidings bring us together. My condolences in your grief. If there is anything you or Eliza need, you have only to ask."

"Thank you, but I am well provided for and have been blessed with such lovely company." She turned her head to smile at Anne and Margret.

"Ladies," he grinned at them. "I hope they have not led you astray, Lady Phoebe."

"We have not," Lady Anne protested, her eyes twinkling. "Why did you not tell us you were coming?"

"I was not sure I was. I went to Maidenhead first to locate Ware." He kept a straight face while adding, "He was bemoaning the fact he had left you alone and insisted I hasten to protect you from further intruders."

"What!" Mrs. Wycliff exclaimed. "We managed that incident quite well without him."

"He is teasing you," Lady Anne said with composure. "It is good to see you, my lord. I hope you have come to tell us what Lucien has not and will share the latest news from London."

"I shall willingly accede to your request, although I believe you know everything about the inquiry except my reports from London."

Lady Phoebe rang for wine and tea, and Sherry accommodated the ladies' curiosity by relating recent events regarding the inquiry but only in the broadest strokes. He agreed with Lucien that Lady Phoebe need not suffer through all the details. He would find a private time to talk with Lady Anne, and no doubt Mrs. Wycliff would join them.

"As I told Lord Ware, none of the things he learned sound like Lord Audley," Lady Phoebe protested. "He never gambled, and I cannot comprehend why he would attend something so dreadful as a duel. He would have abhorred the incivility of it all."

"We don't know his thinking, but it is clear a horse seller took him to the card game, a man by the name of Donnelly. Perhaps they were discussing business. According to what Lucien was told, Audley mostly watched rather than gamble. His attendance at the duel is another matter, but the calling card that was stolen from here belonged to one of the gentleman involved."

"Then Lord Audley knew him," Mrs. Wycliff said. "Perhaps from London."

"It is possible." Sherry hesitated, glancing at Lady Phoebe. "Did he have friends or close associates in London? His prior acquaintance with Raven may have been under a different name."

Phoebe's brow wrinkled. "You mean a title?"

"Not exactly," he said slowly.

She appeared worried by his hesitation. "A false name? Why would that be? Is this man a criminal?"

"My lady, do not be concerned. It is not unheard of for gentlemen who wish to avoid recognition for various good reasons to travel incognito." It was an exaggeration. Nonetheless, Sherry had done it himself. "As we haven't yet located Charles Raven, it is possible the name is an alias he regularly uses."

"I see," she said doubtfully, "but why was Graham involved with him?"

"We are looking into it," Sherry said, desperately searching for a way to turn this conversation to safer ground.

Lady Anne, whether by design or happenstance, came to his rescue. "Perhaps the rest of this conversation can wait until tomorrow. After his travels the last day or two, his lordship must be wishing for his bed. I admit I am rather tired myself."

"Oh, dear, of course. How remiss of me." Lady Phoebe rose, immediately the concerned hostess. "All of this affair will no doubt make more sense in the morning."

It wouldn't, of course, but perhaps by then Sherry could come up with better answers.

• • •

Audley Manor, Thursday, 31 March 1814

It stormed that night, the lightning and loud thunder keeping the Audley household awake until the early morning hours. It was a weary-eyed group that assembled at the breakfast table.

"What a racket the storm made," Margret said, hiding a yawn. "I think I shall need a nap to get through the day." She looked toward the window where rain continued to run down the panes. "It is so gloomy, I doubt we shall have visitors."

"All the better for sorting and packing," Lady Anne said. "We shall not be distracted by a desire to wander through the garden or go for a ride."

"I must beg pardon for our task dragging on so long," Lady Phoebe said, regret in her voice, "but I still think we shall finish today. We'd already be done if I had not forgotten the unopened trunks in the attic I brought with me when I married. They need to be sorted again and repacked." She turned to Anne and Margret with a warm smile. "This would have taken weeks or months without your help."

"What is all this talk of packing?" Sherry asked, setting his coffee cup down. "Are you planning to travel?"

"Well, no," Lady Phoebe said. "You shall be wanting the manor, and I did not wish to delay you."

"There is no need to rush about," he said, appalled that she should feel this way. "I have no plans for taking up permanent residence in the foreseeable future and certainly not until satisfactory arrangements have been made for you. Naturally, the Dower House is yours for as long as you desire."

"That is very generous, my lord."

"Nothing of the sort. It is yours by right."

She smiled, clearly pleased. "Some of my things and most of Eliza's are already there, and I shall begin moving the other trunks that are filled."

"There is plenty of time," Sherry protested.

"I would rather be settled somewhere, my lord. I am uncomfortable playing hostess in a house that is no longer mine."

"Nonsense." Sherry frowned. "My lady, I had hoped you would continue to be my hostess until such time as I take a wife or you choose to live away from the estate."

She blushed with pleasure. "I shall be delighted to do whatever you wish, my lord."

"Thank you." Assuming the matter had been settled, he picked up his coffee again and drained the cup.

"Nonetheless," she continued, "I would rather reside at the Dower House with Eliza. Its smaller size is more suited for a child, and I can still come up to the manor on those occasions you require a hostess."

"I shall not argue with you," Sherry said with a slight shake of his head, "but allow me to clarify that both you and Eliza are welcome to reside in the main house. I shall leave the decision to you, however." Having finished his meal, he rose. "If you will pardon me, ladies, I believe I shall look around and become acquainted with the servants."

"Perhaps you would like me to show you the house?" Lady Phoebe asked.

"Thank you for offering, but it is not necessary. It sounds as though you have plans, and I can find my way." Not only did he want to introduce himself, but he had a few questions about Graham's reputation and behavior in the community. He hoped the servants would be more candid without their mistress present.

Mindful of the hierarchy in any household, he started with Godwin, the butler, and found him overseeing the polishing of the silver in the Butler's Pantry. "If that is on my account, I do not require such fancy service," Sherry said, "but I would like a few moments of your time."

"Very good, my lord."

"Perhaps you could come to the study when you are finished here."

"I am at your service now, my lord."

"Excellent." Sherry led the way knowing Godwin would never do so unless Sherry was lost. When he entered the study, he lifted a brow to see his brother's private things had been removed. Lady Phoebe truly was determined to have everything ready for him. While he appreciated her efforts, they were not necessary. He had willingly taken on the duties of the viscounty, but he was far from eager to assume its rights, privileges, and property.

He took a seat and motioned Godwin to a chair.

"If you do not mind, I would prefer to stand, my lord."

"As you please," Sherry said pleasantly. "Have you enjoyed working here, Godwin?"

"Very much so, my lord."

"Does that mean you wish to continue?"

"It does, my lord. Audley has come to be home, but I serve at your pleasure."

"Are you satisfied with the rest of the household servants?"

"Why yes, my lord. Has someone displeased you?"

"Far from it. Indeed, I do not foresee any changes in the immediate future unless we need to hire additional servants, particularly at the Dower House. You may so inform the others."

"Very good, my lord." Godwin unbent enough to smile. "I know they shall be as pleased as I am."

"I hope so. Now that is out of the way…are you aware Lord Audley's death was not an accident?"

"I am, my lord. It is a dreadful thing."

"Indeed. Is there anything regarding your master's habits, his friends, possible enemies…that might rise to such animosity?" Godwin dropped his gaze, clearly reluctant to talk about his deceased master, and Sherry added, "My brother would want his killer brought to justice."

Godwin looked up. "I believe he would, my lord." Still, he hesitated, finally clearing his throat. "His lordship held strong opinions and could be…inflexible in expressing them. His attitude may have led to occasional bad feelings with neighbors or even friends but nothing that would justify murder."

"It seems unlikely. Was there someone with whom he habitually had these intense discussions?"

"No one comes to mind. Nor does any pertinent event. I wish I could be of greater assistance, my lord, and shall continue to think on it. Shall you be speaking with the rest of the household and those in the stable?"

"Mostly to introduce myself. Is there anyone among the servants I should ask the same questions about Audley that I have put to you?"

"The first footman, William. He acted as valet for his lordship upon occasion and might know something of his activities that I do not."

"I shall make note of that." Sherry smiled. "Thank you, Godwin. I hope I have not disturbed your schedule too much."

"Not at all, my lord." The butler gave a respectful bow and withdrew.

Sherry leaned back in his chair. Could Graham's obstinacy and strong opinions have gotten him in trouble in Maidenhead? The card game, the duel, and the horse trickery could all have resulted in heated arguments…but murder?

He sighed and got up to meet the rest of the Audley household.

• • •

Within the hour, Sherry had spoken with everyone in service at the manor except the footman William who was absent on an errand to the village. While waiting for the young man's return, Sherry walked down to the Dower House to meet the four attendants there—and to make the acquaintance of Eliza, a delightful child. He spent so much time playing peek-a-boo with her that an hour and a half passed before he walked back up the hill.

To his satisfaction, the servants at both houses were a respectful, hardworking group. His half-brother's accident had been mentioned only briefly, when Sherry thanked them for their diligent care of Lady Phoebe.

Upon his arrival at the main house, Godwin informed him William had returned, and Sherry asked that he be sent to the study. On his way there, Sherry met the ladies in the hall.

"We are about to have a spot of tea," Lady Phoebe said. "Will you join us?"

"I'm meeting with someone first, but I shall see if you are still in the drawing room when I'm finished."

"I am confident you will find us still lingering over our tea," Lady Anne said. "The sorting and packing that can be done prior to the move is complete, and we have no immediate task to hurry us away. Besides, we were discussing things among ourselves and have a few questions for you."

"I look forward to joining you." Nonetheless, he wouldn't rush his interview with William. In addition to asking about Graham, he wanted to hear what the footman had to say regarding the intruder. He knew Lucien had already questioned the lad, but witnesses occasionally recalled small details hours or days later.

Sherry was rather impressed with William. He was a steady, forthcoming young man, although Sherry was disappointed he couldn't add much to Sherry's understanding of his half-brother.

"He didn't talk about a whole lot except his books," William said. "And other than Squire Levington and Mr. Wheatley, visitors to the house were usually ladies from the village who came to see her ladyship."

"Would Mr. Wheatley be Jasper Wheatley, Lady Phoebe's brother? He seems an unlikely confidant of your master."

"Oh, not that, my lord. I, uh, believe Lord Audley was urging him to mend his ways."

"Debts or women?"

William flushed, dropping his gaze, clearly uncomfortable. "I believe it was debts, my lord."

Sherry nodded and changed the subject. "Did Lord Audley say anything about his two recent trips to Maidenhead?"

"Not to me. I know he bought two horses the first trip. Oh, he had me pack an extra shirt for his last trip because he was going to see his solicitor."

Doubtless it was nothing more than ordinary estate matters. Although, if he recalled correctly, Lucien had had some questions about it and was going to follow-up with the law office.

"Tell me what you can of the housebreaking and the intruder."

William repeated what Sherry had already heard about the incident, from Elsie's baying to Mrs. Wycliff's discovery of the culprit, the chase, the firing of the pistol, and collecting the contents of the undertaker's box.

"Did you get a glimpse of the thief's face? What about his size, his age, his horse? Anything?"

"Never had a good look at him." He mentioned the cap and large coat. "I've thought about it as Lord Ware asked. I can only say he was pretty nimble-footed, going out the window the way he did."

Sherry smiled. "And reckless, I'd say. You've done very well, William. Thank you. Oh, yes, I nearly forgot. I believe you are carrying a pistol."

"Yes, my lord. I know it's not usually allowed, but—"

Sherry interrupted. "For now, you may continue as you have. In fact, if the thief makes another appearance while I am here, perhaps we can catch him together."

William grinned. "I hope so, my lord. I assure you I shall be watchful but very careful."

With the young footman out the door, Sherry rose and hurried downstairs to join the ladies. His interview had taken longer than intended, but they were still talking in the drawing room. Lady Phoebe immediately sent for more hot tea.

"I beg pardon," he said, "but William was my last interview, and I was keen to finish today." He turned to Lady Phoebe. "You have an excellent household, and I will be pleased to employ any of them who wish to stay."

"How wonderful," she said, a smile lighting up her green eyes. "I shall not need so many at the Dower House or wherever I go from there, and the others will be grateful to know they still have employment."

"I have already informed Godwin so that no one need worry. You can tell me later whom you wish to take with you." He turned to Lady Anne, whose curiosity had doubtless kept the ladies lingering over their tea. "Now, I believe you mentioned you had questions."

Chapter Seventeen

Maidenhead, Buckinghamshire, Thursday 31 March 1814

With Sherry watching over events at Audley Manor, Lucien went about his inquiries in Maidenhead with less distraction. He started the following morning by making a return trip to Terrell Stables. If Lord Audley had confronted Donnelly over the horse sale, Lucien wanted to know what happened and why Donnelly had denied seeing the viscount again.

When Lucien arrived at the horse farm, he couldn't find Donnelly right away, and a stable boy suggested he talk with Mr. Terrell up at the manor. Since he was already curious about a man with such a dubious reputation, Lucien climbed the path to the Georgian house.

The footman who answered the door took Lucien's card and disappeared into the back. A heavy-set man with bushy sideburns and a large nose appeared almost immediately and came toward Lucien with an affable smile.

"Lord Ware, I am honored by your visit. What may I do for you? Are you interested in purchasing a horse?"

"Not today. I am looking for John Donnelly. I wanted to talk about a horse he sold Lord Audley."

Terrell's lip curled. "You're too late. I dismissed him yesterday. I heard how he cheated his lordship and a couple of others at the spring sale. It wasn't the first complaint of his trickery, and I don't want a man using deceitful practices working for me. I sent him on his way."

"How did you hear about it? Did Audley come here a week ago to complain?"

Terrell looked surprised. "No, who told you that? As I recall, a stable boy told me what Donnelly had done."

Lucien doubted that. More likely Donnelly bragged about it, and Terrell would have approved. "What was the real reason you dismissed him? Did he cheat you? Keep more than his share of the sale?"

The stable owner rubbed his whiskers. "As a matter of fact, he lied about the actual selling prices and stole a portion of the latest sales. But the Audley sale was the last straw. You can't go swindling the nobility and stay in business."

So swindling common folk was all right? Lucien struggled to suppress his scorn. He'd come there for information not to rail at a man who wouldn't listen.

"Do you know where Donnelly went?" he asked.

"I do not. When he was off my property, I put him out of my mind. If that's all you wanted, my lord…" Terrell was clearly done with the conversation.

Lucien persisted. "Perhaps you might tell me where he worked before coming here."

"I would if I could, but I don't know. His reference was false. When I confronted him on it, he said he couldn't use his prior employer because he'd been dismissed for kissing the owner's daughter." Terrell shrugged indifferently. "I suppose that was a lie too, but at the time I accepted his story, and it didn't worry me because I have no daughters. He was good with horses. I suppose you'll find him at another stable. If you'll pardon me, my lord, I *must* attend to other business."

"By all means." Lucien turned and left.

It was a dry and dusty day, and on the ride back to Maidenhead, he kept one hand on his hat while he pondered the odd amount of deception surrounding this inquiry—false references, misleading sales practices, false names, card cheating—and yet he hadn't found a thread among them that explained Audley's death.

Still in a pensive mood, he entered the Goose & Gander a bit over an hour later. The public room was only mildly busy, and Sam looked up immediately. "A message for you, milord," he called before Lucien got to the stairs.

"Yes, Sam. What is it?"

"A boy was here to see you. He was all excited. Said his name was Joey, and that he and Eddie found the stable where some man kept his horse." Sam shrugged. "I hope that means something to you."

"It certainly does. Is Joey coming back? Or did he say where I could find him?"

Sam nodded. "He'll be here tonight. I couldn't pin him down on a time."

"It doesn't matter. That's great, Sam. Thank you."

Lucien rapidly climbed the stairs with a grin on his face. Joey could only be talking about the "small man" seen near Audley's horses, and this could be the break he needed. In the meantime, once he washed off the dust, he intended to talk with Edward Marchant again, and this time he'd insist the solicitor tell him what he was hiding.

• • •

Lucien mounted the steps of the white stone building and entered the suite where the Marchant Brothers had their legal offices.

Edward Marchant, solicitor, as neatly dressed as before, this time in dark blue, stood at the front desk talking with the secretary. He looked up when he heard the door and smiled. "Lord Ware, are you here to see me again?"

"If I could have a few more minutes of your time."

"Certainly. Right this way." As he closed his office door behind them, he asked, "May I pour you a glass of port?"

"Thank you. It would be most welcome."

After tasting the wine and expressing his approval, Lucien broached the subject of Phoebe's brother. "I appreciated your candor regarding Jasper Wheatley when we met previously, but I cannot get it out of my head that there was something you withheld, something you thought about telling me but didn't."

Silence stretched for a long moment. "You are perceptive, my lord," Marchant said. "I am still hesitant to reveal the truth, for I'm sorry to confess I disagree with Lord Audley's stated intent. It poses an ethical dilemma for me."

Lucien frowned. "To what do you refer?"

"His proposed disposal of certain bills and IOUs."

"Not Audley's debts, I assume." Lucien cocked his head. "I'd wager they belong to Jasper Wheatley."

"Yes, they do." Marchant sighed as though making up his mind. "His lordship bought Wheatley's debts from his creditors a year ago, mostly gambling IOUs. The rest were unpaid bills from his tailor and boot maker. They total nearly forty thousand pounds."

Lucien shook his head. "You are not joking, are you?"

"I never joke about money."

"No, I suppose not. So, Audley was holding Wheatley's debt. What is it you disapprove?"

"They made a bargain in my presence. If Wheatley stayed within his allowance for three years, Audley would burn the notes of debt. Of course, Wheatley failed to do so, not even complying for six months."

"What happens to the notes now?"

Marchant sighed audibly. "That is the problem. Against my advice, Lord Audley wanted them destroyed upon his death. Naturally, he assumed that would be years from now. I have examined Wheatley's current debts—acquired since their agreement—and I can tell you that he does not deserve such generosity."

"I thought as much, but if those were Audley's instructions, what choice do you have?"

"It was his intent—I know that from our conversations—but he never got around to asking for the paperwork to be written. Their original three-year agreement was done but not the additional clause allowing forgiveness of debt upon his lordship's death."

"So, nothing that is legal and binding," Lucien finished.

"Exactly. I have been torn by what to do."

"I see your quandary. Did Wheatley know of Audley's intent?"

"Not directly. He may have suspected it. When he came to see me right after the carriage wreck, the first thing he asked was what happens to my debt now?"

"Unseemly behavior but not criminal."

"Very true, my lord."

"Where are these bills and IOUs?"

"In our vault. I daresay, our thief may have been hoping to recover them."

"There has also been a housebreaking at Audley Manor. Wheatley remains a suspect in Audley's death, and his debts might tell me something useful. May I see the notes?"

"Of course." Marchant rose and left the office, returning promptly. He set a small box on the desk and opened it with a key. Inside, Lucien found a stack of bills from tailors, shoemakers and the like, even the village butcher, but an even thicker stack was composed of gambling IOUs. From the dates, the debt had been accumulated in less than a year, and Marchant had indicated Wheatley's behavior had not changed. So his current debts might also be close to forty thousand,

"Even if the estate forgives these," Lucien said, "he may find himself in debtors' prison in a year or two."

"Yes, it appears inevitable. Lord and Lady Audley had both been paying various bills of his for two years before these."

"I am surprised the estate has not suffered."

Marchant was slow in responding. "Lord Audley was careful in his expenditures, but to accommodate Wheatley's debts he was forced to cut back...sometimes in the wrong places. He should have hired an estate manager."

"Are you saying he was a poor landlord?"

"No, no. Well, not exactly, but the tenant farms were not his priority."

"I see." And he did. Due to Audley's intense interest in history books and his written treatises, his tenants had been neglected, just as his wife had. Lucien handed the box back to Marchant. "What are you going to recommend be done with these?"

"I honestly do not know. I shall consult with Lady Phoebe and the new Lord Audley, of course, but ultimately, the magistrate may have to decide." Marchant produced a grim smile. "I doubt Wheatley could ever pay these debts, but I would not care to make it too easy on him, not after all Lord and Lady Audley have already done."

Lucien stood with a nod. "I cannot agree more, sir."

He left the law office wondering if they'd been mistaken in thinking Wheatley was incapable of committing murder. Desperate men do desperate things, and he clearly had a compelling motive. Sherry's brother should have known better than attempt to reform a scapegrace and gambler, particularly when Wheatley's actions made it clear he had no wish to be reformed.

Even though Wheatley oozed motive, did he have the nerve or the skills? It wasn't likely he had the ease around horses to cut the harness, nor could he have made the leap out the window at Audley Manor. If he was guilty, he'd need an accomplice—possibly the man Eddie had seen? The thought made Lucien even more keen to speak with Joey that night.

• • •

Sitting in the public room of the Goose & Gander, Lucien watched the door and sipped a tankard of ale with little enthusiasm. He'd been waiting for Joey since six, and it was approaching seven. He was growing bored and tired of ale. This was his third glass.

With little else to do, he'd been thinking about Ponsonby and Raven, wondering who they were and why they'd been in Maidenhead using false names. Well, to be accurate, he was wondering why Raven had been there. It was pretty clear Ponsonby had followed Raven there…and more than likely with the intent to kill him in a way that murder wouldn't be suspected.

That could explain why Raven was using a false name—he knew someone was looking for him and had hoped to throw them off his trail. Lucien scowled. So, how did that help find them? It didn't. The reasons why one man might hunt another were too numerous to even speculate.

"Hey, Lord Ware, it's Joey."

Lucien looked up with relief and smiled. "Have a seat, lad." He motioned him to the other bench at the table. "Would you like something to eat or drink while we talk?"

Joey's face lit up. "One-na them pies 'd be good."

Lucien raised a hand for the barmaid and ordered a meat pie and a glass of small beer for Joey. While the lad wrinkled his nose at the children's drink, Lucien chuckled and refused to buy him the regular version containing much more alcohol.

Watching Joey dig into the pie, Lucien wondered when the lad had last had a decent meal. Several minutes passed before Joey wiped his mouth with the back of his hand, took a long drink, and sighed. "Thanks. Was really good. S'pose y' want to know what me and Eddie found. It's where he kept his horse."

"You mean the man Eddie saw with Gordon's horses?"

Joey nodded, finishing off his drink.

"Can you take me to the stable?"

"'Course." Joey jumped up from the table and was halfway across the room before Lucien could grab his hat and follow.

While Lucien had been waiting, dark had fallen, and Joey led him through parts of town that were poorly lit and had such a strong odor of unmentionable things that it wrinkled his nose. An occasional squish underfoot had Lucien wishing he'd brought a pair of old boots to town.

The boy finally pointed ahead to a decrepit shed with a slight lean. "There. Ol' Dobbs runs it."

"Are you coming in?"

"Sure. He likes me."

"Well, that may be, but I'll give you this now, so you can leave when you want." He handed Joey a quid, and then held up another. "This is for Eddie. Will you give it to him?"

The lad nodded. "Promise. Me and 'im be friends now."

"That is good to hear. Let's go inside."

Dobbs, a man of fifty or so, whose muscles had run to fat with age, was sleeping sprawled across a mound of straw. The shed held four stalls and all were filled with horses that Finn wouldn't have allowed in the stable at Hays Mews.

Lucien nudged the man with his boot. "Are you Dobbs?"

The fellow sat up and blinked at him. "Wot you want? Me stalls are full."

"I'm looking for information, and I'll pay well for it." He pulled several shillings from his pocket.

Dobbs struggled to his feet, his eyes fixed on the coins. "Wot y' want to know?"

"T'at fella me and Eddie talked 'bout," Joey chimed in. "Tell 'im."

"Oh, him." Dobbs dipped his hands in a water bucket and rubbed his face. "So all right." He slumped onto a harness box.

Assuming that meant Dobbs was ready to talk, Lucien asked, "Was this man here on the eighteenth and nineteenth?"

"Yep. Paid up front for two days. Left in a hurry jist before dark on Saturday."

"Did he give you a name?"

Dobbs shrugged. "Dint ask."

Clearly all Dobbs had cared about was getting paid. "Did he mention where he was from or why he was here?"

"Up from London to finish a job. T'at's all he said 'an aye dint ask no more."

Lucien suppressed his eagerness and kept his voice casual. "No hint what kind of job? Or who it was for?"

"Nope."

"Did you get the impression he'd finished it?"

"Could be." Dobbs frowned. "Took outta here in a hurry headed south."

South to London, Lucien wondered, or south to Audley to see if his tampering had been successful?

"Describe him to me."

"Like Eddie say. Small, skinny, brown hair. Maybe thirty or forty."

"What about his horse?"

He jerked a dismissive hand. "Brown mare."

"Anything else you remember?" Lucien prodded.

"Nope."

Dobbs was looking impatient, even wary. Lucien had learned all he would get. He handed over the coins, then he and Joey left.

"Did that help?" Joey asked as they walked back toward main street.

"It sure did, Joey. Thank you." He eyed the lad. "How would you like a more permanent job away from Maidenhead?"

Joey pushed out his lips in thought, then slowly shook his head. "Nah. This is wot I know."

"You could learn something else, working on a farm, or maybe as a stable boy?"

Joey shrugged.

"If you change your mind, I'll be at the inn another day or so."

"Got it, sir."

When they reached the town's main street, Joey waved goodbye and disappeared into the dark streets behind them. Nice lad, he thought. His offer had been impulsive, but if he heard from Joey again, he'd find him a place with Sherry at Audley Manor or take him to London when they left.

He turned and strolled toward the inn, reviewing his conversation with Dobbs. How confident could he be that this man was the one who tampered with the harness? These street boys were very observant—it was how they earned their coins—so this man *had* been near the horses. If he'd also cut the belly straps, then the killer and the one who paid him must be in London.

Yet, Lucien still felt something could be learned here in Maidenhead—such as a motive for murder. Without it or something else to go on, where would they look once they got to London? The small man wasn't tied to any known trouble here, and the only other link Lucien had found to London wasn't Wheatley or Donnelly or a farmer with a grudge—it was that scandalous card game and duel.

Chapter Eighteen

Audley Manor, Saturday, 31 March 1814

Lady Anne and the other ladies joined Sherry for a ride on horseback Saturday morning. It was a beautiful spring day with the land turning green. Wildflowers peeked out here and there, and the sweet scent of bluebells floated in the breeze. Lady Phoebe pointed out the boundaries of the estate and each of the tenant farms. They didn't approach the farmers, but Sherry spoke of his plans to do so one day soon.

"If I am to be a responsible land owner," he added, "I need to learn all I can about my tenants and what they expect of me."

"They are good people who work hard," Lady Phoebe said. "I know they shall welcome your interest."

When they returned to the manor it was nearly midday. After freshening up and changing clothes, they met in the drawing room for tea and lemonade and were just comfortably settled when they heard the pounding hooves of a galloping horse. As they rushed to the window, Sherry saw a one-horse gig with two women aboard.

"My sisters," Phoebe exclaimed. "With Papa's gig. Why have they come this time? Could something be wrong?"

The horse and simple two-wheeled carriage came to an abrupt stop at the manor's entrance, and the young women climbed down the moment a stable boy grabbed the horse's reins. They brushed past Godwin and hastened toward the group that had just come into the hallway from the drawing room.

"Oh, Phoebe, surely you cannot turn us away this time," Charlotte blurted. "We are in peril of our lives."

"Good Heavens, whatever is the matter? What peril?" Phoebe asked.

But her sisters seemed momentarily speechless having taken in that Phoebe and her lady visitors were not alone. Lady Anne hid a smile at Charlotte's dismayed reaction upon sight of Sherry that quickly turned to speculation. Apparently the girl's peril didn't keep her from wondering if an attractive man was eligible.

Sherry stepped forward and smiled at the two young women. "Perhaps you would be so good as to introduce us, Lady Phoebe."

"Yes, of course, my lord. These are my sisters, Miss Charlotte Wheatley and Miss Dorothea Wheatley. Charlotte, Dora, this is Lord Audley, the new viscount."

If Anne harbored any doubts of Charlotte's thoughts regarding Sherry, they were dispelled by the girl's coquettish smile as she and Dora dropped him a curtsey. "*Very* pleased to meet you, my lord."

Her ingratiating manner was unbecoming and rather off-putting, Anne thought, but Sherry, as usual, was very much the gentleman.

Her gave the sisters a formal nod. "My pleasure entirely, young ladies. Is there some way in which we can assist you? You appear quite flustered."

"Oh, yes," Charlotte said, suddenly recalling their great peril. "A man came after Jasper with a rifle."

"Good Gracious. What did he want?" Phoebe took Charlotte's hands. "Were you and Dora present?"

Charlotte nodded. "It was dreadful, Phoebe. Jasper said to run and come here, so we did. We don't know exactly why the stranger was so angry, but Jasper said he'd try to get away and join us. Is that not what he said, Dora?"

Dora bobbed her head. "Yes, so we got the gig, and Charlotte whipped the horse all the way here."

Anne slipped behind the group and looked outside. The horse and gig had already been taken away, and she assumed the horse would be properly tended. If Charlotte had truly galloped the poor animal for most of an hour, they'd be fortunate if it wasn't wind broke or worse.

While still listening to the conversation behind her, Anne was increasingly skeptical of Charlotte's story. According to her, Jasper had bravely stayed behind so his sisters could escape. Not to belittle him unduly, but that didn't sound like the Jasper Wheatley Anne had met.

She turned now and interrupted. "Lady Phoebe, perhaps we should return to our tea. I'm sure Charlotte and Dora could use a cup after such a narrow escape."

"Yes, of course." Phoebe urged Charlotte toward the drawing room.

"That would be delightful," Charlotte agreed. "Come, Dora, I'm certain you would like a biscuit or two."

"And then we must hear every detail of your close escape," Sherry said, with a lifted brow at Anne.

She lightly shook her head; he grinned in return. So, she wasn't the only one who suspected this was a Banbury tale, but she hadn't yet decided to what purpose.

Two cups of tea and two biscuits later, Charlotte resumed her tale while Dora, already pleasingly plump, continued to eat.

"I suppose it has something to do with Jasper's gambling. He had hoped to win enough funds to keep up the house and other expenses. Lately, his luck has not been so good, and we have had to cut back."

On what? Anne wondered, eyeing the latest fashions the girls were wearing. Perhaps it was food, as Dora had already consumed four biscuits. She caught Anne's eye, and as though remembering her manners, she drew her hand back from taking a fifth.

"I hadn't realized how indebted he'd become until last night," Charlotte continued, warming to her story. "That's when he explained he owed a large sum to a very bad man, and someone might be coming to collect. Since he had nothing to pay them with, he would be in grave danger. That's when he said we should come to you, dear Phoebe, if anything happened to him. Did he not say so, Dora?"

Thus appealed to, the younger girl bobbed her head as before. "We packed our bags, just to be ready."

Sherry had been listening in silence. Now he turned to Dora. "Tell me about this man with the rifle. What did he look like?"

"Well," Dora shot a look at Charlotte, "he was big and scary. And had a deep scar on his face, and—"

"He looked very serious, "Charlotte said, interrupting her sister's description. She gave Dora a severe look.

"And very mean," Dora added, getting in a last word before she subsided.

What a plumper. Anne now knew they were lying. While the part about Jasper's large gambling loses rang true, she doubted the girls had seen any man with a rifle and certainly not one who sounded like a villain from a fairy tale. She waited to see whether there would be more to the story, but Charlotte had succeeded in silencing her sister.

"That's all we know," Charlotte said. "The stranger had just reached the front door when we sprung the gig from the stable."

"He did not fire at you or chase you?" Anne asked.

"No, thank goodness. I suppose he was mostly angry with Jasper."

Sherry arched a brow. "If your brother is in such danger, we should contact Squire Levington or our constable immediately and arrange for someone in authority to assist him."

"Oh, no," Charlotte said. "Jasper said that would make things worse. We are to wait several hours to hear from him before sending help."

"Sounds risky to me, but very well. No doubt he knows the situation best. We shall wait." Sherry rose. "I must excuse myself. I have the accounts waiting my attention in the study. Lady Phoebe, perhaps you could arrange a room for your sisters and have one prepared for your brother. If he arrives, I assume he will be in need of rest and a safe place to hide after such a harrowing experience."

Phoebe appeared startled by this request, and Anne witnessed an exchange of looks between Phoebe and Sherry. He nodded and smiled to reassure her.

Anne suppressed a chuckled. While it was obvious Jasper was after money or an excuse to stay at Audley, perhaps both, she knew Sherry could be cunning when the occasion arose. He was already planning how to deal with Jasper Wheatley. And she could hardly wait to see the outcome.

Regardless of his stated intent to work on the accounts, Sherry lingered until Phoebe and her sisters left the drawing room, and then he turned to Anne and Margret with a wry smile. "No, I have not lost my mind. When Jasper arrives, I shall welcome him into my home. Whatever he is up to, he is still a suspect in Graham's murder, and I shall take this opportunity to learn what I can about him and assess the likelihood he was involved. And, of course, I intend to catch him out in his latest scheme to cozen Lady Phoebe or me of further funds—and to make certain this is his last attempt."

Margret laughed. "I *did* wonder. I shall help any way I can."

"It's clear he primed Charlotte to inform us of his dire straits," Anne said. "But they appeared very eager to stay here, and I cannot but wonder why."

Sherry nodded. "So do I."

• • •

Sometime later, Anne was sitting in the parlor with Margret, Phoebe, and Phoebe's sisters when they heard another arrival at the front entrance. Charlotte jumped up, scattering the cards in the game of Vingt-Un that she and Dora had been playing.

"Oh, that must be Jasper." She fled the room while Dora stayed to pick up the cards.

"She and Jasper are very close," Dora said, attempting to explain her sister's less than lady-like behavior. "I do hope he is all right. May I go?"

"Of course, you may," Lady Phoebe said, as she, Anne, and Margret put down their embroidery. "I believe we are all going."

As they reached the drawing room, Sherry and Charlotte were already talking with Jasper Wheatley. He was dressed to the nines—

high shirt points and intricately tied cravat—with not a hair out of place, nor any sign of injury or distress.

Jasper turned as they entered and bowed. "Ladies, I beg pardon for coming at such an unfashionable hour, but I was anxious to learn of my sisters' fate."

"I am relieved to see you are well," Phoebe said.

"As are we all," Anne added. "Your sisters' account had led us to fear for your life."

Jasper had the grace to redden a bit. "Well, I doubt it would have gone that far, but I was concerned he meant to use that rifle. I was just explaining to his lordship and Charlotte that I was able to outrun him. Fortunately, my horse was fresh, and he had just ridden from London."

"What will you do now?" Margret asked. "Keep running? If this terrible man came so far to find you, he may not discourage easily."

Sherry cleared his throat. "That thought had occurred to me too and is exactly why I have invited Wheatley to stay overnight until it is safe to return home."

"Oh, how delightful." Charlotte clapped her hands twice. "It will be wonderful to know we shall not be murdered in our beds."

"Hush, Charlotte," Jasper said. "He only wants money, not our lives, although I feared how he might treat ladies. He is not a gentleman. I am convinced, however, that he will return to London within a few days."

"Might he not follow you to this house?" Anne asked to see what he'd say. Any self-respecting ruffian should be able to ask around and make the family connection.

"No, my lady. You need have no fear," he said as though indulging a child. "I took a long way around, so I would not be followed."

"Then we shall all rest easy," she murmured.

• • •

By the time dinner was over that evening, Anne was more than ready to retire with the ladies. While Phoebe's sister Charlotte was gushing over Sherry or making sly remarks—mostly at her brother's behest—and Dora was often giddy and childish, they were much preferred company over Jasper. Perhaps his role as head of the household had made him so self-centered and vain, but Anne suspected he had always been patronizing and shallow. She'd had enough of him for one evening and hoped he and Sherry had a nice long chat over their port before rejoining the ladies. After that, well, she could plead the headache, but then what would she say tomorrow night and the night after? Although Sherry had spoken of an overnight stay, she'd heard Jasper mention "a few days." It might be difficult to remove the unwanted guests.

Anne sighed and picked up the handkerchief she was embroidering with her father's initials. She hoped to give him a set of six next Christmastide and had made little progress thus far. She had sufficient skill for the task but found little time while in London due to their busy social life. She was taking advantage of the quiet countryside to get as much done as possible.

She glanced at the clock on the parlor's mantel over the hearth. Oh, my, nearly an hour had gone by since dinner. While she welcomed the respite, what on earth was Sherry finding to discuss with Jasper Wheatley for so long?

• • •

Audley Manor dining room, an hour after dinner

Sherry stifled a bored sigh. After listening to Wheatley all through dinner and for nearly an hour over cigars and port, he had no better idea why Phoebe's brother had invented such a wild deception to push himself and his sisters onto the hospitality of Audley Manor.

He had swiftly taken measure of Wheatley's character and could say without hesitation that whatever motivated him, it was entirely self-serving. Instead of talking about the alleged debt collector with a rifle, his sisters, or his small estate—all things that would be uppermost in the minds of most gentlemen during such a crisis, Wheatley had given Sherry his opinion on the latest fashions—

spending an inordinate amount of time on the various colors and quality of deerskin gloves—the best horses for impressing the ladies, and sports' betting. He appeared quite fond of cock fights, which Sherry detested, and local boxing events, the style that was little more than a tavern brawl.

They had little in common, but Sherry knew the longer Wheatley talked, the more likely he was to give himself away.

"And so I told Graham that he was too kind but I could pay my own debts."

"Sorry, I didn't quite follow that," Sherry said in surprise, realizing he'd missed a shift in the conversation. "My brother was in the habit of paying your debts?"

"Oh, no, of course not. He offered, but I said no."

Sherry frowned, knowing Jasper was lying, but encouraged him to continue. "Why would you decline when you are so obviously in need? Had he asked something burdensome in return?"

"No. Nothing." Wheatley shrugged and finished his second glass of port. "I believe he was offering for the sake of Phoebe and her sisters. Charlotte and Dora have so many expenses with one being of marriageable age and the other approaching it."

Before Wheatley embarrassed them both by asking for money, Sherry rose. "I see. Well, I am sure you will devise a way to cope." He waved his hand toward the door. "I believe it is time we joined the ladies. Shall we?"

"Certainly, my lord. I am a bit tired by the day's events. Perhaps a few rounds of Whist with my younger sisters, and then I shall be off to bed. I'm sure I shall sleep soundly indeed."

● ● ●

Audley Manor, early morning, Friday, 1 April, 1814

The clock in the hall chimed two, and Sherry stretched and yawned in his chair by the study fireplace. A wasted night. Perhaps Wheatley had meant it when he said he would sleep soundly... or he was biding his time. Sherry had felt sure his guest would be looking around tonight for whatever he had hoped to find at Audley Manor, but William was watching the library, so no activity there either, or the lad would have shouted.

Sherry had hinted he expected Wheatley to leave tomorrow and thought that might be enough to encourage him to take immediate action. So, why hadn't the dratted fellow appeared? Was Sherry overly suspicious of his intent? Had he merely sought to stay at the manor for a greater opportunity to ask for money? He and his sisters had mentioned his debts often enough.

Sherry stood, stretched again, and started for the library door that he'd left partially open so he could hear anyone up and about. He was just about to enter the hall when he heard faint footsteps on the stairs.

He stepped back, retreating into the study's darker shadows. Unless his night prowler was hoping for a late snack from the kitchen, he or she must be headed for the study or library, the only rooms on the main floor likely to contain anything of interest.

The smell of candle smoke reached him first, then a candle appeared in an outstretched hand and a figure slipped into the room. Sherry slid behind him and closed the door with a loud click.

"What! Who's there?"

"Ah, Wheatley. Is that you?"

The figure held up his candle revealing his own face and Sherry's.

"Audley, what are you doing in the dark?"

"Waiting for you." Sherry lit a lantern that illuminated most of the room. "What are *you* doing up so late?"

"I...I was looking for a book. Yes, I couldn't sleep and wanted something to read. I must have chosen the wrong room." Having regained his composure, Wheatley added indignantly, "You nearly frightened me out of my wits."

Sherry ignored his grievance. "You should know the layout of the house by now. This is far from your first visit."

"I was confused in the dark." Wheatley lifted his nose in a haughty gesture. "I believe I shall return to my room."

"Without a book?" Sherry moved toward the door. "Let us step into the library. What do you like to read? Fiction—Sir Walter Scott, Jane Austen? Or perhaps travel, history, farming? What strikes your fancy?" He turned to give Wheatley a hard look. "None of those? I suspected not. I don't know what you hope to find or achieve by coming to Audley Manor under false pretenses. Perhaps you'd like to tell me?" When Wheatley only glared at him, his lips pressed in a stubborn line, Sherry sighed audibly, but his voice hardened. "I feared not. I dare say you will understand why I suggest you and your younger sisters should return to your own home without delay."

"Well, I never—"

"You have now," Sherry interrupted, losing patience. "I don't for a minute believe you were looking for a book tonight, nor do I think your home was invaded by a man with a rifle. Debts, I believe, for that is your unfortunate pattern of which my brother was well aware. Phoebe will not be paying them again, not ever, and don't even bother asking me. I could care less if you end up in debtors' prison." He was being severe, but nothing else had worked in the past, and he wanted Wheatley to get the clear message that he needed to fend for himself.

"We shall be gone by mid-morning," Wheatley said stiffly, "but don't expect Phoebe to thank you for abandoning her sisters."

"They are welcome at Audley at such times as Lady Phoebe invites them."

"But I am not?" Wheatley's eyes widened in surprise and resentment.

"Not at present. Perhaps, I shall change my mind if I observe you are taking proper responsibility for yourself."

Wheatley brushed by him and left in a huff.

Sherry gazed after him. He still didn't know what Wheatley was after. Perhaps it didn't matter as long as the n'er-do-well stayed away. He couldn't prevent the man from visiting Lady Phoebe—not indefinitely—but egad, Sherry found him annoying.

Chapter Nineteen

Maidenhead, Friday, 1 April 1814

With Lucien's inquiry now focused on the card cheat and duel, he realized there was one important source he hadn't yet found—the men who acted as seconds in the duel. Their task was to try to reconcile the two parties, and failing in that, they must ensure a fair duel by examining the weapons and reminding their principals of the twenty-seven rules set down in the Code Duello in 1777. In the performance of their duties, they may have picked up vital information that would help Lucien locate the duelers.

He hurried downstairs to the Goose & Gander's public room the next morning and after ordering breakfast, he asked Sam if he knew the names of the two men who had served as seconds for the dueling parties.

"I know one of them. Tom Newsome has been a friend for ten years or more." Sam huffed in his throat. "I doubt he'll be so quick to say yes to an appeal from a stranger again. Ponsonby said he knew no one locally and asked Newsome to stand for him. Tom was appalled with Ponsonby's later actions. Why do you ask?"

"It appears that Audley had some connection to that affair or one of the men involved. I hope the seconds can help me locate either Raven or Ponsonby."

"I doubt he knows much—both men were strangers to town—but maybe I'm wrong. Newsome is a banker and savvy enough he should have known better than to get involved in a duel. He is pretty embarrassed by Ponsonby's disgraceful show, so I don't know if he will talk about it, but you can try."

"Thanks, Sam. I'll do that…after breakfast and strong coffee."

• • •

Knowing the bank wouldn't open until ten, Lucien ate a leisurely meal before strolling down main street to the bank, only four buildings away from the Goose & Gander Inn. The financial institution was housed in a distinguished white stucco, one-story, square structure with black window frames and a black door set off by white columns on each side.

When he entered, a clerk immediately looked up. "Good morning, sir. How may I help you?"

"Is Mr. Newsome available?"

"Do you have an appointment?"

Lucien handed him his card. "I do not, but I will only take a few minutes of his time."

"Of course, my lord." The clerk gave a respectful nod and disappeared into the back. He reappeared shortly with a gentleman by his side. If this was Newsome, he looked to be in his late thirties, neatly and conservatively dressed in a gray coat and long trousers. He held Lucien's card in one hand and came forward with a genial smile.

"I'm Thomas Newsome, Lord Ware. May I be of assistance?"

"I certainly hope so. Might we speak privately?"

"Certainly." Newsome gave a nod. "Please step into by office. Would you care for tea or coffee?"

Lucien declined, and they settled into a well-appointed office with a gleaming mahogany desk and upholstered chairs. It was apparent that the bank was doing well.

"What brings you to Maidenhead?" Newsome asked conversationally.

"Business I'm afraid. I am inquiring into the death of Lord Audley and was hoping you could answer a few questions for me."

"I am sorry, my lord, I don't know what I can tell you." Newsome looked bewildered but cautious.

"He was present at the card game and the Raven-Ponsonby duel. I was hoping you could tell me more about it."

"Why? No, don't tell me," the banker said hastily. "I have nothing to say about that sordid affair."

"I'm not asking out of curiosity," Lucien said. "The incident may be connected to Lord Audley's murder."

"Murder?" Newsome's face paled with shock. "I heard his lordship died in a coach accident."

"The investigation is on-going, and I'm assisting the family and Squire Levington, the local magistrate. Lord Audley was at the duel and was acquainted with at least one of the duelers. Two weeks later he's dead, his harness cut, and he is carrying Raven's calling card."

"Good God," Newsome murmured.

"Naturally," Lucien continued, "I wish to speak with Raven, but thus far I've failed to locate either man. As Ponsonby's second, I hoped you could give me the details of the affair and how I may reach him."

The banker folded his hands on his desk. "I regret I can be of little assistance, my lord. I barely knew Ponsonby…obviously not well enough, or I would not have agreed to act for him. Raven's second and I met as required, but Ponsonby had no interest in a peaceful resolution. All Jack and I talked about was where, when, and the weapons involved. As for how to reach them, I had the impression both men were from London. I am fairly certain Ponsonby was."

"Did he say so?"

"Not exactly, but when I said I was a banker, he mentioned doing business with a London bank, Barclay & Son on Piccadilly."

"That is helpful, indeed. Did you see Audley speak with Ponsonby or Raven that night?"

"I did not, but I only saw the two men at Galloway's Pub that one time and the following morning at the duel. What Ponsonby did before or after is unknown to me, and I am pleased to have it that way."

"You referred to Raven's second as Jack. Do you know his surname or anything about him?"

Newsome shrugged. "He may have said his full name, but I don't recall. A nice young gentleman. He said he was a visitor to our town. From the way he talked and his polished manners, I presumed he came up from London for the sale, and I'd wager he and Raven were previously acquainted. I could be wrong, of course. Perhaps he was dragged into the affair same as I was."

Lucien turned his attention to the game. "Did you observe Raven cheating?"

"No, I just assumed he had." Newsome shrugged. "Who would lie about it? But others have since told me they thought Ponsonby set it up. Honestly, my lord, I was…and still am mortified by the whole affair." Newsome sat back and sighed heavily.

"By all accounts, a distasteful affair," Lucien agreed sympathetically, having heard that assessment of the event repeated several times. "Only one more question or two, and I shall let you get back to the more dignified business of banking."

Newsome gave him a wry smile. "I would appreciate that."

"You said Jack and Raven might have known each other before that night. What about Ponsonby and Raven? Did you have a similar impression?"

"I did, sir. Ponsonby's animosity felt calculated and extreme under the circumstances. Even at the time, I thought his actions were prompted by a problem from the past rather than a card game."

"Any guess what that might be?"

Newsome shook his head. "No, Ponsonby didn't say much to me, except when I handed him the loaded pistol. He muttered something that sounded like 'he'll regret it now.' Seemed to me he was referring to something in the past, but I suppose it could have been the game."

Lucien lifted a shoulder. "First impressions are often born out, and it gives me a place to look. If I'm to locate these gentleman, good descriptions might help. If you wouldn't mind indulging me another minute or two…"

"Of course." Newsome nodded thoughtfully. "Ponsonby was a bit of a rough fellow—a short man with dark brown hair and a mustache. He was near my age, I'd say, and although he was dressed as a gentleman, his language and demeanor left much to be desired. Having thought about it more than I like, I believe he falsely represented himself and was not a gentleman at all," he added in annoyance. "Raven, on the other hand, was a quiet gentleman, soft spoken, clean shaven, light brown hair, and of average stature. He was an experienced card player but a bit intense."

"Scars, war injuries, an unusual manner of speaking or walking?"

"Not that I noticed." Newsome spread his hands. "I'm afraid I have not been very helpful."

"To the contrary, I know more than I did an hour ago. Thank you, sir. I apologize for interrupting your day."

Newsome rose when Lucien did, and his friendly smile returned. "I hope you get it sorted out, my lord."

• • •

Lucien spent the rest of the day and evening hanging out in the back rooms of pubs and taverns. Everywhere he went, he asked about the Ponsonby-Raven affair, hoping someone would come up with details he hadn't yet learned. When he heard nothing but the same story over and over, he gave up around eleven and returned to his lodgings.

He lay on the bed staring at the ceiling. If Ponsonby had attempted to murder Raven over something that happened in London, was it possible Audley knew Raven or both men when he'd lived there or met them on one of his rare trips from Audley to London? If so, the motive for Audley's death might have nothing to do with Buckinghamshire but with something from his past in London.

Or maybe not. And speculation was worthless unless it helped Lucien locate the missing men. With a huff of frustration, he reached over and snuffed out the candle.

Chapter Twenty

Audley and thereabouts, Friday, 1 April 1814

Breakfast the morning Sherry caught Jasper Wheatley in the study was a rather awkward affair. Wheatley, Charlotte, and Dora huddled at one end of the table, rarely speaking, but Phoebe's brother darted angry looks at Sherry now and then. Sherry ignored them, and when the younger sisters had emptied their plates, Wheatley hustled them out of the room, shouting for someone to send for his horse and gig.

A footman promptly sent word to the stable, but he needn't have hurried. For nearly an hour, the mare stood quietly in the traces of the gig, and a stable boy held the reins of Wheatley's gelding while the two sisters scrambled to collect their belongings. Every time it appeared they were ready to depart, the girls kept running back into the house for forgotten items.

Finally they were ready. Lady Phoebe hugged her sisters. "Give me time to get settled at the Dower House, and I'll have you come for a visit. I wish for Eliza to know her aunts."

Dora looked at Sherry. "Truly, may we come?"

"Yes, you may." Sherry smiled at her, wondering what Wheatley had said. "You are welcome whenever Lady Phoebe invites you."

Jasper Wheatley left without saying goodbye.

As soon as Sherry had watched Wheatley reach the main road, he muttered, "Good riddance," to himself and set about his tasks for the day, beginning with a visit to the stables where he talked with the head groom about hiring a new coachman and purchasing a small carriage for Lady Phoebe's personal use. His father was selecting two carriage horses for her from Tattersall's in London, and they should arrive soon.

Once that discussion was over, Sherry spent the next hour learning everything he never thought he'd need to know about stable management. And this was only one facet of the knowledge he'd need to be a good steward of the estate, its lands and tenants. As swiftly as possible, he had to acquaint himself with what was running smoothly and what needed attention.

Once he had a good handle on the situation, he'd need to hire an estate manager. Sherry didn't expect to live at Audley Manor year-round—mostly holidays and an autumn stay during hunting season, if his work for Whitehall permitted—and thus, he'd need an estate steward who was both competent and trustworthy—hopefully a local man with an established reputation.

With that thought in mind, Sherry planned to ride into the village this morning. It was time he made the acquaintance of the villagers and neighbors, beginning with the squire.

The sound of hoofbeats on the cobblestone courtyard brought Sherry and his head groom to the stable door. They stepped outside as four strangers reined their mounts to a halt. One of them dismounted, and a stable boy ran forward to grab the reins.

"That's the squire," the stable-man said quietly.

"We'll finish our talk later." Sherry went forward to meet his guest. "Squire Levington, I believe. I'm Andrew Sherbourne."

"A pleasure to meet you, Lord Audley," the squire said, as the two men assessed each other. "I heard you were here, and after my discussions with Lord Ware, I felt you should be part of this."

Part of what? Sherry cocked his head and looked at the men still seated on their horses. "Perhaps we should all go inside where we can talk more comfortably."

"I'm afraid we are pressed for time. Did Ware mention Percy Slade to you?"

"The land dispute?"

Levington looked relieved. "Yes, that's the fellow. His wife says he's become violent, ranting about his stolen property, acting a bit addled, and she is terrified he may shoot someone. He's torn down your hedge fence at the berry patch and is guarding the property with a musket. If you'll ride with us, I'll tell you the rest on the way."

"Give me time to make a quick change," Sherry said.

Hurrying inside to pull on riding breeches and boots, he told Godwin to inform the ladies of his departure, and within ten minutes, the party was on its way, moving at a steady canter.

The squire introduced the other riders: Constable Holt and two villagers he'd recruited, Robert Franklin and Jed Harris.

Sherry nodded at each. "I take it this is unusual behavior for Slade," he said. "Ware thought he was rather good natured."

"So did I." Levington cleared his throat. "I unwittingly gave Lord Ware the wrong impression. Not only did Slade tear up the fence, he actually threatened to shoot a neighbor passing by."

"Why? What had the neighbor done?"

"Merely suggested it was Audley property, and Slade set off raving…and waving that musket, ordering him to leave," the squire said grimly. "This is a side of him I've not seen before."

"Could he be castaway by strong spirits? Or overcome by a family malady?"

"I've seen him foxed now and then. His father was overly fond of whiskey, but I never knew it to make him mean. 'Course, the family doesn't socialize much. Never has. if you're suggesting a family madness, not to my knowledge."

"Well, he sounds all about in the head to me," Constable Holt said.

• • •

The disputed berry patch, Audley estate, Friday, 1 April 1814

Slade's square Georgian country house with its gray stone façade was of moderate size but well-maintained, as were the surrounding yard and farm fields. The property contained a small stable and a barn for cattle and grain storage. A nice property for a gentleman farmer, Sherry thought.

When he, Levington, and the others reined to a halt in front of the country house, Mrs. Slade came running out to meet them. She was wearing an apron over her everyday dark blue gown and was wringing one corner of the apron in her hands.

"Squire Levington, I'm ever so glad you've come. He's not hisself, acting like a man possessed. And he won't come home. I took him up some food and water, but he just isn't thinking right. Not right at all. He'd been brooding a couple of days, talking about property thieves, and, Jed Harris, you were no help," she said, glaring at Harris before she turned back to Levington. "He won't like you coming up there, Squire, and I got to tell you—that musket of his is loaded. I seen him do it, and he took all the extra shot he had."

"All right, Mrs. Slade. Send your stable boy for the doc. It looks as though we're going to need him. Then you stay inside."

As soon as she entered the house, Harris said, "Slade sounds upset and rather determined. Maybe we should leave him be."

"You know we can't do that." Levington turned and frowned at him. "What did she mean by saying you were no help?"

Harris shrugged. "Slade and I are friends. When he's been drinkin', he likes to talk. I just listen. But I don't think we should be doin' this. He has his rights."

"Is that so? Well, then, you stay here and guard the wife."

He turned to Sherry. "Any suggestion how we approach him? I've known the man for years, but I'm not sure that will make a difference. He may shoot us on sight."

"Perhaps a bit of artfulness with you taking the lead," Sherry said, recalling an approach he and Lucien had once used in France and changing the details as he talked. "What if we pretend to just run into him? Tell him we're chasing a thief who broke into Audley Manor. That would explain my presence and give him something to think about other than his grievance. If we can keep him talking, we can assess how dangerous he is. And hopefully get close enough to grab that musket."

"It might work. Anybody have a better idea?" Levington asked. When no one spoke up he nodded to Sherry. "Let's give it a try."

They nudged their horses forward and discussed exactly what they'd say and do when they reached Slade's location. They agreed

Levington would do the initial talking, and they'd see how it developed from there.

Since the berry patch was near the bottom of a hill, they rode to the top, pulled up abruptly, and Levington called out, "Hey, Slade, is that you down there?"

"Go away, Squire." Slade came out of a make-shift shelter of tree branches and blankets carrying the musket.

"Have you seen a stranger come by riding hard?" Levington called as though Slade hadn't spoken. "A thief crept into a nearby house and frightened the ladies."

Slade acted confused and looked warily around as though the thief might be hiding in the berry bushes. "A stranger, you say? What's he look like?"

The group slowly rode down the hill with Levington describing the imaginary intruder and his horse. As they drew closer, Sherry grew tense at what he saw. The man who'd been described to him as a gentleman farmer was filthy, his hands and face covered with grime, his clothes rumpled and torn, but it was the look in Slade's eyes that worried Sherry—angry and intense one moment, unfocused and befuddled the next. Either state was dangerous in a man carrying a loaded musket.

"I don't think…I don't know. Hey, Franklin," he said, spotting the villager. "What are you doing out here?"

"Looking for this thief," Franklin said.

"Oh, uh, what thief is that?"

"The house breaker," Levington said. "I told you we were looking for one, a stranger. Are you living out here, Percy?"

Slade frowned. "I'm protecting what's mine." He lifted the musket and motioned toward Sherry. "Who's this fellow?"

Apprehension shimmered through the air as Slade stared at Sherry.

"Name's Andrew," Sherry said calmly, his hand sliding to the pistol in his coat pocket. "I just moved to the neighborhood." If anyone introduced him as Lord Audley, the disputed owner of the berry patch, Slade might start shooting. He needed to get Slade's attention away from him. "I'll just ride back up the hill a bit and keep watch for the thief."

Levington nodded. "All right, Andrew. We'll join you shortly."

Sherry walked his horse a few yards away, and Slade seemed to lose interest in him as though he'd become invisible. He stopped and sat quietly watching the scene unfold.

"You got anything to drink, Slade?" Franklin asked, dismounting. "My throat's mighty dry."

The farmer looked at his shelter and the ground around it that was scattered with the evidence of rough living. "Oh, sorry, I think it's all gone. The wife will bring some, if you wait a while, but, uh, don't know when."

"I'm mighty thirsty now. Maybe we could all walk back to the house for tea before we ride out again."

"Well, I don't know." Slade frowned, rubbing the back of his neck with one hand, allowing the musket to dangle from the other. "I suppose we could do that, if I wasn't gone too long. Who is this fellow you're chasing?"

"We don't know his name," Franklin said patiently, keeping his voice low and level. The others fell silent as Slade appeared to be responding favorably to Franklin. "Come on Percy, let's walk back together." When he reached the glassy-eyed man, he took hold of the musket by the barrel. "You don't need this, my friend."

Slade offered token resistance, tightening his hold, then he let go as the villager continued to talk matter-of-factly. "The squire can carry it for you."

Franklin handed the gun to Levington, and they started back to the house. Sherry stayed behind at the shelter long enough to see if anything should be retrieved. It was scattered with uneaten food, a few pots, and the extra ammunition the wife had mentioned. He collected the lead shot and left the rest. Wild animals would take care of the food, and the pots and blankets could be picked up later with a wagon. He nudged his horse to catch up with the others but stayed well in the rear.

Slade remained calm under Franklin's handling, and by the time they'd covered the two miles to the farmer's home, Slade was quiet and somewhat submissive. They found the doctor waiting, and Slade agreed to an examination with only a mild protest.

Oddly enough, Jed Harris had left.

"Where's Harris?" Levington asked Mrs. Slade. "I wanted to talk with him."

"I sent him away," she said. "I blame him for getting Percy so wrought up. They been drinkin' and complainin' most every night."

"I'll have a talk with him," Levington said. "And tell him to stay away for now."

Concerned Slade could become belligerent again, the four men waited to talk with the doctor, and Levington seized two pistols from the house to add to the musket he would be taking with him. Mrs. Slade slipped into the kitchen, soon filling the house with the savory aroma of baking bread and some kind of soup.

Sherry hadn't realized he was hungry, but the kitchen aromas made him grateful for the tea and fresh biscuits Mrs. Slade served them. The bowl of chicken broth went to her husband on the doctor's orders. Almost three-quarters of an hour past before the doctor was finished, and Slade had been put to bed.

The doc met with the men and Mrs. Slade in the front parlor. "I've given him a dose of laudanum, and he should sleep until morning. He was a bit better after the broth. I don't think he'd eaten much of the food you brought him," he said, addressing the wife. "Your husband's body is out of harmony with itself, ma'am. Good food and plenty of ale and tea may help, along with bed rest. I shall return in the morning to bleed him. He has agreed to my remedies, and I'm hopeful he'll recover with a sparing use of laudanum and occasional blood-letting. Try to keep him as quiet as you can."

"What if he doesn't get better?" Mrs. Slade's voice trembled.

"We won't worry about that yet. I shall watch him closely and hope for the best."

"What do I do if he becomes violent again?"

"Send for me, but it won't happen if he responds to treatment." The doctor sighed as though reluctant to go on. "If he becomes so irrational and violent we cannot care for him, he would have to be confined in a hospital such as St. Mary's in London."

Sherry grimaced. St. Mary's of Bethlehem hospital was better known as Bedlam. It had a long and inconsistent history of patient care. Currently it was overcrowded, and its primary purpose was confinement rather than treatment. The lunatics sent there were considered chronic and were locked away for society's protection. If Slade needed to be held somewhere, Sherry hoped other madhouses would be considered. A few were even humane.

The somber party rode away from the Slade farm a short time later. Such family turmoil was difficult to witness. Sherry broke the silence. "Mr. Franklin, you were remarkable with him."

"I had a cousin like that," Franklin explained. "He wasn't exactly a lunatic, and he'd never been threatening, but he could be loud and unruly. We learned to talk softly and be patient with him."

"Your experience was sorely needed today."

Levington nodded in agreement. "I'm not sure how or if we would have gotten the musket if you hadn't known what to do."

Franklin looked away, his neck reddening. "It was nothing, sir."

"I disagree, but enough said."

When the riders reached the turnoff for the village, Levington and Sherry thanked Constable Holt and Franklin for their help and then rode together another mile until they reached the fork that led to the squire's manor in one direction and the Audley estate in the other.

Sherry pulled up. "Slade was fixated on his property grievance with Audley, but I don't believe he's capable of planning the coach accident and cutting the harness. In his agitated state, he'd never get it done."

Levington gave a brief snort. "I'll say. He's confused and unpredictable, that's for sure, and for a moment there I thought he might shoot you. I'd haul him to gaol, but he clearly needs a doctor's care…and he didn't actually hurt anyone."

"Not yet," Sherry said. "But he is still dangerous. I hope Doc's treatment works. If he gets any worse, his wife may be in danger."

"I'll see that the constable and Doc are out there every day," Levington said. "And then…we'll do whatever needs to be done."

• • •

Upon reaching the manor house, Sherry found the ladies in the music room. Lady Phoebe was playing the pianoforte and playing it well. He paused in the doorway to listen before his arrival interrupted the impromptu performance.

Then Lady Anne turned as though sensing his presence. "My lord, Godwin said you had gone to Mr. Slade's with the squire and three other riders. Is something amiss?"

"It's a long story, and I'd rather be enjoying Lady Phoebe's playing," he said, crossing the room to join them.

"Oh, come now. You can do better than that," Margret said. "We have been waiting for ages. Is he the murderer? Did you go to arrest him?"

"Egad, I am sure Godwin did not say that," Sherry exclaimed. "This had nothing to do with Graham's death. We had a few tense moments—eased by Robert Franklin's experience—but mostly it was rather sad." He explained the situation, including the doctor's diagnosis and his own concern for Mrs. Slade. "We saw how quickly he can go from confused to angry. The constable and doctor will visit daily, and I hope that is enough."

"What a heartbreaking state of affairs," Lady Anne exclaimed. She turned to Phoebe. "We should talk it over with the vicar and see what can be done to help them. To get the villagers involved, we may need to set an example. Too many are afraid of people thus afflicted."

"In his case, it may be warranted," Sherry said. "No one should go inside the house, particularly the ladies. Any deliveries should be made by male servants. If treatment doesn't work or if Slade stops cooperating with Doc, I fear Slade could be a serious threat."

"And his wife is alone with him," Margret marveled.

"She wasn't afraid of him, only of losing her husband. Doc told her if he gets worse, he'll end up in a madhouse."

"Oh, no, this just gets worse and worse," Phoebe said in dismay."What a horrid future."

"It does sound bad, but don't despair yet. Mrs. Slade is a determined woman, and I would not count her out. Doc was hopeful, and he should be able to tell us more within a few days."

"We must find ways to help her," Anne said. "His condition should be treated as any other tragedy or illness–and the village ladies could bake bread, collect supplies. "

"We could provide all the meat they'll need," Phoebe said, looking at Sherry for approval.

"By all means," he said, "as long as none of the ladies deliver it."

"I have a wonderful idea," Margret said, getting into the spirit of things. "What about a ladies' tea for Mrs. Slade out on their lawn?"

Anne hid a smile. Margret's upper class breeding was showing.

Chapter Twenty One

Audley Manor and village, Saturday, 2 April 1814

Sherry spent Saturday morning visiting his tenant farms, meeting tenants, listening to their needs and concerns. Graham had apparently replaced two tenant farmers who hadn't been producing, and everyone else Sherry met appeared to be experienced farmers, doing well.

"I could be doing better," one of them told him.

"What's holding you back?"

That was when Sherry started learning the drawbacks of neglecting the on-going needs of an estate. He assured the farmer and each of the subsequent ones he met that he would pay heed to their concerns and that he would be employing an estate manager to take over in his absence.

"Thank the lord," was one farmer's relieved response.

By midday Sherry had a long list of repairs, including leaking roofs, broken equipment, and a failing water well requiring replacement. He was pensive as he headed back to the manor. Lacking the interest to be a good steward, Graham hadn't done everything he should, but he hadn't let the estate fall into ruin either. Sherry had already studied the account books, and he doubted if the property would make much profit for the next two or three years, not with everything that needed to be done, but after that… He smiled and nodded to himself. Yes, after that it should be just fine.

As he approached the turn off to Levington's manor, he wondered how Slade was doing. On an impulse, he made the turn to see if the squire was home, and, as it happened, he was outside talking with his gardener.

"Audley," Levington said striding toward him with a smile. "Out for a ride? Do you have time for a drink?"

"I cannot stay. My tenants have given me a long list of things to do. Pardon me for just dropping by like this," Sherry said. "But I was on my way home and wondered about Slade…and his wife. What have you heard?"

"He is doing better. Doc and Constable Holt were both out there this morning. Since Doc plans to continue that routine for a while, I told Holt that starting tomorrow he should go in the evening. That way we'll have eyes on the situation twice a day."

"A good plan, Squire. I hope it all works out."

"So do I." Levington nudged a rock with his boot and frowned. "I kept thinking about Jed Harris last evening, and I asked Holt to see if Mrs. Slade would tell him more about the fellow's talks with her husband. She said Harris encouraged Percy's drinking and his outrageous beliefs, particularly about the berry patch. She hadn't even met him until a few months ago and wants me to tell Harris to stay away. I agree that friends like that would only interfere with Slade's recovery."

"Some men just get mean with drink. I wonder what made Harris encourage Slade's madness."

"I'll ask him…after I warn him away from Slade and his wife. If he doesn't heed my warning, I'm sure I can find a few criminal charges that fit the situation."

"If you decide Harris has a worthy grievance of his own, let me know," Sherry said. "My brother may have simply overlooked something."

"I shall do that, but he strikes me as a man who is ever blaming the other fellow."

• • •

After dinner that evening, Sherry retired to the study and went over the books again to confirm his earlier estimates that the estate could bear the charges of all the repairs and new equipment he was considering. He was nodding with satisfaction at what he'd found when there was a tap on the door.

"Lord Sherry, it's Lady Anne."

He leapt to his feet and crossed the room. "Yes, my lady, do come in." He reached the door in time to hold it open as she entered.

"I hope I'm not interrupting at a bad moment, but I was wondering if Lord Ware should be told about the situations with Jasper and Mr. Slade."

"Please, sit down, my lady," he said, guiding her to a chair. "Of course, you're right. I've been caught up with estate affairs, and your reminder is well-timed. I shall write to him tonight." He peered at her as he seated himself. "Unless you want to take on that task?"

"Oh, I should not. It truly is not proper. I had to write about the break-in because there was no one else to do it, but you are here now."

"I hardly think you need regard society's dictates with Lucien, Lady Anne. You two are nearly engaged, and in any event, who is to know other than the two of you?"

"We are *not* nearly engaged." She sighed. "Lucien loves the inquiries he does, and my curiosity about them gets me into situations that worry him, and, if I am being totally honest, I am uneasy about the work he does for Whitehall. Neither of us is going to change. How could we live like that, always worrying about the other, wondering if we'll both survive?" She lifted her hands in an uncertain gesture. "I fail to see an answer."

"Far be it from me to advise you," Sherry said. "And I know Lucien would tell me to stay out of it, but…why not embrace what the two of you have, accept it as what it is, and get on with your life together."

"A life of constant fear?"

"I cannot deny the risks, but what about the excitement, the adventure, and your regard for one another?" Sherry gave a heavy sigh and shook his head. "But what do I know? And if you tell Lucien we had this conversation, I shall deny it." He swiftly moved the conversation away from the personal. "If you would be so kind as to write and post your letter tonight, please tell him that regardless of all that has happened, I don't believe Wheatley or Slade is the murderer. On the other hand, a man named Jed Harris has become a potential suspect. I'll explain it all when I see him."

"Very well. I shall do so…at your request." She gave him a saucy grin and rose. "And thank you for the conversation we did not have."

• • •

Late that night, Sherry was still in the study going over the improvements he planned and writing letters to set some of the process in motion. He wanted to get these things done before Lucien arrived, and he expected him in the next few days. Although he intended to take a better look at Harris, Sherry was concerned they were running out of suspects. How ironic it would be if his brother's death was the one murder they could not solve.

"What the—?" Sherry straightened in his chair at sudden loud shouts from the courtyard. He leapt to the window and distinctly heard the word," Fire."

Bolting from the study, he shouted to wake the household. Godwin met him in the hall in his nightshirt and robe. "Wake everyone," Sherry said as he ran past. "Until we know more, assume the worst and clear the house."

"Yes, my lord. I shall take care of it." Godwin's final words floated down the staircase as he was already knocking on bedchamber doors.

Sherry ran toward the side door into the courtyard and burst into a scene of organized chaos. Smoke billowed from the rear of the stables. Horses whinnied in fear as Finn and two stable lads trotted them out to safety. The head groom and Lucien's coachman, Gregory, had already rolled the travel coach outside and were carrying out harness and other small equipment. Servants poured from the house and rolled out more hoses while others had already started pumping water from the well. Two lads were emptying the horse watering trough and the rain barrel into buckets and racing with them toward the stable. Three kitchen maids had grabbed empty buckets and were filling them at the well.

Once Sherry was sure the fire was not presently threatening the house and the horses were safe, he stripped off his coat and grabbed a hose, sending the footman he replaced back to the pump. When the women brought sheets and rags that had been soaked in water, he turned the hose over to the footman who'd arrived from the Dower House, grabbed two of the wet sheets, and started beating out the flames.

Within minutes, the household was soaked, filthy from smeared soot, and boots and slippers were soaked or caked with mud, but the fire was out. The smoke was clearing, but its pungent smell was still strong enough to tickle Sherry's nose. He glanced up at the stable roof. Most of the back wall on the north end was gone, but they'd only lost a small portion of the roof above it. The rest of the stable had been saved and the damage could be easily repaired. A timely alarm had been raised before the fire got a good start or reached the stored grain and piles of hay and straw.

"Is General all right?" Sherry asked, confirming what he already knew, as he saw Finn standing off to one side with his bay gelding.

"Gor. Give 'im a fright but he good now." Finn gave the horse a pat. "Good thing John were awake."

General blew softly against Sherry's hand as though to reassure them both. "Did John discover the fire?" he asked.

"Sure did." Finn pointed to a black-haired lad in his early twenties who was clearing out an area for the horses away from the fire damage. "That's 'im."

"Thank you, Finn, for keeping this fellow safe. What about your carriage team?"

"They be good, m'lord."

"Excellent."

Sherry made his way over to John. "Thanks for sounding a warning, lad. Did you see how it started?"

"I was asleep, but an odd noise woke me. I was goin' to see what it was when I smelled the smoke and yelled fire."

"What kind of noise?" Sherry asked.

John shrugged. "Like a stick snapping. You know, as though someone stepped on it and broke it. Not a dog or fox sniffing around, something bigger, heavier. I didn't get a chance to look around though. We had to get the horses out."

"Thanks to your quick warning, everyone and all the horses are safe. No harm was done that cannot be fixed." Sherry smiled at the lad's serious face. "I shall speak to the head groom, but I'd say we can work out an extra day off for you. How does that sound?"

"By Jove. It's jolly." The boy's eyes danced.

Sherry laughed. "Be off with you then. There is still much to do." When the lad ran to join those who were cleaning the stables and putting down fresh bedding, Sherry's smile faded. It sounded as though the fire had been set. A human boot likely broke the stick John heard.

Cooper, the head groom, came toward Sherry shaking his head.

"Everyone is all right? And the horses?" Sherry asked, just to be sure he hadn't missed something.

"Yes, my lord," Cooper said quickly. "All is good. But this wasn't an accident to my reckoning. There was nothing close by to start a fire."

"Let's take a look to be certain." They walked around to the back of the stables where the fire had started, but it was too dark to make a thorough inspection, even with a lantern. Sherry stepped inside the stable to look for a lantern or candle-stick knocked over on the floor. "I don't see anything that would start a fire, but we can get a better look outside in the morning light."

"Yeh, but I'm still laying my bet on a two-legged varlet," Cooper fairly growled. "Someone was up to no good."

"A safe wager, I'm sorry to say."

Another hour slipped by before the horses were bedded down and the household was settled for the night. After a much needed bath, Sherry lay awake in bed, attempting to make sense of the fire. Why the stable? Why not the house? Was the culprit afraid he'd be seen crossing the yard? And just who the devil set it?

Was this connected to Graham's death? How could it not be? And yet, most of the local suspects had been eliminated. Was Harris a genuine suspect? Or could this be something or someone else? Such as?

Sherry could think of two possibilities—this might be Jasper's idea of revenge for having been ejected from the property, or Slade had slipped back into lunacy and escaped from his wife.

Chapter Twenty Two

Maidenhead, Saturday, 2 April 1814

Determined to find *something* that would point him in the direction of Ponsonby or Raven, Lucien returned to the Sleeping Pig Inn on Saturday morning.

He handed the innkeeper his card. "I need to reach Charles Raven. I understand he stayed here during the Spring Horse Sale. Did he leave an address or anything else that might help me locate him?"

"I heard you were asking questions around town, something about Lord Audley's accident being suspicious. I don't need the particulars," the innkeeper said, lifting a hand, "None of my business, but I'll tell you what I can. Raven didn't give an address, but he and that young fellow Jack Smith come in together."

"Jack *Smith*?" Lucien repeated doubtfully.

"Yeh, that's what he said." The publican lifted his brows and shrugged.

"Did he say anything about being from London?"

"Not directly, but when they were leaving, he mentioned they needed to hurry to get back to town for a big meeting at three, so it couldn't have been too far."

Lucien cocked his head. Jack's use of the word *town* might be significant, as that was generally how people referred to London— they were going to town. No one called it a city. Of course, he might also have meant any other town.

"Do you know if they were on horseback or in a carriage?"

"A carriage, I believe. Beg pardon, but I need to get back to paying customers." And he walked off.

Lucien went directly to the stables. A carriage meant a driver. And the stable lads knew immediately who he was asking about. Card cheating and duels drew everyone's attention, and the lads had questioned Herbert, Raven's driver, but found little joy in his answers. They knew he'd worked for Raven for several years, and it was clear he lived in London because he'd mentioned several places and events he'd attended.

"He talked about himself," the head groom said, "but not about Mr. Raven. If you asked about Raven, he'd go quiet."

"Did he say anything that might help me find them?"

The groom raised a careless shoulder. "It may not help, but Herbert was laughing about the reaction of Mr. Smith, the younger gentleman, to the rat-baiting a friend took him to."

"Did he mention the friend's name or where they went?"

"Nothing about the friend, but the baiting was held at a pub near Piccadilly…called, uh, something to do with the Queen, but I doubt you'll find Smith there, 'cause he didn't like it much."

Lucien thanked him and left. It wasn't what he'd call a great clue to follow, but he'd worked with less.

• • •

The one thing Lucien couldn't find was where Ponsonby had stayed overnight or stabled his horse, and over dinner at the Goose & Gander that evening, Lucien pondered why that would be true. The man might have had friends in or near Maidenhead, but if so, why would he not have turned to them as seconds for the duel? If he had stayed in one of the small boarding houses with a single stall or two for boarders, how would Lucien ever find such a place in a town this large? And how would Ponsonby have found one? They weren't widely known or advertized.

He pushed his plate away and glared at his tankard of ale. Why was every path he looked down in this case so complicated?

All right, assuming Ponsonby came to Maidenhead with the sole purpose of challenging Raven, he might have ridden from London just that day, but he still would have needed to stable his horse—unless, oh, devil it, he could have arrived on the mail coach. Even so, wouldn't he need a room for the night because of the morning duel? Or had he gambled all night at one of the clubs and gone straight from there to meet Raven at daybreak? He wouldn't be the first nervous dueler to have done it that way.

"Lord Ware?"

Lucien lifted his gaze to find a large, fashionable gentleman in his forties, holding his hat in his hand and looking rather uneasy.

"Yes, do I know you, sir?"

"No, my lord. My name is Roger Coyne. I would not have accosted you in this manner had I not heard you were inquiring into the particulars of the Ponsonby-Raven duel."

"This is true." Lucien raised a brow. "Have you new information?"

"I may have. I doubt if anyone else heard it."

Lucien hesitated only an instant. He'd be a fool to pass by a chance to gather even a small piece of this puzzle. "Please join me. May I buy you a brandy?"

"Thank you. I could use a pint of ale."

Coyne slid onto the opposite bench while Lucien lifted a hand and ordered their drinks.

"Do you live in Maidenhead?" Lucien asked conversationally while they were waiting for the barmaid.

"I do, my lord. I was born just a few miles away and have lived in town nearly twenty years."

"So, you are well-acquainted with the area's residents. Had you seen either of the two gentlemen involved in the duel except during the horse sale?"

"Nary a once, my lord."

Lucien paused while the barmaid delivered the tankard of ale and glass of brandy before focusing his gaze on Coyne. "What is it you have come to tell me, sir?"

"I was at Galloway's Pub that night. In truth, it isn't what I saw but a conversation I overheard. I was not trying to listen, I assure you, my lord, but nonetheless, I heard it quite distinctly." Coyne's brows pinched together as though he feared he would be thought a busy-body.

Lucien curbed his impatience. "I accept that you are a proper gentleman, Mr. Coyne, and I would very much like to know what you heard."

"Yes, well, it was after the card game was over. As it happened, I was leaving the pub right behind Mr. Raven—merely by chance, you understand—when Ponsonby pushed by me. As he reached Raven, he leaned over, and I heard him whisper, 'You were warned.' Raven looked startled, as well he might, but it was obvious that it meant something to him." Coyne leaned closer, his voice more confiding. "There was menace in his voice, I tell you. I thought his remark most telling."

"Very astute of you, sir," Lucien said. "A strong hint that the trouble began before that night."

"I thought so, my lord…as do others. There has been talk."

Lucien gave a nod. "I had heard the conjecture, but this is the first confirmation."

"I hope you find it useful." Coyne set down his empty tankard. "I shall be on my way, my lord."

"Just one more moment, sir. Did you observe Lord Audley talking with either man?"

"I don't know his lordship, so I cannot speak to that."

"A tall, thin man. Rather distinguishing looking with dark hair and side whiskers."

Coyne raise his brows. "Say, now, I do recall the side whiskers. He acted a bit reserved and somewhat ill-at-ease in that crowd. I *did* see him talking with someone, rather earnestly, I thought. It was outside shortly after the conversation I overheard. I know the other man wasn't Ponsonby, but it could have been Raven. They were standing in the shadows, however, and I'm not at all sure."

What could he make of that, Lucien wondered? If anything at all?

"Thank you, Mr. Coyne. I'm much obliged to you for coming forward." Lucien returned the gentleman's polite nod and watched him hurry out the door—a man prompted by conscience to speak out but not comfortable in doing so. He'd given Lucien another hint or two regarding this complicated affair—although it wasn't clear if they would lead anywhere.

What was certain was the situation was more serious than a simple card dispute. The game was the set-up and the duel nothing less than a failed murder attempt.

What the bloody hell had happened after that night? Had Raven gone into hiding and Ponsonby was still hunting him? Is that why they couldn't be found?

He finished his brandy and stood, asking himself for the hundredth time, what did any part of the Ponsonby-Raven disagreement have to do with Audley? Had he been the one talking to Raven in the dark that night? If so, what had they talked about?

If not for the calling card and someone's apparent determination to retrieve it, Lucien would have dismissed the affair as irrelevant. He couldn't do that now. Was it the key to understanding why Audley was killed? Was the matter still a risk to Audley's good name and thus to the reputations of Lady Phoebe and the Sherbourne family?

As Lucien climbed the stairs to his room, he acknowledged his inquiry had broadened—Ponsonby and Raven had to be found to prevent Raven's murder, a task more suited for Bow Street than Whitehall, but the calling card in Audley's possession changed everything. It looked as though Lucien's next stop might be London.

• • •

Maidenhead, shortly after one in the morning, 3 April 1814

Lucien woke with a start. Shots were being fired and voices shouted in the street. He grabbed his pistol and ran to the window. The road beneath him was filled with men who were spilling from the inn's public room and from other inns and late night establishments along the street. He frowned, having expected to see a brawl in progress or a major quarrel of some kind, but this appeared to be a celebration.

He opened the window and leaned out. "What's going on?" he shouted. He tried twice before someone finally looked up.

"Paris has fallen, sir."

Another man elaborated. "The Frogs surrendered, and they're gonna vote out Boney."

Good lord! Could this be the end of the long war? He pulled his head in and stood a moment in disbelief, the memories of those who hadn't lived to see this day flashing through his head.

Then he slipped into his clothes and went downstairs where merry-making was in full swing. The ale was freely flowing; men were laughing and slapping each other on the back. Lucien cornered Sam.

"It's true," the publican said. "We just got word. Paris surrendered three days ago, and the French senate was voting today to remove Napoleon in favor of King Louie."

"Has Napoleon surrendered or been captured?"

"Not that we've heard, but he can't hold out for long." Sam turned away in response to more shouts for ale.

Lucien wondered if Sam was right. Boney's history suggested he'd hang on as long as he could, and they didn't yet know what the Senate had done. Politicians were fickle, and many Frenchmen would oppose Napoleon's removal. Regardless of Lucien's reservations, he held out hope the news boded well for the future. The long war had to end someday…did it not?

After a celebratory tankard of ale, he returned to bed. But not to get much sleep. The crowd gradually diminished, returning inside, but a few, either ecstatic over the news or simply drunk, carried on until near dawn.

Chapter Twenty Three

Maidenhead to Audley, Sunday, 3 April 1814

Due to the short night, Lucien came down to breakfast later than usual carrying his bag. When he set it near Sam's counter, the innkeeper nodded toward the front door.

Joey was sitting on the floor, holding a tattered bag in his lap, a look on his face both hopeful and wary. Not confident at all, Lucien thought. Doubtless anyone would have difficulty believing a stranger's promises if everyone in your life so far kept letting you down…and yet, here he was.

Lucien grinned and waved him over. "Come, lad. I'll buy you breakfast."

While they ate and talked about Joey's future, Lucien was considering how he was going to get the lad to Audley. He discovered Joey had never been on a horse, except once on a dare, and that was only a few minutes three years ago. Hiring a horse was out, not to mention the difficulty of getting it back to Maidenhead. Aziz, being highbred, was also prone to high spirits, and Lucien wondered how the stallion would act with a second rider. Nonetheless, that was the best answer, if he could just convince Aziz.

"Good heavens, Lord Ware, I nearly forgot," Sam said, hurrying over to their table. "My apologies. This came for you overnight." He handed him a letter.

"Thanks, Sam. It was a rather chaotic night."

"That it was, my lord. That it was."

As Sam returned to his counter, Lucien glanced at the letter. Lady Anne.

"It is from a lady I know," he said, smiling at Joey. He swiftly ripped it open, but his smile faded and turned into a frown the longer he read. Jasper was still hanging around, and Slade had turned into a dangerous madman. And Sherry had discovered another local suspect. What the devil was happening around Audley village? Lucien didn't envy Sherry inheriting the muddle his absent-minded brother had at least partially created. Nonetheless, it was past the time Lady Anne should return to London.

"Somethin' wrong, sir?" Joey asked tentatively.

"Nothing to worry you, lad, but we should get on our way."

As if Aziz understood Lucien was in no mood for tomfoolery, his only protest to Joey's added weight was a few stiff-legged hops and a shake of his head. Afterward he settled into a steady ground-eating pace, and they arrived at Audley Manor's stable around midday. Finn ran out to grab Aziz's bridle, while Lucien dismounted and swung Joey to the ground.

"Joey, this fellow is my groom. Finn, can Joey stay with you for a while?"

"'Course, milord." Finn gave the boy a big grin.

Lucien sniffed the burnt smell in the air and noticed his coach sitting outside. "What has happed here?" he asked rather sharply. Before Finn could answer, he strode into the stable where the acrid smell got stronger as he walked toward the far end. Then he saw the charred wall and roof. "Good Lord! Was anyone hurt?" he called out to anyone listening.

"No, my lord." Cooper, the head groom, appeared behind him. "We caught it pretty quickly. Everyone got out, and we got all the horses to safety."

"How'd it happen? Was a lantern kicked over?"

Cooper shook his head. "I don't think so."

"Lucien," Sherry called, hurrying toward them. "I saw you ride in. We had quite a night."

"I can see that. A dropped candle?"

"Oh, no. Someone set the fire."

"Bloody hell, Sherry. There's way too much trouble around here. First Graham dies, then Jasper sniffing around, a bold daylight intruder, Slade's crazy threats, and now an arsonist? It's time we took the ladies to London," he said in exasperation.

"I'm not arguing with you," Sherry said. "But I do think we should talk it over. There is unfinished business here." He turned and looked behind him. "Who is the lad you brought with you?"

"His name is Joey. Long story. I'll explain later." Lucien started toward the house, then stopped and turned back. No matter how annoyed he was with the world, Joey wasn't at fault, and the child needed gentle handling. "Come here, lad," he called to the young boy standing at the other end watching Finn rub down Aziz. "I want you to meet my friend," he added, noting the child's reluctance. "Joey, this is Lord Audley."

"But I thought…" Joey looked confused.

"That I was dead?" Sherry asked gently. "That was my brother."

"Oh, sorry, sir."

"I appreciate your concern, Joey."

"This lad is tired of living on the streets," Lucien said putting a hand on Joey's thin shoulder. "I promised we'd give him a better job."

"A splendid idea. We'll find something you like, lad."

"Mighty fine, sir."

Sherry laughed, and Lucien hid a smile at Joey's response. "Go on with you now. You stick with Finn."

"Yessir." Joey nodded and ran back to join the small Irishman.

Lucien chuckled when he heard Finn admonish him, "Slow down, boy. Dunna run in here and give the horses a fright."

"Shall we go to the house?" Sherry asked. "The ladies will be eager to hear anything you learned in Maidenhead."

"No doubt." Lucien had already seen the drapes move at the drawing room window. "I believe we both have much to tell, and I could use a bit of ale or wine."

• • •

Nearly two hours passed before everyone had shared their stories and opinions of events at Audley and in Maidenhead and exclaimed over the war news from Paris. Sherry had just ordered up a bottle of champagne to celebrate the fall of Paris when Squire Levington was announced.

"Levington, do join us in a salute to our troops," Sherry said. "Ware has just told us about Paris."

"Gladly. I heard the news in the village. I hope to hear soon that Napoleon is dead," he added grimly. "Too many good men died because of him."

His remark brought a sober note to the celebration. "In remembrance of that, we should drink to those who have fallen to bring this day about," Lucien said, lifting his champagne in a toast.

Everyone raised their glass and drank.

Levington set his empty goblet on the table. "Actually, the war news is not what brought me here. It's about the fire. When I left here earlier after viewing the damage, I went directly to the Slade farm, but he had not left the house. And by the by, Doc was there, and he's much encouraged."

"That is excellent news," Sherry said.

"Very much so. While I was there, I took the opportunity to talk with Slade and his wife about Jed Harris, and then I tracked down Harris to question him about the fire. He was drunk and didn't bother to deny setting it. Immediately confessed. In truth, he was rather pleased with himself."

"Why?" Sherry demanded. "Why my stables?"

At the flood of exclamations and questions from everyone, the Squire held up his hands. "I can explain. He's a disgruntled former tenant farmer who Audley dismissed."

"Now I recall the name," Lady Phoebe said. "Lord Audley gave the tenant farm to someone else because of Mr. Harris's poor management, but that was over a year ago. Why burn the stable now?"

"He and Slade have been feeding each other's grievances for weeks, sitting around drinking blue ruin at night, and blaming Audley for their problems. Harris had already been angry, and then his wife left him. He blamed Audley for that too, instead of admitting his drunkenness was at fault. And then—already looking for a fight, I suppose—he took offense to our recent dealings with Slade. The fool convinced himself we me meant to put Slade in a madhouse so you could keep the berry patch, and when he got totally jug-bitten last night, he decided to take his revenge."

"By burning the stable?" Lucien said in disbelief.

"Good Grief," Margret added. "He must be as crazy as Slade."

"Well, maybe close to it thanks to the whiskey," Levington said. "He sure wasn't thinking clearly." He turned to Sherry and shrugged. "Don't expect any reparation for the stable. He's got nothing to his name."

Sherry waved a dismissive hand. "No matter. The damage can be repaired. I'm relieved you caught him so quickly before he did something worse."

"After talking with Mrs. Slade, I was nearly certain who the culprit was. He was foxed when we found him and blurted everything. Even as he's begun to sober, he's still angry and not denying a thing."

"If he's so angry he is void of reason, might he be responsible for my brother's death?" Sherry asked.

Levington heaved a sigh. "I thought about that, but he denies it, and Mrs. Slade said he was drinking with Percy most nights the last few weeks."

"What happens to him now?" Lady Phoebe asked.

"A few days in gaol will sober him up, and then we'll see if we can get him a job somewhere. Maybe outside of Buckinghamshire. In any event, he shouldn't be bothering you again."

"Well, that accounts for my last suspect," Sherry said as he and Lucien stood outside and watched the squire put his horse into a canter.

Lucien frowned. "That brings us back to Ponsonby and Raven. I don't know how or why your brother was involved with them, but when we find them, I believe we'll know the answer to his death.

I'm going to London to hunt for them and shall take the ladies with me if they agree to go."

"We're all going," Sherry said. "Clearly we need to locate these men, not only to learn the truth but to prevent another murder. I have unfinished business here regarding the estate and in particular, dealing with Jasper Wheatley and the IOU's Graham was holding. I'm not going to forgive the debts as long as he bothers Lady Phoebe, but those problems can wait until I return."

• • •

As it turned out, the ladies were delighted by the prospect of returning to London. Mrs. Wycliff said she missed her husband, and she probably did, theirs had been a love match, but Lucien suspected she and Lady Anne were also missing the busy social life they enjoyed in town.

Privately, Anne mentioned she'd had a letter from her father, asking about her return. "I think he is getting a bit concerned," she said.

"About what? Surely he cannot deny you've been well-chaperoned, and I have not been here most of the time." He grinned as he added, "Unless you think he is planning to marry you off to Sherry. After all, he too will be an earl someday."

"Do not talk nonsense," she said, rather sternly but her lips twitched. "Father does not have designs on Lord Sherry, but he is worried Society will remark that his marriageable daughter has been staying in the home of a bachelor for nearly a fortnight. He thinks it is time for me to come home."

Good lord. He had not thought of Audley Manor as a bachelor's home. And he should have. A short stay would be overlooked, but tongues would soon be wagging—not here, but in London—and that was the last thing he wanted.

"Your father is quite right. We shall leave for London as soon as you are ready."

"Let me talk it over with Margret, but I believe we'll be ready tomorrow."

Over tea that afternoon, Lady Anne and Margret urged Lady Phoebe to come to London with Eliza for a visit at Chadley House. "You need mourning and half-mourning clothes," Lady Anne said. "What better place to buy them than London?"

"That's true. Just looking through the London shops would be a delight," Lady Phoebe said.

"Oh, we'd do more than look," Lady Anne laughed. "Few people would know you by sight, and you'd be free to attend a few small dinner parties or other discreet social events without the village gossips looking askance at you."

"I'm not sure I would do so, not often at least, but it would be nice to know I could. And to walk in Hyde Park *would* be a treat."

"We have many parks," Anne coaxed. "We could go for walks every day."

"And visits to the museum," Margret said. "I could come into town and join you."

"Think of the bookstores, the theatre," Lady Anne said.

"All right," Lady Phoebe said with a smile. "How can I resist such temptation? I shall tell Nanny immediately. I don't want to hold up your departure."

"This is going to be so much fun," Lady Anne declared.

• • •

Return to London, Tuesday, 5 April 1814

Having made such exciting plans, the ladies eagerly set about packing, and on Tuesday they left for London. Eliza and her nanny rode with the ladies in Lucien's travel coach. He and Sherry rode astride. Joey, who'd begged to come with them, and Finn were sitting up top beside Gregory, Lucien's coachman.

They arrived in London mid-afternoon, where Sherry took his leave, headed for the Sherbourne town house, and Lucien returned Lady Anne to the Earl of Chadley, along with her guests. Since Margret had sent a note to her husband the night before, they also found Capt. Wycliff waiting.

After the first greetings were over, Lord Chadley announced the city was agog with the latest reports from the Continent. "Napoleon has abdicated."

"I never thought he'd do it," Lucien said.

"He did not have much choice, since the French senate voted him out," Wycliff said.

"Nonetheless," Chadley cautioned, "he is still attempting to dictate the terms. He agreed to step down in favor of his son taking his place, but in a bold move of solidarity—which I'm sure surprised him—the allies refused to accept his condition. They're drawing up the treaty now, and the rest of us are holding our breath to see if the negotiations fall apart."

In spite of the interesting news, Lucien wanted nothing more than to get home, have a long bath, and a night in his own bed, so he didn't linger at Chadley House. He conferred briefly with Wycliff, and they arranged to meet at Hays Mews the following morning at eleven.

"I'll send a note to Sherry tonight. We need to know everything you've already done in searching for these men so we don't waste time going over the same possibilities. I'm sorry to take you away from your wife so soon, but if we don't get to Raven before Ponsonby murders him, we may never learn what happened to Audley."

Chapter Twenty Four

London, Wednesday, 6 April 1814

Lucien shifted in his chair and leaned forward. "They have certainly taken great efforts to hide their identities."

It was near midday, and he, Sherry, and Wycliff had been talking for nearly an hour in his study. While most of Wycliff's time during the last two weeks had been taken up with a blackmail inquiry for Whitehall, he had continued to search for Ponsonby and Raven when he could. Their names were not found on the property and tax rolls, thanks to a search by Sloane, Rothe's secretary at Whitehall, and Bow Street station had no knowledge of or recorded arrests of either person.

Nor was the Quality aware of either man as far as Wycliff could ascertain by inquiring of his own friends and acquaintances. "You might have better fortune than I in looking for Raven within polite circles," he said with a shrug. "A captaincy gets me only so far."

Neither Lucien nor Sherry contradicted him as they were both aware of Society's haughty reservations.

"Since I turned up a hint of political interests by Raven, I'll ask Salcott if he knows him," Lucien said. "He represents the more serious-minded of the haute ton and political circles, but I doubt if he'll know either man by the names we have. It's obvious to me that Raven is a gentleman using a false name. I assume Ponsonby is a false name too, although I'm not as confident about it."

"Why so convinced of one and not the other?" Wycliff asked.

"Everyone described Raven as a gentleman. If that was his name, you would have found him by now. Ponsonby, on the other hand, may be out of the docks or at least the lower classes. If he has avoided Bow Street's attention, how would we have heard of him? He would have little need of an alias."

"Unless he's just cautious," Sherry crossed his arms and eyed Lucien. "Cade might know him."

Lucien sighed, shaking his head to reject the idea. "It's possible, yes. But we don't even know if Ponsonby is the man's name. Until we do, I'd rather pursue other lines of inquiry. Frankly, I've run up too much personal debt with Cade."

Neither Sherry nor Wycliff made any further comment, and Lucien was relieved. Charles Cade was a London crime lord who ran a respectable gentlemen's club and was known as the "Gentleman Thief" by a quixotic Society who had received him into their ranks. Regardless of the haute ton's acceptance, Cade was a dangerous man, and Lucien was uncomfortable with his acquaintance.

One day Cade would call in favors for the assistance he had given to Lucien and Whitehall from time to time, and Lucien couldn't help wondering what would happen if those favors were something he couldn't stomach. If Lucien refused, would he then become expendable? Marked for an assassin's bullet or a knife in the dark? Just another of those unanswered questions that thus far had kept him a bachelor.

He shrugged it off…concerns for another moment, another day.

"Lucien picked up a bit more information about the missing men in the last few days," Sherry said, filling the awkward silence. "We know Ponsonby was working for someone in London, and we have a decent description—rough fellow, short, late thirties, dark brown hair and a mustache—and he'd done some kind of business with the Barclay & Son bank on Piccadilly."

"Let's hope the *business* wasn't robbing it," Wycliff said.

Lucien gave a wry laugh. "Not entirely impossible."

"Why don't you visit the bank?" Sherry suggested to Lucien. "Your title may get you somewhere, and I don't have new calling cards yet. Although they may be ready." He frowned rather uneasily. "Father ordered them when we first came to town."

"Go pick them up," Lucien advised. "Those cards will open doors, and there is no sense in avoiding what is rightfully yours."

"Yes, I know," Sherry muttered. "I know."

Lucien let it drop at that. Sherry was struggling with his new standing in Society, but Lucien knew from experience that the sooner you accepted the change in your fortune, the sooner you set aside the guilt of having what you had never expected to be yours.

"We don't know much about Raven—I'll come back to him—but we have a possible link to Jack," Lucien said. "He talked about a friend taking him to rat-baiting at a pub near Piccadilly, and Queen was part of the pub's name."

"Queen's Head Pub," Wycliff said.

"Has to be," Sherry agreed. "Why don't Wycliff and I take that. It's usually a large and rough crowd so two is better."

"You'll be looking for Jack's friend, not Jack, who expressed distaste for the sport. It is unlikely he'd go back."

"Got it. Friend of Jack," Sherry said. "Not much to go on, except I bet the friend is young like Jack and probably from the gentry."

"I agree," Lucien said. "Now about Raven. Every person I spoke with referred to him as a gentleman, reserved and soft spoken. He's either Quality or rubs shoulders with polite society. We have a general description—early thirties, average stature, clean shaven with light brown hair. The only hints I have to where we might look are a vague remark about politics and a suggestion he was an experienced card player."

"We need to visit the gambling dens," Wycliff said. "Shall we go together or separately?"

"We could cover each club faster if at least two of us went to cover the main floor and the back rooms," Sherry suggested.

"That's true," Lucien said. "And I forgot to mention, Jack and Raven appear to have arrived in Maidenhead together. If we find one, I believe we'll have both."

"I cannot assist you tonight," Wycliff said. "I promised Margret I'd take her to Allenby's dinner party. Since she's been away and I was busy several nights before she left, I need to keep that promise."

Lucien and Sherry laughed and teased him a bit, but Lucien understood, and he was certain Sherry did too. Family had to be a priority.

Wycliff took off for a meeting at Whitehall on his other on-going inquiry, and Lucien and Sherry discussed their own commitments.

"I can meet you about ten tonight," Sherry said. "Sherbourne is in town, and we're headed to Tattersall's as soon as I get back. He still hasn't found those carriage horses for Lady Phoebe, and we'll also take a look at carriages. After dinner, he'll make an early night as he leaves for home in the morning. In fact, with Emily at her parents in the country, I should be available most of the week."

"Give your father my best," Lucien said. "I too should have a limited number of commitments. Lady Anne has her guest to keep her entertained— I believe they are shopping this morning—but I am taking them to the museum this afternoon."

"Better you than me. See you this evening." Sherry tipped his hat and disappeared down the stairs.

• • •

After seeing Lady Anne and Lady Phoebe home from the museum, Lucien ordered his coachman to stop at the Earl of Salcott's London home. The large cream-colored, two-winged mansion with dark gold trim sat well back from the road, surrounded by iron railing that enclosed expansive lawns, elegant gardens, and a large wooded area at the back. A circular drive led to the mansion and the cobblestone courtyard with its stable and coach house. They entered the main gate and his coachman Gregory stopped at the front entrance.

Lucien found his father in the study. Looking at him was like seeing himself in another thirty years—the same gray eyes and fine features, the black wavy hair with streaks of silver that only made Salcott more distinguished. The earl was seated at his desk with papers all around him, and yet, he had pushed back his chair and was staring out the window with an empty brandy glass in one hand.

"Lucien," his father straightened and smiled. "I am afraid you caught me woolgathering. It's these confounded Luddites. Lord Ashley thinks he can legislate them away, but making more laws will not cure the problems."

"I hope I have not interrupted your thoughts."

Salcott smiled. "A welcome interruption. Always, my son. Brandy?"

There was a time when Salcott's greeting would have been forced, but father and son had done much over the past year or more to ease their long estrangement. While Lucien didn't have those warm childhood memories that were the foundation of most father-son relationships, he and Salcott had formed an adult friendship which appeared to suit them well.

"I shall pass on the brandy as I won't stay long. I have plans for tonight." Lucien dropped into a chair, suddenly feeling more discouraged than he'd thought.

"Are you just returned from Audley?"

"Last night. We brought Audley's widow and child with us, and I've been escorting the ladies around the museum." He grinned. "Not that spending time with Lady Anne is ever a hardship."

"I would hope not."

Salcott wisely did not pursue the matter. Lucien already knew Anne had his father's heartfelt approval.

Instead, the earl changed the subject. "Did you learn what happened to Audley?"

"Not yet, although I know it was murder." He gave his father a short summary of his investigation so far, including what he knew about Raven. "I'm convinced Charles Raven is an alias, but I was hoping you might recognize the description, particularly as he may have a connection with political circles."

Salcott shook his head. "He does not sound familiar, but are you aware how many people work in government?"

Lucien gave him a wry look. "It was worth asking."

Salcott's brows were still lowered in thought. "Raven could be a shortened version of Ravencoff or Ravenhill. Yet, the men I know are older than you describe, and dueling would not be their style. I can ask around, if you like."

"That would be good of you, sir. We could use the help. Sherry and Capt. Wycliff have exhausted the normal avenues for finding these men, although we have new angles to explore on Ponsonby and this young man Jack who was Raven's second at the duel."

"Cade might know Ponsonby."

Lucien gave his father a sharp look. "Not you too. Why does everyone bring up his name?"

"Now you are being obtuse." Salcott gave him an indulgent look. "Whether you approve of Charles Cade's business dealings or not, you cannot deny he has provided valuable assistance to you and to Whitehall in the past."

"Yes, that is true…but I don't know why, or what he wants from me in return… and that worries me."

"There may be no rhyme or reason to it, simply a quirk of the man."

"You sound as though you approve of him."

The earl frowned at him. "He is who he is, Lucien. You have to admit he is unique."

"I grant you that. I'd still prefer to keep my distance."

Salcott shrugged. "Do as you see fit, but he may well be the only person in Society who knows the right people to find a man like Ponsonby."

"I am aware, but I hope to find Raven first. Then, if I'm right that Ponsonby intends to murder Raven, he will find us." Lucien straightened and rose. "I should be going. You have work to do, and I'm meeting Sherry to begin a search of the gambling dens. Good evening, sir. I shall find my way out."

"If I hear anything of Raven, I shall send word. Take care, Lucien."

As he sat in his coach on the way to his townhouse to change clothes, Lucien frowned, wondering if Sherry and Salcott were correct, that he needed to swallow his misgivings and ask for Cade's assistance. The man had a web of information that was second to none, not even Whitehall, particularly when it came to London's underbelly.

Perhaps he should send a note to Cade, merely asking if he knew Ponsonby but not to pursue the matter further. Surely such minimal contact would keep them at arm's length. He could always reach out again if necessary. Having made peace with his reservations, Lucien wrote the note as soon as he got home and sent it off.

• • •

London, Wednesday night, 6 April 1814

As pre-arranged, Lucien drove his curricle with Finn aboard to Sherbourne House at ten that evening. Sherry was waiting, wearing his favorite colors, a brown coat and top hat with fawn trousers.

He hopped up beside Lucien with a grin. "How were the ladies?"

"Lady Phoebe was delighted by everything at the museum. It was rather entertaining just to watch her. Afterward we went for ices, and by that time she was worrying about Eliza, so I took them home. Honestly, I think she was tired from all the shops they'd visited in the morning."

Sherry lifted his brows. "I believe we're fortunate they didn't ask us to accompany them on that excursion."

Lucien laughed. "Lady Anne would never ask. She knows I have little patience for extended shopping. A bonnet, a piece of jewelry, are fine, but beyond that, I am hopeless. She is better off with a footman to fetch and carry, and she knows it."

"When Emily comes to town, I hope Lady Anne will pass on her wisdom."

"I'll tell her you said so. By the by, I talked with Salcott earlier this evening. The names meant nothing to him, but he offered to ask around Parliament today in hopes Raven's description or Jack's name would bring some results."

"Capital idea. I've been wondering if Lady Julia could make sketches from the descriptions as she did on the kidnapping case."

"I had not thought of that, but none of us have seen these men. We cannot provide the details she needs. No, I'm afraid we just have to hope that something will turn up if we look long enough. My strategy for tonight is to mention Maidenhead and the duel frequently on the chance Raven or Jack may have talked about the affair."

And so they drove from club to club, mingling, playing a game of cards now and then, and having entirely too many drinks. When they were too tired to continue in the early hours of the morning, Lucien turned the reins over to Finn. They made plans to try again the next night, and Lucien vowed to pace the drinks a bit better.

"If you hadn't talked to so many witnesses who saw these men in Maidenhead, I'd swear they didn't exist," Sherry said as they pulled up to Sherbourne House and he climbed down. "I say, do you know what the ladies have planned for tomorrow?"

"Fittings, I believe. I'm staying far away from that."

"Good Lord, yes. I had thought I might take Lady Phoebe for a walk in the park, but I'm sure another day would be better."

"Wise decision." Lucien chuckled. "Until tomorrow night."

Chapter Twenty Five

London, Thursday, 7 April 1814

The morning began early with the ringing of bells and the news Napoleon had abdicated unconditionally to be exiled to the Isle of Elba. The long war spanning twenty years was over. Even Lucien's valet Talbot was smiling when he brought him the news with his morning coffee.

Regardless of the short night and too many brandies, Lucien was out and about by mid-morning. He stopped at Whitehall to hear the latest details from France and was pleased to learn from Sloane that a formal treaty would be signed within three or four days.

"I wonder if they can hold him on Elba," Lucien said.

"They must think so." Sloane gave him a worried look. "I'd be more confident of peace if he was in prison or dead."

"You are not the first to say that. While I'm here, I suppose you haven't heard anything about Charles Raven?"

"Not a word, my lord." Sloane pushed his wire-rimmed glasses up on his nose. "I'd say he is not who he says he is."

"It appears so. We'll just keep looking."

After leaving Whitehall, Lucien drove to the Barclay & Son banking establishment on Piccadilly. Leaving Finn with the horses, he entered the front door, presented his card, and was introduced to Alexander Barclay, the slender, neatly dressed son in the bank's title. As his hair was already gray, Lucien assumed the original Barclay had retired or passed on.

"My lord, please step into my office. I am delighted to serve you in any way I can. Are you looking to open an account?"

"Not today," Lucien said. "I'm attempting to locate a man calling himself George Ponsonby. He claims to have done business with your bank." Lucien seated himself, and Barclay settled behind his desk.

Barclay's look was speculative. "I am sorry, my lord, but the name is not familiar. As you said 'calling himself,' you must have a reason to believe Ponsonby is not his true name."

"That is correct." Lucien gave him Ponsonby's description. "Witnesses have suggested he was merely disguised as a gentleman."

Barclay frowned. "What has this man done?"

Lucien hesitated. "He is suspected of murder."

"Good gracious." The banker stiffened in dismay. "We shall, of course, do everything we can to assist you. While I do not recognized this man's name or description, perhaps one of my clerks will. If it suits you, my lord, I shall send them in one at a time to speak with you." He stepped to the door, and within moments the first of four clerks arrived.

Not until the third clerk, a young man with red hair and freckles, did Ponsonby's description engender a positive nod of the head. "It could be him. I recall the mustache, but he wasn't using that name. He was a scruffy fellow, all right, dressed like a laborer when he was here. He was trying to cash a bank note for twelve pounds. He got unpleasant when I questioned him about where he got it and told me I'd best remember him because he'd be back with another note just like it."

"What name did he give?"

"Uh, well, that was a while back, my lord." The young clerk shook his head slowly. "It may have started with T. Tate, Talbot? No, that's not right. Sorry, I just don't recall."

"When was this?" Lucien asked. If it was recently they might be able to locate the bank note, which just might lead to Ponsonby's employer. But those hopes were swiftly dashed.

"Three, maybe four weeks ago."

"And he hasn't been back?" Lucien persisted. If Ponsonby had been paid half up front and promised the other half when the job was done, then Raven might still be alive.

"No, sir. I haven't seen him."

"Was there anything about him that could help us locate him?"

The clerk stared at the desk in thought. "He had a gold ring on his pinkie finger, right hand. Just a plain band, but it was real gold, I'm sure. I wondered if he had stolen it." He flushed at the admission. "I cannot recall anything else. I wish I had paid more attention."

"You have done very well, sir, particularly after so long."

The clerk smiled. "He wasn't our usual type of customer, my lord."

Lucien nodded. "I suppose not." He thanked the clerk and Mr. Barclay for their cooperation before returning to his curricle.

Finn handed over the reins. "Any luck, milord?"

"I believe Ponsonby was there, but otherwise, no."

"Ye'll find 'im, m'lord," Finn said with a shrug. "Ye a'ways do. Where to now?"

Lucien flicked the reins. "Home, Finn. Until tonight I have nothing but thinking to do."

• • •

Deep in thought, Lucien walked into his townhouse, still trying to determine if there was something he learned at the bank that could be put to use. There was the ring, of course, but it wasn't unusual enough for most people to notice. He absently handed Hughes his hat, and the butler handed him a note.

"The boy who delivered it said you should open it immediately." Hughes sniffed as though he found the directive offensive.

Lucien couldn't mistake the bold writing. It was from Cade.

A body at the Wapping ferrymen's stairs may be of interest to you. I believe it to be that of Owen Tulk, known to you as George Ponsonby.

And, no, I did not have him killed."

C"

Lucien read it twice, thinking rapidly. For once, he hoped Cade had made a mistake. If Ponsonby was dead, how would they ever find the person who paid him to murder Raven and possibly Audley?

After a moment, he retrieved his hat from Hughes, and called for his curricle to be brought around again. Within twenty minutes he'd notified Dr. Pettigrew, the physician/surgeon used on death cases by Rothe and many at Bow Street, and he had picked up Sherry. They headed into east London to the Wapping docks south east of Whitehall and below the notorious Radcliffe Road.

Lucien and Sherry waited at the top of the Wapping ferrymen steps used by those accessing the ferries on the Thames River. This particular set of steps was known as the Dead Man Stairs. It was one of the places along the river where bodies were pulled ashore and left to be identified by relatives or until a coroner had them removed.

The stench rising from the bodies and the river itself was overwhelming and the scene made all the more eerie by the calls of seagulls hunting for food. Lucien was grateful that John Pettigrew arrived only minutes behind them. The three men proceeded down the steps with handkerchiefs held over their noses.

"That must be him," Lucien said, pointing to a male corpse that was still recognizable in spite of decomposition. The figure fit the general description of Ponsonby—right age and height, right hair color, mustache—and although the gold ring had been removed, presumably by a thief, Pettigrew found the distinctive mark on his little finger where one had been. If Ponsonby, or rather Owen Tulk, had any funds left of the twelve pounds, that too was gone, as were his coat and shoes. His other garments, not yet snatched by the rag-pickers, were torn and soaked with dried blood.

"He was stabbed at least twice," Pettigrew said as he squatted next to the body and brushed the flies away. "Abdomen and chest."

"Facing his attacker," Lucien said. "He saw it coming."

"I'd say so," Pettigrew agreed. "But not in time to fight back. There are no other signs of injury. It was quick and unexpected. He has been dead three or four days, probably pulled out of the water yesterday." The young doctor stood. "Does the family know?"

Lucien shrugged. "Unknown, but we'll attempt to locate them and get a positive identification. And we'll notify Bow Street."

"Very good. Then I'll return to my living patients."

They climbed the steps rather swiftly, eager to get away from the terrible smell. Ponsonby/Tulk had been only one of five bodies on the stairs. The others had been there longer and were unlikely to ever be identified by sight.

As they drew close to their carriages, Lucien thanked Pettigrew for coming. "I owe you a good bottle of brandy."

The young doctor smiled. "I shall look forward to it. Always a pleasure to see you, gentlemen. Someday you'll have to stop by, and tell me what this was all about."

• • •

Surprisingly, it didn't take long to locate Owen Tulk's family—a wife and a girl who looked no more than ten. They lived in a rundown row house not far from the docks where her husband's body was found.

Mrs. Tulk might once have been an attractive woman, but life had beaten her down. She regarded them solemnly with tired eyes when the news was delivered and nodded her head. "He'd been away too long. I reckoned he weren't comin' back this time."

"We'd like you to identify the body," Lucien said.

She shot her daughter a worried glance. "Her bein' a girl, I don't like leavin' her alone."

"It won't take long."

"I'll stay with her," Sherry offered. "It would be crowded on the curricle with three of us, and I'll make sure your girl stays safe."

After staring at Sherry a moment as though assessing whether he could be trusted, Mrs. Tulk climbed aboard the curricle, tucked the strands of her mouse-brown hair behind her ears, and clutched the seat as Lucien flicked the reins.

The identification was brief. She recognized her husband immediately, then turned away with slumped shoulders and asked about the ring.

"I'm afraid it was stolen," Lucien said. "What do you want done with the body?"

"I'll have his kin come get 'im and bring 'im home. He weren't a good man, but he provided fer us, and we'll do right by 'im."

"Since he was stabbed, I'll have to report this to Bow Street. Someone may come to talk with you." And then again, they might not. Bodies pulled from the Thames and of those who lived in this area weren't always high priority for the constables or for the Thames River Police, and their murders were rarely solved.

She nodded again, a woman who appeared to face life by accepting whatever came her way. When they returned to her house, Lucien handed her several quid from his pocket. She hesitated, giving him a questioning look.

"For your daughter. Take care of her."

The woman nodded once again, apparently reassured that his interest was kindly. She took her daughter by the hand and entered the house without a backward glance.

"Well, was it Owen Tulk?" Sherry asked as he climbed aboard the curricle.

"It was. Next stop Bow Street." Lucien paused and sighed. "And then, I have to talk with Cade. He may know who Tulk's employer was…and likely the person who killed him."

"Unless it's Cade himself."

"That's a possibility, yes, but he denied it. We need the answers, no matter where they take us, and, in all truth, I doubt this is Cade's work or he wouldn't have sent us to the body."

"I concede the point, but why was Tulk killed?"

Lucien lifted a brow. "Perhaps because he failed to kill Raven. Or because the duel and Audley's death drew too attention to him. His employer may have feared Tulk would be found and that he'd talk."

"He'd become more of a risk than he was useful."

"Very aptly stated."

• • •

Cade's Gentleman's Club was quiet at five in the afternoon, and Lucien's presence was noted the moment he walked in the door. Reginald, the house manager, met him before he was halfway across the lounge.

"Lord Ware, what may we do for your today?"

"Is he in?" Lucien asked.

"He is. Shall I inquire if he will see you?"

Lucien sighed. "Yes, Reginald, I would appreciate it."

"Very good, my lord." Reginald disappeared up the stairs only to return moments later and gesture for Lucien to come ahead. They passed on the stairs. "I believe you know the way."

Lucien gave a single nod.

As usual Charles Cade was seated behind the desk in his spacious office furnished in gleaming mahogany. He was sipping a brandy, and a second poured glass had been placed on a small table set between two chairs.

"I hope you'll join me in a drink," Cade said.

"If you insist. I would not want to waste a good brandy." Lucien seated himself, took a small drink, and eyed the club owner. Cade had shaved off the small mustache he'd worn for the last two years. It made him look younger. In all other aspects he remained the same, a man in his mid-thirties, physically fit, a few inches shorter than Lucien, with fashionably styled brown hair, and a charming manner much more suited to the gentleman he appeared to be than the crime lord Lucien knew he was. Lucien had seen those light blue eyes turn hard as stone.

"Thank you for the note. Tulk's wife appreciated knowing what had happened to him. How did you know he'd been using the name Ponsonby?"

"So you came here to interrogate me?" Cade asked, a hint of amusement on his lips.

Lucien smiled in response. "I would not dare, but I am pushed for time, and I know you are a busy man. I thought it was best to get right to it."

Cade chuckled. "I do like a man who speaks his mind, although I cannot decide whether you are so by nature or if you're highly adaptable. Tulk was not very inventive. He had used the alias before. I had already been informed of his death when I received your note."

That did not sound good. "I dislike asking, but I sincerely hope he had not fallen afoul of your business interests."

Cade took a sip of his brandy. "What a refined way of asking if I had him killed, but I already told you I did not. Do you take me for a fool? I would not have informed you of his death if I had."

Lucien nodded. "Do you know who he worked for?"

"What is your interest?"

Lucien sighed inwardly. He loathed giving Cade information about himself or his friends, but as usual, it was unavoidable if Cade was to understand the situation. He related the basics of his search for Audley's killer and how that had led him to Ponsonby and Raven.

"And you have yet to identify Raven?"

"I had hoped Ponsonby could give me Raven's true name…and the name of who hired him."

"Yes, I see. Tulk's death is a double blow, leaving you with a number of unanswered questions."

"And little to go on," Lucien admitted

Cade set his glass down. "Tulk worked for Manny McCarty, but Manny would not have ordered a murder as refined as a duel or tampering with harness. Tulk must have picked up a side job on his own."

"Would he have been killed for stepping out of line?"

"By Manny? No, he wouldn't care."

Lucien emptied his glass, set it down, and stood. "Thank you for pointing me to the body," he said, reluctantly acknowledging his growing debt. "It'll save us from wasting additional hours looking for a dead man."

"While a corpse is not what you hoped to find, his death may allow you to locate Raven in time to prevent another murder."

"How so?"

Cade lifted a brow. "The real murderer, the man holding the purse strings, will need time to hire another killer."

Chapter Twenty Six

London, Thursday night, 7 April 1814

Sherry's plans for another night of visiting the gambling dens with Lucien changed at seven that evening when Wycliff sent word he was available to attend the rat baiting at the Queen's Head Pub. Consequently, they split tasks, with Sherry meeting Wycliff at the pub and Lucien continuing alone to the gambling clubs.

Sherry and Wycliff entered the smoke-filled room below the public rooms of the well-known Queen's Head tavern. Rat-baiting was a fairly new betting sport, but it still drew a good crowd. While ratting had begun as an occupation for the lower classes to rid homes and establishments of the recent invasion of the brown "Norway" rats, the specialized breeding of dogs for the rat hunts had eventually led to men betting on whose dog was the best. As the ratters also bred rats in secret to keep business flowing by deliberately releasing them, the competition grew and rat-baiting moved indoors to pit the best rats against the best dogs—and the best dogs against each other. It eventually became a gentleman's sport to bet on the fastest time and the highest number of kills.

The room Sherry and Wycliff stood in had a large 12 by 12 feet pit in the middle, originally built for cock fighting. The floor inside the circle had been whitened so the rats would be easier to see and count. At one side were cages of rats, and two small terrier-type dogs whined and barked in excitement.

Sherry searched the crowd where bets were furiously being placed. How was he supposed to find this friend of Jack's? He moved through the crowd in one direction and Wycliff went the other. He decided his best approach was to inquire if anyone had seen Jack. If the friend was present, perhaps he'd come forward to see why Sherry was asking.

When the rats were turned loose in the pit and the first dog began his frenzied attack, Sherry was forced to suspend his questioning because he couldn't hear or be heard. The fight was over quickly—30 rats killed in 3 minutes. While they were preparing the pit for the next competitor, Sherry resumed moving through the crowd. Thus far, no one admitted knowing Jack, although a few had asked, "Jack who?" He was prepared for that.

"Sorry, I don't have his surname. We met here a few weeks ago. He talked about a friend with carriage horses for sale, but I've forgotten the friend's name. I was hoping to find Jack again." Everyone had accepted his explanation, but it hadn't gotten him to Jack's friend or Jack's full name.

Just before the second match started, Sherry saw Wycliff raise his hands and gesture he'd learned something. Hastening toward them, Sherry lost sight of Wycliff as pandemonium broke loose with the renewed frenzied mayhem in the pit by dog number two. Cheers and grumbling greeted the latest time: 30 rats in 3.1 minutes. The first dog had won the match by six seconds.

While those who'd placed wagers were happily collecting winnings or bemoaning their loses, set up and betting began for the next match. Sherry pushed through the crowd and finally spotted Wycliff with a round-faced, rather pudgy young man.

"This gentleman knows Jack," Wycliff said when Sherry arrived.

The young man smiled jovially as Wycliff introduced them. Robin Goode was bracing his feet to remain steady, and his breath smelled of Blue Ruin gin. Nevertheless, he appeared coherent.

"I know Jack Ridout, but I haven't heard of any carriage horses for sale. Are you sure this is the right fellow?"

"He fits the description," Wycliff said.

"Does the Jack you know work in government?" Sherry asked.

"Yes, he does," the young man's face lit up. "Not exactly sure where. He's a junior clerk for some fellow in Parliament. I don't pay much attention to that stuff, and I don't know Jack well. We've done a bit of drinking together, but that's all." He shrugged affably. "You won't find him here. He didn't care for it. Hey, sorry, but I got to go and get my bet down before it's too late."

"Wait, tell me where you met him."

Goode shrugged. "One of the clubs."

Sherry would have pursued the matter, but the young man had already faded into the crowd.

Well, they had a name, and Sherry was more than ready to get out of there and away from the persistent smell of blood. Wycliff's pinched face said he too had had enough of rat-baiting. It was an ugly, bloody event without much sport to it, certainly not for the rats.

"It's still early," Sherry said, as they reached the top of the stairs where noise was at a minimum. "I'm going to locate Ware, if I can, and let him know we have a name. Want to join me?"

"No. If I hurry, I can escort my wife to a ball she plans to attend." He grinned. "Much as I enjoy your company, my friend, after the last couple of hours I believe I'd rather enjoy a bit of music and dancing."

• • •

An hour later Lucien was playing Faro in a rather disreputable gambling den on the far east side of London when he looked up and was surprised to see Sherry in the crowd of on-lookers. He gave up his seat at the first opportunity and joined his partner. "I had not expected to see you tonight."

"Rat-baiting is a disgusting event, not one I wish to spend much time around, but we have Jack's name. It's Ridout. And he is a junior clerk somewhere in government."

Lucien grinned and slapped Sherry on the back. "Excellent! It may take a day or so, but I'd wager Sloane will find his name on government rolls. And Ridout should take us to Raven. I'm keen to hear their story."

"So, are we done for tonight?" Sherry asked.

Lucien hesitated. "Yes, I suppose so. I was following the trail of a gambler who I thought might be Raven, but it looks as though Ridout is a more reliable path to that end. So, yes, let us go home."

"I'll follow you out. I found you by looking for Finn, and I left General with him."

They stepped into a heavy fog and a black night lit only by lights from the gambling establishment. The moon was hidden behind clouds that had threatened rain all day. Lucien frowned, not seeing Finn right away. Then he spotted a grove of trees off to the right where his groom might have sought shelter to keep the open carriage dry. He saw his grays and walked in that direction.

In addition to asking about Raven and Jack, Lucien had made tentative inquiries regarding how he might have a word with crime boss Manny McCarty. He and Sherry were discussing whether they should continue or delay attempts to reach McCarty until they'd spoken with Ridout.

At an odd sound from the shadows of the building, Lucien broke off in mid-sentence and spun in that direction while he heard Sherry turn to face running steps from behind them. A hard bat missed Lucien's head but hit his back, and pain shot across his ribs. He stumbled, caught himself, and kicked out with one boot, connecting with the assailant's knee. It buckled, and the man went down, just as two more ruffians leapt from the shadows.

Lucien cursed the fact that his pistols were in the curricle, but he pulled the knife from his right boot, took a slash at the arm of the first man regaining his feet, and then side-stepped to the left to meet the next threat. The new assailants were giving a wary eye to Lucien's blade, but their clubs had a longer reach, and they were circling ever closer.

Sherry moved behind him, and they stood back to back as the four cutthroats grew bolder. Then a light carriage with a team of gray horses charged toward them. Finn was yelling something Lucien couldn't understand, but he turned pulling Sherry with him. As their attackers scrambled to get out of the way of those flashing hooves, Lucien and Sherry swung aboard the curricle, Finn flicked the whip, and the grays leapt forward.

The bloody devils hadn't yet given up. A big man grabbed the back of the carriage and hung on. Another one snagged General's stirrup as the big bay galloped behind, still tied to the carriage, and the ruffian was slowly pulling himself into the saddle. While Sherry stomped on the hands clinging to carriage until the man let go, Lucien retrieved one of his pistols and shot the ruffian attempting to mount General.

Lucien took over the reins, and only minutes later he pulled the galloping team to a halt a half mile away. They'd left their attackers far behind.

"What was that about?" Sherry demanded. "We've stirred up enough people lately that those ugly customers might belong to Tulk's employer, Raven, Manny McCarty or God knows who else."

Lucien flinched as he stretched his bruised back, and he handed the reins back to Finn. "Appreciate the timely rescue, lad. I'll let you get us home if you don't mind." At the small man's wide grin, Lucien turned to Sherry now aboard General. "I'm relieved we are relatively unscathed so we have the opportunity to discover who they were."

• • •

London, Friday, 8 April 1814

After Talbot fussed over him and taped his ribs the following morning, Lucien escaped the house and went straight to Whitehall.

"Mr. Sloane, I have a name. Jack Ridout, possibly John or Jonathan. He is a junior clerk in government employment, and I desperately need to find him. I think he will lead us to Charles Raven."

"Good news, indeed, sir. I have a few things I must finish for Lord Rothe, but I should be able to tell you where he works by tomorrow. Sooner, if other things fall into place."

"Sloane, I am in awe of you." Lucien grinned at him and left. In spite of his injured ribs, he was in excellent spirits, knowing they were getting closer to untangling the truth.

• • •

Lucien had not seen Lady Anne since they went to the museum, and he certainly owed her and Lady Phoebe a report on their progress. He stopped by Chadley's London house in hopes he might catch the ladies before they ventured out on whatever they had planned for the day.

As good fortune would have it, he found them taking tea with a guest, Mrs. Wycliff.

"My Lord Ware," Anne said, giving him a warm smile. "Thank heavens you have come to interrupt this very gruesome tale from Margret regarding rat-baiting."

"Ah, a re-telling of the captain's adventures. I understand he and Lord Sherry had quite an interesting night."

"A dreadful night, I'd say. But now that you have this young man's name, do you truly believe you will find the murderer soon?" Lady Phoebe asked.

"I dearly hope so." He turned to Anne with a smile. "Since you've already heard of our activities, tell me what you have been doing."

"Mostly we have visited the shops," she said.

"Oh, my, yes," Lady Phoebe added. "I am embarrassed at the number of gowns I now own. I'm not sure I shall wear them all in Buckinghamshire. A widow being out and about is not so readily accepted there."

"Then you must stay here," Anne said. "As long as you wish."

"And when you grow tired of Anne's company," Mrs. Wycliff said with a chuckle, "you may visit with the captain and me. You needn't go home to Audley for months."

"Oh, I could not. Thank you both for your gracious offers, but I must go home soon. London is delightful to visit, but it is not my home." She looked at Anne and Margret. "You have been wonderful to me, but I am already missing the country...just a bit, but it will grow stronger."

"You cannot fault her for that," Lucien said. "Think of all the fresh country air and the open fields of flowers. Parts of London are not very appealing in the summer."

"That is true," Mrs. Wycliff said, making a face. "That is when I am most grateful our home is outside the city. It may be inconvenient to drive an hour to attend social events, but it's well worth it in the heat of summer."

"If you love the country so much, I hope all of you will visit Lord Audley's manor from time to time so that I may see you again."

"I'm sure we shall," Lucien said, although he had no certainty it would happen soon or very often. He had trouble finding time to visit his own estate at Waring in Lincolnshire once a year. It was a two-day trip by coach.

He took an inadvertent glance at Lady Anne. If he were to have a family, he would have to make the effort to visit Waring more often. Children thrived on the freedoms in the countryside, as he had done at his uncle's estate. Something more to think about.

After spending another half hour talking with Lady Anne and secretly holding her hand, he took his leave, and was nearly home when he was overtaken by a closed coach. The driver gestured for him to pull over. Lucien glanced at the shield on the carriage door and sighed. What did Cade want with him?

Lucien halted his team and stepped down, handing Finn the reins. He reached for the door on Cade's coach, and it flew open.

"Get in here," Cade said through gritted teeth. He was obviously angry, an emotional display Lucien had not witnessed before.

"Good day, sir. Is there a problem?"

"Sit down, you damn fool. Did I not tell you to stay away from Manny McCarty?"

Lucien's good humor fled swiftly. "I am not one of your men, Cade, nor have you any other right to dictate to me. I do as I see fit."

"And it nearly got you killed."

"Ah, you heard about last night's attack. I assure you, sir, Sherbourne, that is, Lord Audley, and I have been in worse scrapes."

"Perhaps, but this one was unnecessary," Cade said grimly. "I have expended considerable good will today in persuading Manny to call off his cutthroats."

"Who asked you to?" Lucien snapped. "Why do you insist on intervening like this? More to the point, what is your interest in me?"

The two men stared at one another for long seconds. Cade was likely deciding what, if anything, to tell him. Lucian's thoughts were more murderous, wondering if he could just choke the truth out of him.

Cade finally sighed and leaned back. "I owe your brother Arthur a debt I cannot repay."

Taken aback, Lucien's eyes widened, his anger dissipating. "You knew Art? When? What kind of debt?"

"I have said all you need to know. Now get out, and leave McCarty alone. He can't help you, nor would he if he could."

Chapter Twenty Seven

London, Saturday morning, 9 April 1814

While Lucien was still at breakfast the following morning, he received a note from his father.

> *Nothing of worth to pass on from Parliament. I hear you have created a mystery for the gossips, and speculation over your interest in Raven is spreading rapidly. Perhaps it will bring him into the open or reveal the witness you seek.*
> *Salcott*

It was not what he'd hoped to hear, but he had to chuckle that Salcott had understood why his only son and heir had been so strangely garrulous the last few nights. He could only hope his efforts to reach out for information had not indelibly tagged him as a gabster, besmirching his reputation beyond redemption.

He had just sent word to the stables to bring his curricle around and was walking toward the back hall, when he heard voices at the front entrance. He turned to see what the commotion was when Sherry hurried toward him.

"Have you heard from Rothe? I received this note just moments ago." Sherry waved a message in the air. "He is telling us to halt our investigation."

"What are you talking about? Let us step into the study."

"It's regarding Raven," Sherry said in exasperation the moment Lucien closed the door. "We've been ordered to stop looking for him."

"You say Rothe sent this? What the devil does Charles Raven have to do with Whitehall?"

"Exactly what I want to know."

Hughes tapped on the door and stepped inside. "My lord, an urgent message from Lord Rothe."

"Your similar orders, I assume," Sherry said derisively.

Hughes handed Lucien a note. It was indeed in Rothe's handwriting. The marquess must have been in a hurry to write it himself. He ripped it open, and, as Sherry had predicted, it advised him to halt his search for Raven but offered no reason why. Lucien frowned. Such high-handedness was not typical of the marquess.

"Have we stumbled into some secret operation?" Lucien wondered aloud.

Sherry dropped his note on the desk. "Whatever the case, Rothe owes us an explanation—certainly more than this."

"And I suggest we go ask."

"Excellent idea, Lucien. Get your hat, and let us be on our way."

Before either man had a chance to move, another knock on the study door was followed by Hughes announcing, "Two gentlemen are asking to see you, my lord. Mr. Blackbourne and Mr. Ridout."

"I was just on my way out. Ridout, you say?" Lucien looked at Sherry. "Jack Ridout?"

"I cannot say, my lord. Do you wish me to inquire? Mr. Blackbourne indicated it was urgent." Hughes paused. "He also asked if Lord Audley was here. He expressed a wish to speak with you both."

Lucien and Sherry exchanged another look.

"Are they in the drawing room?"

"Yes, my lord."

Lucien straightened his cravat. "Then we shall see them directly. Thank you, Hughes."

"Very good, my lord."

"Well, Sherry, this is an interesting development. Let us not keep our guests waiting."

When they entered the drawing room, they found two men standing near the front windows and talking quietly. The older man was in his mid-thirties, wearing well-made but conventional attire, his light brown hair carefully brushed into the windswept style. He came forward promptly, his blue eyes assessing them. His companion, no more than two or three and twenty, hung back, allowing the older man to take the lead.

"I am Charles Blackbourne," the man said. "And this is my junior clerk, Jack Ridout."

Lucien introduced himself and Sherry. "I assume this is about Maidenhead."

"Partially. It will take some time to explain. May we be seated?"

"Yes, of course," Lucien said. "Would you like tea or coffee?"

"Not for me." Blackbourne looked at his companion. "Jack?"

"No, thank you, my lord," the younger man said, lapsing back into silence.

Lucien drew up a chair and sat opposite his guests, who'd chosen the couch. Sherry elected to stand, his arm resting on the fireplace mantel.

Blackbourne cleared his throat. "Let me first state, I am also known as Charles Raven. I serve as a senior clerk to the Foreign Secretary, Viscount Castlereagh, and Jack is my very loyal assistant." He gave a heavy sigh. "Where to begin… To my shame and regret, I am excessively fond of gambling, mostly card games of chance. For the last two years it has consumed much of my time and funds. More than twelve months ago, Castlereagh learned of my weakness and deepening debts, and he was rightfully concerned they could lead to a scandal. He offered me the option of curtailing my habit or resigning. Naturally, I was grateful for the opportunity to prove myself worthy, and I stayed away from the tables for three long months. I say long because it was a daily struggle, in spite of my improving finances. Then I started playing again—just a game now and then at first. I thought I could control it, but soon it was every night."

When Blackbourne hesitated, Lucien prodded him. "Castlereagh was not aware you were gambling again?"

"No, I adopted the name of Charles Raven and sought games on the outskirts of London. I thought I was being careful, but someone noticed, and I received a letter from a Mr. Brown. He said he would remain silent if I provided him with certain information on Castlereagh and Liverpool, including their private opinions on proposed laws and their activities."

"He is blackmailing you," Sherry said. "And I'd wager Brown is not his name."

Blackbourne nodded. "I assume he is a political opponent, seeking a means to discredit Castlereagh or Liverpool, but I've been unable to learn who he truly is. Eventually, I agreed to his demands, thinking I could satisfy him by mentioning a few minor things, mostly confirming gossip that was already out there."

"But even facing blackmail, you went on gambling," Sherry said incredulously.

"Yes, I couldn't seem to stop."

Lucien shot Sherry a look to hold back on the censure. Shaming Blackbourne wouldn't help the situation, and Lucien wanted to keep the politician talking until he'd told them everything, even the smallest details.

"Hence the game in Maidenhead," Lucien said, keeping his voice level.

Blackbourne nodded. "I moved further from London hoping to keep my secret, and I knew the horse sale would bring in a large crowd. There were sure to be many gamblers among them."

"I don't understand how this ended in a duel," Sherry said.

"As I mentioned before, this is a long story. Around Christmastide, Brown asked for information regarding Castlereagh's trip abroad to negotiate a peace with Napoleon—the date of his departure, the name of the ship. I was alarmed by the request, fearing he meant to do harm or serious mischief to Castlereagh, whom I admire very much. When Brown's letters continued to press me, I provided him with information on a ship sailing two days after Castlereagh's actual departure."

Lucien lifted his brows. "I'd wager this did not sit well with Brown."

"Not at all. I knew he'd be outraged, but I could not think what else to do. After the news broke that Castlereagh had sailed, Brown left several threatening messages, which I ignored, and with Castlereagh out of the country, I spent more and more time outside of London, gambling…and avoiding Brown. A week before the game in Maidenhead, I receive a letter ordering me to turn over the terms of peace proposed in Castlereagh's negotiations with Napoleon. I was given forty-eight hours."

"Or else what?" Sherry asked.

"The note didn't say. I assumed he was planning to expose me, not have me murdered. But I couldn't have given him the papers if I'd wanted to. I didn't have them. With Castlereagh out of England, he was corresponding directly with Liverpool. Nothing was going through our office."

"So, what happened in Maidenhead? Did you know Ponsonby before that night, perhaps as Owen Tulk, his actual name?"

"He was using a false name too? Egad, this was a muddled affair. But no, I didn't know him by either name. I was baffled by the man's hostile attitude. It had not occurred to me he had been sent by Brown until after he had forced the duel upon me."

"When he said, 'You were warned.'"

Blackbourne's head jerked back with a shocked stare. "How could you know?"

"A witness overheard him."

The politician sighed. "I knew you would dig out the truth when I first heard you were asking about the affair."

Lucien ignored the remark for the moment, returning to the card game. "He accused you of cheating. Did you?"

"Absolutely not. Lord knows, I have my faults, too many to count, but cheating is not one of them. Ponsonby, or whoever he is, planted the extra card to force the duel."

"Did you see him do so?"

"I did and was puzzled because it did not fit with his card hand. I should have said something, but then it was too late—he accused *me*. I'd been played for a fool."

"How did the former Lord Audley get involved?"

"He wasn't, not truly." He shifted his gaze to Sherry. "I was sorry to hear of his death, but I barely knew your brother. We only spoke twice. The first was at the horse sale where we discovered a mutual interest in history. I mentioned a few books and maps I had, and he wanted to see them the next time he was in London. When he asked for my calling card, I had no recourse but to hand him Charles Raven's card. Other than thinking it was too bad we would not be continuing our acquaintance in London, I forgot about it. Until I heard of Audley's death and that you were asking questions. I had no part in his accident, but I knew I'd be exposed if you saw the card, that you'd keep looking until you found Charles Raven. That's why I asked Jack to retrieve it, but I guess we were too late."

Only because of Lady Anne's remarkable memory, Lucien thought.

Lucien shifted his gaze to Jack. "That was quite a jump you made. I commend you on such a well-trained horse."

"I've had him for years," Jack said, breaking out of his shyness. "While still living at home, I used to escape in the same manner when my father had forbidden an evening out."

Sherry looked back at Blackbourne. "This all sounds like motive to me."

"You cannot believe I had anything to do with Audley's death," Blackbourne said anxiously. "I would never."

"You said you spoke to him a second time. When was that?" Sherry asked, making it clear he wasn't yet satisfied.

"After the card game. When I realized Ponsonby might be planning to kill me at the duel, I wanted a reliable witness to attend. Audley was the only face I recognized in the crowd, so I asked him to be present. As it turned out, we had plenty of witnesses. His mere presence could not have placed him at risk."

"Unless Tulk thought you'd told him about Mr. Brown and the blackmail."

"Egad, sir. Even if I had—which I assure you, I did not—it would not be reason enough to kill him," Blackbourne said.

"You think not?" Lucien studied Blackbourne's face, wondering if he was that naïve or just self-serving, not wanting to own his request might have resulted in Audley's death. "I suspected Mr. Brown would not want to be exposed either. Nonetheless, you both were safe from discovery until Jack was so persistent in retrieving the card."

Ridout looked mystified. "Sorry, sir, I do not understand. Persistent in what way?"

"Did you not also enter my room at the Goose & Gander Inn?"

"No, sir. I swear. I was only in Audley Manor. I retrieved the calling card, but they nearly caught me. By the by," Jack took a cuff link from his pocket, "would you return this to the widow? I found it in my greatcoat with the cards."

Lucien absently placed it in his own pocket, but he was focused on Jack's denial, and he gave Sherry a look. "Then there had to be a second intruder."

"With all the inquiries you made, someone may have sought information on exactly who you were," Blackbourne said. "I might have done so myself, except I already knew you by your reputation."

Plausible, Lucien granted. His penchant for delving into murders and other clandestine inquiries was becoming all to well-known in London but would not be commonly known in Buckinghamshire. So, who had the prowler been? The most likely suspect was Audley's killer.

"What do you intend to do about Mr. Brown?" Lucien asked.

"I have resigned. When I heard Whitehall was asking about Jack, I spoke with Lord Rothe early this morning. He knows I posed as Charles Raven to conceal my gambling, but I told him only enough to explain my resignation. I shall, however, do whatever I can to avoid gossip that reflects badly on Castlereagh or Lord Liverpool, and I hope to preserve Jack's position. He had no fault in this other than his loyalty to me."

Lucien doubted if Castlereagh would see it that way. As an assistant in the Foreign Secretary's department, Jack owed his loyalty to Castlereagh first, not Blackbourne.

"You should tell Rothe everything. Brown is not only a danger to you but to Castlereagh, Liverpool, and England. Your resignation won't stop him. He'll expose you, thereby creating the scandal he wanted, and then he'll find someone else to blackmail."

Blackbourne met Lucien's gaze while the clock on the mantel continued to tick, then he nodded. "Yes, you are right. I see that now. I was thinking of myself again and my reputation, but it is too late for that." He sighed and stood, Jack popping up beside him. "I shall do as you advise, my lord. It might be a start to putting my life back together and regaining a bit of self-respect."

Lucien waited until Hughes had shown their guests out before turning to Sherry. "I'm relieved that your family reputation is not at risk and your brother was not part of Blackbourne's deception… but Tulk must have thought he was."

"So, Graham was killed for nothing." Sherry's face darkened. "What do we do about Brown? He was responsible for my brother's death, and what if he thinks Lady Phoebe knows something she shouldn't? It sounds as though you are turning the inquiry over to Rothe, but I cannot put it behind me until I know Brown has been punished and won't bother Lady Phoebe."

"As though I would do such a thing," Lucien said in surprise. "Blackbourne needs to confess the whole to Rothe, but I am quite certain Rothe will expect us to sort it out. Shall we make our way to Whitehall?"

• • •

When they entered Rothe's outer office, Mr. Sloane met them. "If you are here to see Lord Rothe, you shall have to wait or come back. He is meeting with someone."

"Mr. Blackbourne? And perhaps Mr. Ridout?" Sherry asked.

"Why yes. Did you know they were coming?"

"We urged them to return. Would you ask Lord Rothe if we may join them?" Lucien asked.

"Yes, of course," Sloane said. "Give me a moment." He tapped and entered Rothe's private office, returning promptly. "He said to go through."

Sloane stood aside to allow them to enter. Polite greetings were exchanged, and Blackbourne added, "I do not blame you for doubting I would follow-through, but as you see, my courage has not failed me this time."

"It was not doubt but realization we were the logical agents to continue the inquiry," Lucien said. "Lord Audley has an on-going interest in discovering his brother's murderer, and that person may well be your Mr. Brown. Since we are already involved, I anticipated Lord Rothe might wish us to carry on."

Rothe smiled. "Mr. Blackbourne wasn't quite finished, but as it is likely you are correct, please sit, gentlemen, while I hear the rest of his tale. Afterward, we can discuss what needs to be done."

Lucien and Sherry listened in silence as Blackbourne repeated the details behind his resignation. Rothe showed no emotion or judgment but asked how the blackmail had worked.

"But how did you get in touch with Brown?"

"Jack left my messages at the post office in the Hawthorn Inn, just addressed to Mr. Brown. I assume he picked them up or had someone do it for him."

"You never tried to catch him?" Lucien asked.

"I did once," Jack offered. "I waited for two hours, watching the inn, noting everyone that entered. But at the end of that time, I inquired of the innkeeper, and the message was still there. It seemed rather fruitless to continue. One person could not keep constant watch for long hours or days."

"How did his messages get to you?" Rothe asked Blackbourne.

"They appeared on my doorstep. No one ever knocked, but once my manservant saw a street boy running away. I assume that's how he delivered them."

"Do you have any suspicion who Brown is?"

"None, sir. If I did, I might have come to you sooner. I know Castlereagh is unpopular with the public, but they don't know him as I do. He has an acute mind and is staunchly loyal to the Crown. I would never wish harm to him or his reputation."

Rothe sat back and steepled his hands. "You must attempt to correspond with Brown again. Act frightened by his warning and declare you are now willing to do whatever he says. Ask if he still wants Castlereagh's papers."

Blackbourne sighed. "Very good, sir. Whatever you wish."

Lucien nodded, understanding the trap Rothe was setting. "Audley and I will keep watch on the inn until Brown makes an appearance."

"And then I want you to follow him wherever he goes. I want to know if Brown is in this alone."

Lucien turned to Blackbourne. "One other thing, have you a sense whether Brown's animosity toward Castlereagh is personal or political?"

Blackbourne slowly nodded. "I have given that a great deal of thought. In the beginning, it sounded political, but as he became angrier over the months, it felt personal. I began to fear he might do Castlereagh actual harm."

Lucien looked at Rothe. "Could this be related in some way to the old duel?"

"Castlereagh and Canning?" Rothe looked pensive. "It's been five years, and I cannot believe Canning would resort to murder."

The two men had both served in the cabinet of Prime Minister Portland with constant clashes over political and war policies. Their differences led to a duel on September 21, 1809, in which Canning was injured, and afterward, both men were forced to resign due to public outrage. In the intervening years, both had mellowed and successfully regained their political power but with their differences remaining unchanged.

"Perhaps Canning would not, but what about a political associate or follower?" Sherry asked.

"Did you have someone in mind?" Rothe asked

"No, just thinking aloud."

Rothe gave a nod. "Whether associated with Canning or not, Brown's stance on the war may place him in opposition to the negotiations."

"That might make him either a traitorous supporter of the French or a loyal Englishman who felt any negotiations would be too lenient toward the enemy." Lucien turned to Blackbourne. "Do you have the messages you received?"

"I might have one or two locked in a drawer. I often destroyed them for fear they'd be found."

"We'll need to see what you have and a list of any you recall. They could give us a hint if the war is an issue with him, and if so, which side he is on."

"Does this mean you don't expect to catch him at the Hawthorn Inn?" Ridout asked.

"Not truly. Just being cautious," Sherry said. "If he is a careful man, he won't come himself, and we may need to gather more evidence before we approach him. But you never know."

• • •

Attired as simple hackney drivers in drab, nondescript garments, Lucien and Finn sat atop a coach hired for the evening; Sherry was inside. They were parked across from the entrance to the Hawthorn Inn as though awaiting a customer. In the two hours since Jack had dropped off Blackbourne's note, they'd had to tell two gentlemen they were already committed to wait for another gentleman and his lady.

They'd spoken to the publican earlier, and he had promised to come to the door and wave if the message was retrieved. So far, they hadn't noticed anyone acting suspicious nor sighted the innkeeper.

Lucien shifted and grinned at Finn. "I had not realized the seats were so hard. Hey," he said, suddenly tapping on the coach roof to get Sherry's attention. "There's the innkeeper."

Lucien leaped down, Sherry burst out the door, and they ran across the street.

"A boy picked up the message and went out the back. Long black hair," the publican shouted as they ran past.

The alley behind was empty. They searched the surrounding streets but failed to turn up a likely lad. As they walked back, Lucien was frowning.

"We should have asked the innkeeper how Brown knew he had a message. Does he send someone every day, or does the publican signal him?"

"I guess we'd better find out." Sherry turned to him with an appalled expression. "By Jove, Lucien. I hadn't thought of it before, but if Brown uses this place regularly, do you suppose he is blackmailing others?"

"Another excellent question."

"He got away?" the publican asked as they walked inside.

"For today, but the incident raised a question or two," Sherry said. "How does Brown know he has a message?"

"Why, I, uh, maybe he sends someone to watch."

"Every day?" Sherry persisted. "And what would they watch for?"

"I'm not sure. Guess I've not given it proper thought."

"Come, sir," Lucien admonished, growing more suspicious. "You can be more precise than that. Does a boy come every day, or do you notify Brown?"

The publican appeared flustered for a moment, then firmed his jaw. "I know nothing more than I've told you. Nor am I required to discuss my business matters with you."

"You will unless you want Bow Street coming around," Sherry said.

"But I tried to help you," the publican said, acting affronted.

"Well, you did, and you didn't," Lucien said. "You made sure we wouldn't catch the boy. I believe you signaled Brown that there was a message and to be cautious in retrieving it."

"And now you're going to tell us how you did it," Sherry said leaning over the counter with a stern look.

The publican backed up a step. "Now hold on. I don't want trouble."

"Then you had best explain," Lucien said.

Taking another look at Sherry's scowling face, the innkeeper sighed. "I set a candle in the window to let him know there's a message. I light it if any constables, runners, or the like be around."

"And thus, the boy used the rear entrance. Simple but effective," Sherry remarked.

"How does he pay you for this service?" Lucien asked.

"The boy brings payment when he gets the message."

"Out of curiosity, how many victims did Brown have?" Sherry asked. "You must be making a goodly sum for assisting a blackmailer."

"What? Oh, no, I'm no part of blackmail."

"Ah, but you are. How much per message?" Sherry insisted.

"Two shilling, but nobody mentioned blackmail."

"Well, now you know. And we know your price, so perhaps we can do a little business of our own," Sherry said. "We can pay handsomely if you tell us who Brown is or where we can find him."

The publican shook his head vigorously. "I cannot, because I don't know."

"How did you originally set up this system?" Lucien asked.

"A letter. Honestly, I never met this man, nor did I know he was a blackmailer."

"You knew something wasn't right," Lucien said. "But putting that aside, you didn't say if he is getting messages in more than one handwriting."

"Only the one. There was another but not for months now."

"Has he ever sent you messages to send out?"

The innkeeper raised his hands in denial. "Never. I swear. He must have his own methods of delivery."

They continued to question him until they were satisfied, then they warned him not to mentioned their discussion with anyone or attempt to contact Brown again without their approval. As they were leaving, Lucien lay five quid on the counter to encourage his on-going cooperation, and Sherry again threatened to bring in Bow Street. Lucien hoped their efforts would keep the publican quiet, so they could use the set up again.

Chapter Twenty Eight

London, Chadley House, Monday, 11 April 1814

Lady Anne was having difficulty entertaining Lady Phoebe. As a widow, her guest was not allowed to attend most social events. They had finished their shopping and had visited the museum twice. Anne had even quietly taken her into a play by keeping her in the shadows at the back of Lord Chadley's private box.

After only six days in London, they were running out of things to do. Phoebe was showing signs of missing her country home and community. And in truth, Anne didn't fault her. Phoebe was a country girl, and while she had enjoyed the excitement of London at first, she wasn't exactly comfortable in the city, and she missed the people in her little church. That was obvious yesterday when they had attended the church of Saint Paul, and Phoebe had looked around in dismay at knowing no one.

"Good morning," Anne said as she entered the parlor to find Phoebe sewing a bonnet for Eliza. "What a pretty cap. You have such lovely stitchery."

"We don't have such marvelous seamstresses as you do," Phoebe said. "I've had to learn to make a fine stitch, and I truly do not mind. I rather enjoy it." She paused and laid her work in her lap. "Anne, I hope you will not think me ungrateful, I have so much enjoyed your company, but I must go home soon. Eliza and I need to get settled into the routine of our new situation, and I know I am keeping you from your normal social life."

"Oh, Phoebe, I can attend parties anytime. I love having a friend to talk with staying in my own home, and what a pleasure to see Eliza every day. I know you miss Audley village, but I will very much regret the loss when you go. Please say you'll stay a few more days, at least until the murderer is caught. Otherwise, we shall all worry about your safety."

"Good heavens, I don't want to worry anyone," Phoebe said. "But I cannot stay indefinitely."

Anne laughed warmly. "I would not ask that, my dear. I am sure Lord Ware will have news for us soon. Until then, is there something else in London you would like to do?"

Phoebe gave her a shy grin. "Hatchard's bookstore? I do love to read novels, and winters are long in Buckinghamshire."

"Oh, I should have thought of it before. It is one of my favorite places to spend time browsing the latest offerings. I am always awed by the sight of so many books."

"It sounds lovely."

"As we have guests coming for tea today, let us put that on our list for tomorrow."

"I shall look forward to it," Phoebe said, picking up the unfinished bonnet.

Anne let out a quiet sigh of relief, ensured of entertainment for one more day. Nonetheless, Phoebe would soon insist on leaving, whether the murderer had been caught or not.

• • •

The church ladies they'd entertained for afternoon tea had departed only minutes earlier when Phoebe's father-in-law Lord Sherbourne was announced.

"My lord," Lady Phoebe dropped the stitchery again and rose, smiling with obvious pleasure. "I am delighted to see you."

"And I you, Lady Phoebe." He smiled and nodded at their hostess. "A pleasure, Lady Anne."

"Good to see you, Lord Sherbourne."

He crossed to take Phoebe's hands, leaning down to kiss her cheek. She blushed prettily. "I am returning to Sherbourne Manor in the country tomorrow and wished to take my leave of you and my granddaughter."

"Lady Sherbourne must be eager to see you. Thank you for giving me a last chance to say farewell."

She pulled the bell and sent for Eliza to be brought immediately, then seated herself again. His lordship took a chair across from her and Lady Anne.

"For your convenience, Lady Phoebe, a coach and team of horses are now at your disposal at Sherbourne House whenever you need them. My son has hired a new coachman who will see you home and is eager to take up residence in Buckinghamshire as he was raised in the country."

"You are both so kind. I cannot thank you enough."

"No need to thank us, my dear. And be forewarned, Lady Sherbourne and I shall visit Audley Manor no later than autumn." His eyes lit with a smile. "She is eager to visit and shamelessly indulge her granddaughter."

Phoebe gave a soft laugh. "Eliza and I shall await such a treat with great pleasure. Give your wife my warm wishes when you reach home. Will you make a long stay at Sherbourne Manor this time?"

"I fear not. With Parliament in session, I cannot be gone long for worry they will do something foolish in my absence," he said with a bark of laughter.

They chatted for several minutes, but after he'd held his granddaughter, bounced her on his knee, and given her a kiss, he was on his way again.

Anne feared his visit—conveying the news Phoebe's coach was ready—had given her guest one more excuse to leave London. After a bit of thought, she sat down and wrote a note to Lucien, asking him to accompany them to Hatchard's bookstore. Although a gentleman's escort was not required, she wasn't going to miss an opportunity to see him, and she wanted to share her concern over Phoebe's growing restlessness. Perhaps he could prevail upon the widow to stay. Until the murderer was caught, Phoebe remained at risk.

• • •

London, Tuesday, 12 April 1814

Lucien sat in his study mid-morning, pondering the list of demands that Blackbourne had previously received from the mysterious Mr. Brown. Early ones asked for information on pending laws—provisions, expected vote count, whether the Crown was supporting or opposing. During the past six months, however, they had become more pointed, asking for war secrets and Castlereagh's movements, in particular. No wonder Blackbourne became worried Brown might harm the Secretary. Lucien would have reached the same conclusion, and for all intents and purposes, it truly did not matter whether Brown was a fanatic political opponent or a French sympathizer.

Hughes tapped on the door and entered. "A message for you, my lord."

Lucien held out an eager hand, assuming Blackbourne had heard from Brown already, and then he smiled, recognizing Lady Anne's handwriting. "Thank you, Hughes," he said, dismissing the butler.

His smile grew as he read her message. She didn't need him to dance attendance on a visit to Hatchard's, so she was missing him or something was on her mind. As it happened, he had his afternoon open, assuming Blackbourne didn't hear from Brown for hours yet. Given his past behavior, the blackmailer was the type who preferred doing business in the shadows of night.

• • •

Lady Phoebe was enthralled by Hatchard's Bookstore. Not unexpected, as it had been a favorite with the Quality since it had first opened on Piccadilly in 1797. Even before they went inside, she wandered the length of the store's windows, gazing at the displays and exclaiming over new books she spied. Once they stepped through the doors, she stopped, staring at the floor-to-ceiling shelves, the browsing tables, and the polished, curving staircase. Books on a variety of subjects met the eye in every direction.

"Oh, my," she said. "It is wonderful."

"Yes," Anne agreed. "And you never get used to it."

"I do not know where to begin." But begin she did, running her hands over volumes, large and small, and occasionally opening a book to read a few lines. "How could I ever choose one or two out of all these?"

While Lady Phoebe continued to meander the main floor, oblivious to them, Lucien and Lady Anne had ample opportunity to talk privately.

"What is on your mind, my lady?" Lucien finally asked. "While I always enjoy your company, you seem pensive, and I believe there is more to this outing than a visit to the bookstore."

"You are perceptive, my lord."

He smiled. "I am beginning to know you well."

"Not too well, I hope. A lady needs her secrets. It is true, however, I am worried about Lady Phoebe. She wants to go home, and I don't think I can keep her here much longer. I'm frightened she won't be safe at Audley, not with a murderer out there and a potentially violent neighbor in Slade." She turned to give him an anxious look. "Can you say I am wrong?"

Lucien shook his head. "I cannot. I'm sure Squire Levington would do his best to watch over her if she returns to Audley."

"Of course, he would. That may be part of her eagerness to return, although she doesn't seem to realize it, but he cannot be there to guard her all the time."

"That is true, but it appears Owen Tulk murdered Audley, and Brown may have set it up—one is dead, the other is somewhere in London. She *should* be safe at Audley, but we cannot be certain until Brown is apprehended. You must try hard to keep her with you as long as possible."

"I *have* been." She squeezed his arm reassuringly. "I shall attempt to convince her there are additional places to see and things she must do, but I pray you catch him soon."

Chapter Twenty Nine

London, Wednesday, 13 April 1814

Lucien was woken shortly after eight the following morning by Talbot opening the drapes. "Good Morning, my lord. I beg pardon for the early hour, but you have a very anxious guest downstairs. Mr. Ridout says he has an urgent message."

Bolting upright, Lucien threw off the covers. "Get me my clothes. Swiftly, Talbot. This has to be the news I've been waiting for." He washed his face, shaved and was dressed in record time.

When he appeared in the drawing room, Jack Ridout jumped to his feet. "It came, my lord. Brown is asking for Castlereagh's latest notes to Lord Liverpool. It is a lengthy message, my lord."

"Where is Blackbourne?"

"He was taking the message to Lord Rothe."

"Very good." Lucien sent off a message to Sherry, dismissed Jack's hired carriage, and took the young man up in his curricle. Upon arrival at Whitehall, he left the horses with Finn, and they hurried up the stairs to Rothe's office.

Mr. Sloane waved a hand for them to go inside. "His lordship is expecting you."

The Marquess of Rothe was seated behind his desk, Blackbourne across from him. Rothe handed the written message to Lucien. "Brown's growing anger makes him bold."

"Anger over what?" Lucien read rapidly. Half of the missive was Brown's rant about the treatment of Napoleon, and Castlereagh's refusal to grant Boney's request to be exiled to Britain. He ended by demanding to know the contents of Castlereagh's latest report from Paris.

"Even if we gave him the notes, they would not be helpful. Events are proceeding too rapidly," Rothe said. "Moreover, Castlereagh only reached Paris three days ago. Most of the terms were already decided—but yes, it is true, he refused Boney's request. Can you fathom what would happen if he granted safe entry to England for that barbarian?"

"No, I cannot," Lucien said. He turned toward the door. "Ah, I believe Lord Audley is here." When Sherry entered, Lucien handed him the message from Brown.

Everyone waited while he read it. "By Jove, he doesn't want much, does he? A secret report to the Prime Minister? How does he think Blackbourne would get it?"

"You're exactly right, Audley," Rothe said, straightening in his chair. "It had not yet occurred to me that Blackbourne would not have read it or even had access, not with Castlereagh in Paris. Any report would go directly to Liverpool's office. I wonder if this is a test?"

Rothe and Blackbourne talked that over for quite a while, until Lucien and Sherry exchanged impatient glances.

Lucien finally asked, "Does it really matter? If we succeed in following whoever he uses as a courier, we'll know who Brown is by tonight. He won't even have a chance to read our response to his message." He shrugged. "But in case something goes wrong and he does read it, tell him Blackbourne needs more time and will send the report as soon as he obtains it."

Rothe stared at him, then chuckled. "Perhaps you are right—we are over-thinking this. Makes me wonder if I spend too much time with politicians." He nodded at Blackbourne. "Let's get something drafted along the line Ware suggested."

When it was written, stating Blackbourne should have the information by tomorrow, Sherry took the message to personally deliver it to the inn, with instructions for the publican to put up an unlit candle immediately.

Lucien hurried home to change into working class clothes. He and Finn would keep watch on the inn while Sherry changed after making his delivery, but they weren't using the heavy coach this time. They needed to be unburdened, thus to keep both entrances under surveillance, and they left the curricle in the inn's stable.

They need not have rushed. Nearly three hours passed before a street boy came running down the street and entered Hawthorn Inn. Five minutes later he came out again, and the publican took the candle from the window as agreed. Finn took off after the boy. The small groom was less likely to be noticed, and this gave Lucien the opportunity to circle the building and gesture to Sherry who'd been watching the back door.

Lucien caught sight of Finn nearly a block ahead, and they hurried to keep him in sight. Interesting enough, they were working their way west toward Mayfair, the area populated by the aristocracy and the very wealthy. Lucien grew uneasy, knowing if someone prominent was involved, a scandal might be unavoidable. Finally, Finn stopped, and they caught up with him.

"He be inside there," Finn pointed to a townhouse and started to scamper off.

"Where are you going?"

"Gor, milord. To git t' curricle and General." He had already disappeared into the shadows before Lucien turned to look at the brick townhouse with fancy railing and stained glass over the door.

"Any thought who lives there?" Sherry asked.

Lucien's eyes narrowed. "Good lord, Sherry. I've been to this place. Salcott took me to one of those dull political routs. The residence belongs to Ambrose Wynn."

"*The* Ambrose Wynn."

"Oh, yes, one of the prominent Whigs in the House of Commons. We need to take this to Rothe before further action."

Fifteen minutes later, Finn picked them up in Lucien's curricle with Sherry's horse tied on behind. They drove straight to Rothe's house without changing clothes, spoke briefly, and agreed to meet at Whitehall in an hour. Rothe wanted to confer with Lord Liverpool first. Lucien and Sherry went home to change.

When Lucien arrived at Whitehall, Rothe and the powers that be had already reached a decision—members of the Horse Guards were on the way to escort Wynn to Rothe's office. "We need to tread carefully in handling this," the marquess said. "Every scandal shakes public confidence. It doesn't matter which party it is. Most people don't know the difference."

Lucien turned at the sound of raised voices in the hall outside the meeting room where they had been waiting. Ambrose Wynn, a tall, thin man with unfashionable long brown hair and a hawk nose, arrived in a bluster of threats, escorted by four officers of the Horse Guards.

Over the next hour, Rothe questioned him on his relationships with Tulk and Blackbourne, and why he had been using the alias of Mr. Brown. Wynn switched to indignant retorts and denials. Through it all, Rothe listened calmly, commenting very little on the politician's responses.

Wynn finally said, "I assume I can go now. You cannot just drag me in and throw accusations like this. I shall have much more to say about this indignity tomorrow."

"I certainly hope you will, sir. A night at the Tower should give you an opportunity to consider your answers. Treason is not to be taken lightly."

"Treason?" Wynn sputtered, looking alarmed for the first time. "Is that what this is all about?" He looked at the Horse Guards who stepped forward at Rothe's gesture to remove him. "You cannot take me to the Tower of London."

"If you will come with us, sir," the captain of the guards said.

"Rothe, you *cannot* do this."

Rothe said nothing but waved for the guards to carry on.

Wynn hesitated as though he might offer physical resistance, then he rose without looking at his accusers again and walked out of the room. As soon as the footsteps of the politician and his escorts receded down the hall, Rothe asked, "Well, gentlemen, what do you think?"

"He is frightened but hiding it behind anger," Lucien said. "I assume the Guards seized a sample of his writing to compare with the note Blackbourne received."

"They did, and fortunately for us, his handwriting is distinctive. We can definitely connect him to the blackmail letters."

"And not the murders? You are going to negotiate with him, aren't you?" Sherry asked bitterly. "This happened to us once before, but it wasn't my brother that time. These confounded political things never end the way they should."

"You know we cannot afford a scandal, and Wynn knows it too. In such matters there must always be compromise."

"With no justice for my brother?"

"Can you prove Wynn had him murdered?" Rothe challenged.

Sherry turned away, and Rothe looked at Lucien.

"It's doubtful, unless he confessed," Lucien admitted.

"Which he won't. Not unless we offer to withhold prosecution of the murder charge." Rothe stood and picked up the lantern on his desk. "Shall we take this up again in the morning?"

• • •

Lucien gazed out the window of his bedchamber. Fog had settled over London and the glow of the street lamps was dim, giving little hint of what good or bad might be hidden in the shadows. The brandy glass in his hand was empty. He understood Sherry's bitterness. In his partner's position, he'd be furious. Nonetheless, they'd never change Rothe's position or that of Liverpool, who'd have the final word, but Lucien silently vowed he'd obtain the answers that Sherry needed—that they all needed.

He set the glass down, sat at his desk, and composed two letters, the easy one was to Anne, letting her know Wynn was in custody, and the other to Mrs. Tulk. He rang for Hughes, apologized for the lateness of the hour, but asked that the messages be dispatched immediately.

• • •

London, Thursday, 14 April 1814

Very early the following morning, Lucien knocked on a door in east London that was opened immediately by Tulk's widow. Twenty minutes later, he pocketed a handwritten paper in exchange for a bag of coins, and then stepped outside.

"Thank you for trusting me," he said.

She nodded and closed the door.

Chapter Thirty

Lucien walked into Whitehall at ten that morning, expecting to find everyone ready to continue Wynn's interrogation. Instead, the clerks, Sloane, Rothe, and even Sherry were standing around, smiling and laughing.

"What's going on?"

"Napoleon signed the treaty," Sherry said. "And he is on his way to exile on the Isle of Elba."

Rothe nodded. "A messenger arrived only minutes ago from Paris. The war is truly over."

Lucien and Sherry slapped each other on the back. They'd worked hard on the Continent and more recently here in England to thwart Napoleon and aid the allied cause. At times Lucien had felt the end would never come. It would take time to fully comprehend what this meant for the ordinary Englishmen of every class.

In the meantime, they needed to finish their business with Ambrose Wynn by getting the truth out of him. Lucien grimly patted his pocket, hoping he held the trump card if it was needed. "Is Wynn here yet?"

"On the way," Rothe said. "Your query is a timely reminder we have work to do."

Once they were seated in a room similar to yesterday's, a private meeting room furnished with a single table and several chairs, Lord Rothe related a bit of information on Wynn that Sloane had discovered. Although members of the opposition party were unlikely to share Castlereagh's political views, Wynn had provided the strongest opposition to the Luddite laws supported by Castlereagh that outlawed the smashing of machines. The law's enactment had resulted in the public hanging of Wynn's cousin. It explained the politician's extreme bitterness.

When Ambrose Wynn was brought in, his face was drawn and his clothes rumpled from his night as a guest in the Tower of London. Lucien wished it had been Newgate prison, but a man of Wynn's prominence had been provided more comfortable confinement. Nonetheless, he had not spent an easy night, and it showed. He was still angry and complaining, but his eyes glinted with the fear that lay just beneath the surface. A good omen, Lucien thought.

"Good day, Wynn," Rothe said. "I trust you had a pleasant night."

"You know I did not."

Rothe smiled and got right to the point. He tossed the most recent blackmail letter on the table. "This is the last message you sent to Blackbourne." When Wynn opened his mouth to protest, Rothe interrupted him. "I hope you don't intend to deny it." He put another paper in front of him. "Look for yourself. The handwriting is identical. Go ahead. Look at them."

Wynn stared at the papers for several moments. Lucien suspected he was stalling for time while deciding how to respond. Wynn finally picked up the second letter. "Where did you get this? Have you been in my house?"

"Do you deny you wrote it?"

"No. Why should I? These are my personal notes. You have no right to them."

"What about the message to Blackbourne?" Rothe leaned forward, eyeing him. "Is that personal too? Honestly, Wynn, a child could see the writing is the same."

Wynn worked his jaw back and forth. He wanted to deny it, but the long night since their last interview had taken its toll, and his demeanor said he knew he was caught. As Rothe sat back and allowed the silence to lengthen, Wynn finally said, "All right, I wrote it. But I was just angry. I didn't mean it."

Rothe signaled to Sloane standing beside the door. "Please ask Mr. Blackbourne to join us."

Wynn's face paled, and he sucked in an audible breath.

For the next several minutes, Blackbourne went over the list he'd prepared of blackmail demands made by Mr. Brown over the last year.

"All similar to this message?" Rothe asked, pointing to the last note Blackbourne had received.

"Yes, my lord. They were all signed by Mr. Brown and in the same handwriting."

"In this latest note, he ordered you to commit treason, by intercepting secret war correspondence and providing him with the contents, did he not?"

"He did, my lord."

"Thereby making himself guilty of treason," Rothe said, giving Wynn a scornful look.

Wynn shook his head. "I did not receive the report, so I cannot be guilty of something that never happened."

"The asking was sufficient," Rothe said with calm confidence. "You are caught, Wynn. You might as well get used to it. Blackmail and treason. More than enough to face the gallows."

Wynn swallowed hard and slumped back. "What do you want? What must I do to avoid such a spectacle?"

"You can start by telling the truth, the whole story."

"And if I do? Neither of us wants a scandal."

"Nor can we ignore such serious charges," Rothe countered.

"Including murder," Sherry interjected.

Wynn's face drew into a frown. "Murder? Who do you think I murdered?"

Lucien thought Wynn was wary, perhaps wondering how much they knew…or how much they could prove.

"My half-brother, Graham Sherbourne, the former Lord Audley."

Wynn shook his head. "I don't know him. Never met him. If he has been murdered, I had nothing to do with it."

"We know you didn't commit the murder yourself," Lucien said impatiently, "but can you deny you hired Owen Tulk, alias George

Ponsonby, a known criminal, to work for you? And then," he said, warming to the subject, "you killed Tulk to keep him quiet."

"What the devil? You cannot prove that."

"Are you sure?" Lucien was aware Rothe and Sherry glanced at him, obviously wondering where he was going with this. He hadn't forewarned them, hoping he wouldn't have to go this far. "I can prove you hired Owen Tulk to kill Blackbourne."

"That's impossible," Wynn said with self-assurance. "You have already said this man Tulk is dead."

Lucien's lips curled in a hard smile. "Would you be surprised if Tulk told his wife everything? I spoke to her this morning."

"Whatever she said was a lie." Wynn hesitated before asking, "What *did* she say?"

"You tell me how it happened. I'm willing to listen to your version."

Wynn appeared to consider this. "How do I know she said anything?"

Lucien pulled the paper from his breast pocket. "I asked her to write it all down." He unfolded it so Wynn could see the writing.

"Let me read it." Wynn held out his hand, but Lucien pulled the paper back.

"Oh, no. That is not how this works. I want to hear *your* version."

Wynn eyed the paper and sighed. "I hired Tulk to find Blackbourne—who was not responding to me—and to give him a warning. Nothing more. He was not supposed to get in a duel or try to shoot you," he said, appealing directly to Blackbourne. "The fool was acting on his own." He turned his head to look at Lucien again. "Nor did I kill Tulk. A rough fellow like him must have a number of enemies."

"What about my brother?" Sherry demanded.

"I told you I know nothing about him. When did he die?"

"Two weeks after the duel. Saturday the nineteenth."

Wynn sighed. "Tulk did go back to Maidenhead briefly. I heard he had left something undone, but he came running back the very next day as though he was being chased. He told a mate he feared he might be hung for something he didn't do because someone else got there first." Wynn cocked a brow. "Maybe he was talking about whatever happened to your brother. As I said, it had nothing to do with me. Tulk came around demanding the rest of his money, and I refused. He'd botched the job. He pestered me a couple days, and that was the last I heard of him."

Except when you killed him, Lucien added to himself.

But if Wynn was telling the truth about Tulk's last visit to Maidenhead—which Lucien assumed had mostly come directly from Tulk himself—then Tulk might not have cut the harness. He may have intended to kill Audley for reasons they might never know, but it sounded as though someone else acted before Tulk had the chance. When Eddie saw Tulk near the coach horses, could Tulk have been looking to see what another man had done? It was possible.

If so, who or what had Owen Tulk seen?

Lucien, Sherry, and Rothe continued to press Wynn about the two murders, but Wynn stuck to his story. Lucien would wager he was lying about Tulk's death, knowing they had no proof, but his denials of knowing Audley felt genuine. And if Tulk *had* killed Audley while working on his own, why would Wynn lie about that? He had no reason to protect Tulk's name.

Finally, Rothe said, "I think we are about done." He gave Wynn a stern look. "I need a signed confession from you regarding the blackmail. Afterward, these Guards shall return you to the Tower while I confer with Lord Liverpool, the Prince Regent, and perhaps others regarding how we proceed from this point." He shoved a quill pen, ink, and paper across the table and stood. "If I may speak with the rest of you, gentlemen."

Once in the hallway, Rothe said, "You are all free to go. The blackmail charge is sufficient to require his resignation from the House of Commons. No one will wish to pursue a charge of treason or the murder of Tulk, although I believe he is guilty of both." He turned to Sherry. "On the other hand, I doubt his complicity in your brother's death. I believe you should continue to look elsewhere."

• • •

London, Thursday, 14 April 1814, Chadley House, more than two hours earlier

Lady Anne was just finishing hot chocolate in her bedchamber and deciding what to wear for the day when the butler knocked. She pulled her robe more tightly around her as Jenny let him in.

"My Lady, a rider has just brought a message for Lady Audley. I fear it is bad news."

"What kind of bad news?" Anne turned to him with a worried frown.

"I do not know. That is all the rider said. I thought you would want to know before I deliver it."

"Yes, of course." She stepped into her slippers and held out a hand. "Thank you. I shall take it to her."

"Very good, my lady."

Anne went down the hallway and tapped on Phoebe's door. When the maid answered, Anne stepped inside. Phoebe was already dressed and turned from the looking glass to smile at her.

"I was just trying on one of my new hats. Which do you think goes best with this gown, the blue or the one with green ribbons."

Lady Anne ran her eyes over Phoebe's attire, a white gown trimmed in embroidered blue flowers and green ivy. "Either looks lovely, but I think I prefer the blue."

"I thought so too." Phoebe handed the green one back to the maid. "I am so delighted to return to the museum today. There is just so much to see."

"It is a source of unending delights," Anne agreed. "But before we confirm our plans, you may want to read this." She held out the letter. "It is from Levington, but the rider indicate it might he unhappy news."

Phoebe's eagerness faded as she took the note. "What news?"

Anne shrugged. "I don't know."

Phoebe swiftly broke the seal, read rapidly, and then stumbled backward, sinking into a chair. The note fell to the floor.

"Phoebe, what is it?"

"Jasper."

As the maid snatched up some smelling salts from the dresser, Anne picked up the letter and read it. "He is dead?" she murmured in disbelief, reading on. "A dispute over a gambling debt. Oh, Phoebe, I am so sorry." She put her arm around her friend's shoulder. "I know he could be tiresome, but he was your only brother."

"Yes, he was." Phoebe gave a deep, shaky sigh. "Oh, dear, Anne. Why could he not mend his ways?"

Anne handed her a handkerchief as the tears came. When Phoebe began to sob, Anne sank to her knees in front of her and took her hands. "Some men cannot help themselves, my dear. Perhaps Jasper was one of them."

"Perchance you're right. I knew Jasper wasn't a good man, but I so hoped he might improve as he got older. But now…" She choked back a sob and sniffed. "I'm not crying for the Jasper we knew—he was not an easy brother—but for who he might have been." She suddenly sat up in a start. "Oh, good heavens, the girls. Where are my sisters? What has happened to them?"

"I'm certain they are fine," Anne soothed. "Charlotte is not a child."

"Maybe not in years," Phoebe said, getting to her feet as Anne rose with her. "But she is used to Jasper ever telling her what to do. She won't know how to go on without him. I must go to them immediately."

Anne didn't know what to say. Naturally, Phoebe must see that her sisters were cared for, but it was too soon for her to leave London. Drat, Jasper. Could he not have waited another day or two before getting himself killed? There might still be a killer on the loose. Wynn had not confessed.

"Could you not wait until Lord Ware says it's safe for you to return to Audley?" Anne asked tentatively. "We might write to Squire Levington and asked him to look after your sisters."

Phoebe smiled gently. "Dear Anne, I know you are only thinking of me, but I must think of Charlotte and Dora. I was already homesick and wishing to get settled at the Dower House, and now I must make a home for them too. Besides, Lord Ware has someone under arrest, does he not?"

"For blackmail. They have yet to confirm this politician was the murderer. You need delay only a day, I am sure."

"Nevertheless, I cannot wait." Phoebe wiped her tears. "Thank you for having me in your home. You have been a delightful hostess and a good friend, but it is time for me to go." She went to the wardrobe and threw it open. "I had already begun to pack, so I should be ready to leave in an hour or so. I shall send for my carriage immediately."

Anne couldn't think of an argument to keep her there. After all, if she'd had sisters, she'd insist on confirming their safety too. "I cannot dissuade you, can I?" she said with a sigh of resignation.

Phoebe shook her head with a soft laugh. "My resolve is your own fault, you know. You have shown me how to be a stronger woman, and I can now be strong for those who need me."

Anne gave a rueful smile. "Lucien will not thank me for it. Well, the lady hath spoken, and you leave me no alternative. I shall pack a bag and come with you. I would not forgive myself if I allowed you to go off alone."

Phoebe's eyes widened. "I shall not refuse your company, but how will you get back?"

"I am confident Lord Ware will follow me, and if he does not, my father will send the coach." Anne turned toward the main staircase. "I shall ask the kitchen to prepare a basket for the journey and to set out tea and biscuits before we go. I promise to hurry so we do not keep your coachman waiting."

Anne lifted her skirts and ran up the steps. While her maid Jenny packed a bag, Anne hastily wrote to Lord Ware, sent the footman off to deliver the message, and left another note for her father. Swiftly changing into travel clothes, she put her pistol in the pocket of her gown and hurried downstairs. Jenny followed her carrying the bag.

They barely had time for a quick breakfast before the coach arrived. While they waited for the nanny and Eliza, they watched the loading of Phoebe's trunk.

"Are you certain you want to make such a long trip just to see me safely home?" Phoebe asked one last time.

"Of course, I am sure. You have a difficult few days ahead of you, and there is no need to face them alone. And do not presume you can talk me out of it. Remember who taught you to be so determined."

The corners of Phoebe's eyes misted. "Very well, dear Anne. Then shall we set forth?"

"After you, my friend."

"My Lady, wait." A maid came running toward them with a basket. "Cook sent this for your journey."

Five minutes later, everything was packed on board, and the coach pulled away from the house. Lady Anne knew that her father and Lucien were going to be worried if not annoyed with her for leaving so precipitously, but she really had no choice. Phoebe was her friend and her responsibility. Where she went, Anne just had to follow.

• • •

London, Thursday, 14 April 1814, around midday outside Whitehall

Once Lucien and Sherry left Lord Rothe to sort out Wynn's fate with the other political leaders, they stopped outside Whitehall to discuss what came next for them.

Sherry frowned at Lucien. "Why is it politicians are always above the law?"

"Not all of them, only the well-known and wealthy. Are you still thinking Tulk and Wynn are responsible for Graham's death?"

"I'm not certain what to think. Wynn acted surprised by the accusation, but if the motive for Graham's death was not connected to the duel or somehow to Blackbourne's affairs, then what is left?"

Lucien sighed and stepped up into the curricle, taking up the reins. "I've been mulling that over, and I think I know the answer. If I'm correct, it is fortunate we brought Lady Phoebe to town with us. I'll meet you at Lady Anne's to discuss it with them." He pulled onto the street as Sherry swung into the saddle.

Horse and carriage traffic was light after they left Westminster, mostly men on horseback and a few hired hackneys, and Sherry and Lucien arrived at Chadley House together. The butler looked surprised to see them.

"Were you looking for his lordship?" he asked as he offered to take their hats.

Lucien hesitated, hat in hand. "We hoped to visit with Lady Anne. Is she not at home?"

"I am sorry, my lord, but you have missed her. Did you not receive the message she sent to your residence?"

"Where is she?" he asked, having an uneasy feeling.

"She and Lady Phoebe have gone to Audley Manor."

"Good lord. Why?"

"Lady Phoebe received word her brother had been killed. I do not know the particulars, but she was insistent on returning to Audley in haste to find her sisters. Lady Anne would not let her go alone."

"Bloody hell." Lucien was stunned. "Come, Sherry, we have no time to spare." He grabbed his friend's shoulder and urged him toward the horses. "I'll explain on the way."

Upon reaching Lucien's townhouse, they stayed just long enough to read Lady Anne's message while his four bays were hitched to his fastest coach. He would have preferred the curricle, but on the return trip it would be impossible to accommodate three adults and Finn on a two-seater. Talbot packed fresh clothes in an overnight bag and within minutes they were on their way.

"How could she leave without talking it over with us?" Lucien grumbled.

"It sounded as though Lady Phoebe did not give her a choice. Lady Anne felt she needed to protect her."

"Of course, she did, and that is my fault. I pressed her to keep Phoebe close to her, so naturally she went along."

"Under the circumstances of Jasper's death, I would expect no less." Sherry shot Lucien a puzzled look. "I know their departure was unexpected, but why are we making a panicked dash to Audley?"

"Because the killer is still there. It has to be Jed Harris. All that pent-up anger that has simmered for a year since your brother's dismissal, taking the farm from him and consequently his wife. Graham had good reasons for his action, but Harris doesn't acknowledge it, and he blamed Audley for everything. And then his drinking and ranting with Slade amplified his sense of persecution and rage until he cut the harness. Just look at how he reacted to what he saw as interference with his friend Slade—he tried to burn down your stable. He is carrying around a deep anger, and I doubt if getting thrown in gaol made him any happier."

"Mrs. Slade *did* say they'd been feeding each other's irrational thinking. Is Harris deranged too?"

"Irrational for sure, but I doubt he suffers from lunacy. He is fixated on his misfortunes and has chosen to blame someone else rather than face his own faults. And I'm worried he is not finished with his need to strike out at someone. He could easily transfer his hatred for Graham onto Lady Phoebe and Eliza."

"Egad, Lucien. Levington was going to release Harris when he was sober. What if he is just waiting for her to return?"

"Exactly. Now, you understand. And Lady Anne is with them. Hence, the panicked dash across country."

"Devil take the fiend. Can we go any faster?"

Chapter Thirty One

Approaching Audley Manor, Buckinghamshire, Thursday 14 April 1814, late afternoon

Lady Anne stretched her neck to ease the tension. According to Phoebe, they were only three miles from the manor, and she was looking forward to the opportunity to get out and walk about. Seven hours was a long ride, but with only a team of two, the horses had needed frequent stops and other rests at a walking pace. Anne leaned back, thinking about a stroll around the Audley gardens, followed by a spot of tea, maybe a biscuit or two.

Eliza had slept much of the way or played quietly, but she was getting restless, and Nanny was having trouble entertaining her. So far, the ride had not been unpleasant, but the three women had run out of things to talk about a couple of hours ago. They had speculated on Jasper's death, but the subject only made Phoebe sadder, and Anne soon avoided any reference to the matter. Phoebe was consumed with worry for her sisters, even though Anne assured her that neighbors and Squire Levington would have seen to them. Phoebe nodded but slumped back against the seat unable to hide her anxiety. Since then, they had ridden in weary silence, each deep in her own thoughts. Anne spent much of her time thinking about Lucien and whether there was a future for them.

Phoebe peeked out the window again, a smile lighting her face. "We are getting close. No more than twenty minutes now."

"It will be good to be home," the young nanny said. "I've never been away more than a weekend before."

"As soon as Eliza is put to bed, take the rest of the night off to visit your family," Phoebe said. "I will need you to care for her much of the time in the coming days."

"Thank you, ma'am," Nanny said, clearly pleased by the prospect. "Oh, goodness, there's the turn-off to the village. We *are* close."

A loud shot rang out. The coach came to a sudden halt, throwing Nanny and Eliza onto the floor. The child began to cry.

"Stay down," Lady Anne ordered, as Eliza's wail grew louder and higher-pitched. Anne drew her pistol from her pocket when she heard a man's voice order the coachman to step down. She couldn't hear the reply, but he must have refused or wasn't moving fast enough, because the man repeated his order and this time threatened to shoot.

The carriage rocked as Anne heard the driver descend. She glanced at Phoebe, whose eyes were rounded in fright, as she attempted to help the nanny quiet Eliza.

"Lady Audley," a rough voice called. "Step down and bring your child. The nanny stays behind."

"I'm coming," Phoebe said, her voice only trembling slightly. "But whatever you want, it does not concern Eliza."

"Bring the brat, or your coachman dies."

Phoebe gasped. "What do I do?" she whispered to Anne.

"Do you recognize his voice?" Anne whispered. If the ruffian didn't know she was there, it might work to their advantage.

Phoebe shook her head, terror in her eyes. "What does he want with my baby?"

"I don't know, but for now, do as he asks…only without Eliza. Try to hold it together until I come up with a plan. I promise I won't let him take your daughter."

The two women exchanged a look and a nod.

"Get out here, now," the man demanded. "I'm counting to five."

"Yes, all right, I'm on my way," Phoebe shouted. She opened the door and jumped out, slamming it behind her.

"Where is the child?"

"She is frightened by you." Phoebe stood with her back against the carriage door.

Phoebe might be a gentle woman, soft-spoken and rather shy under normal circumstances, but she was now a fierce mother defending her child. And her defiance was keeping the ruffian talking while Anne was thinking. Confronting a man holding a musket with Anne's pocket pistol was just nonsense, but if she could get over to the other seat, she might be able to catch sight of the fellow and shoot him through the window.

"Sorry, sorry," she murmured as she scrambled over the nanny, keeping her head down and dreading any moment she might hear another shot. She'd almost made it when she heard the click of the door latch. She jerked herself upright on top of the nanny, bringing her pistol up.

"Stop him. Shoot him," Phoebe yelled.

Nanny jerked away, upsetting Anne's balance just as the door snapped open. Seeing a stranger with a musket, Anne pulled the trigger, the bullet hit the door frame, ricocheting, and the man yelped.

Anne righted herself and leaned out the door. The ruffian was down on the ground with his leg bleeding, and the coachman was holding him down. Anne climbed out and pointed her pistol at the man, although it was empty. Fortunately, her bluff wasn't needed. The shooter was engrossed in clutching at and moaning over his injured leg.

"He is bleeding rather badly, my lady," the coachman said. "If we don't do something quickly, he might die."

Anne gaped at them, bringing a hand to her face. She hadn't meant to kill him. *Good heavens.* She didn't even know who he was.

• • •

A second carriage approaches Audley Manor, Thursday, 14 April 1814

Lucien leaned forward, gazing out the window. Upon leaving London, he had ordered Gregory to make all possible haste without harming the horses, and frankly he had expected to overtake the ladies by now. They were getting close to Audley Manor, and he was more than a little worried over what he and Sherry might find at the house.

Suddenly he sprang off the seat and opened the door, startling Sherry from a light doze. "What?" Sherry sputtered.

Lucien hung in the doorway. "Was that a musket shot, Gregory?" he shouted to the coachman.

"I believe so, milord. Could be hunters."

Lucien wasn't so sure, and he wasn't taking a chance. "Spring them, Gregory."

When the coach lurched forward, Lucien tightened his grip on the door, continuing to stare ahead.

"My God, Lucien, what are you doing?" Sherry yelled. "Are you mad? Close the door."

Lucien shook his head. "Something's wrong, Sherry. I'm certain of it." As they came over a rise, his heart lurched at the sight of a coach stopped on the road ahead. He could see at least three figures outside and two of them were crouched over someone on the ground.

Bloody hell. Anne, my dearest Anne, please be safe.

Sherry had shaken off his drowsiness and was hanging out the other door. When Lucien shouted to Gregory to halt the coach, both men leaped out and ran toward the group ahead. The only sounds Lucien heard were Eliza's piercing cries.

"Anne?" He shouted. When she stood and turned toward him, he saw the blood on her gown and swallowed hard. Had she been shot?

"Oh, my lord, I am so glad to see you," she cried out, as shaken as he'd ever seen her. "I didn't mean to kill him."

Reaching her, Lucien gripped her hands, looking her up and down and saw no injury. He swept her into his arms. "Are you all right? Anne, my dear, dear Anne," he murmured into her hair. "I could not bear the thought of losing you."

"Very gratifying, my lord, but I am well," she said softly before turning her head to look at the injured man on the ground. "I'm not so sure about him."

Lucien kissed her hair, not caring who saw them, then released her and stepped away. He frowned down at the injured man. "You," he spat the word and glared at Jed Harris. "What kind of man attacks ladies and children?"

Sherry sent the coachman to quiet Lady Phoebe's frightened horses and squatted beside Harris pressing the man's folded jacket against his leg, attempting to slow the bleeding. Lucien knelt on Harris's other side, pulled off his cravat, and tied it tight around the wounded leg. "That will have to do until we can get a doctor."

Lucien stood and looked at the coachman. "Tell me what happened."

"He fired and ordered me to stop, then shouted for Lady Audley to get out with the infant. She stepped down but left the child inside. He threatened to shoot her or me, or maybe the child…I wasn't sure. Then he yanked the coach door open, and Lady Anne shot him. It all happened very quick."

Lucien nodded. Noting the coachman's steady hands and his concise report, he asked, "Where did you serve, soldier?"

"Southern France, milord."

"Good man. Lord Audley and I shall deal with Harris from here. Take the ladies on to Audley Manor."

The coachman tipped his head. "Yes, milord. I can surely do that."

Sherry already had Lady Anne and Lady Phoebe inside the coach, and as soon as the coachman had them back on the road, he joined Lucien. "How is he?"

"I think he'll live, but he needs a doctor. Let's take him to the house then send someone to get the doc, Levington, and Constable Holt."

• • •

Upon reaching Audley Manor, Lucien and Sherry carried Jed Harris into the stable and laid him on a blanket fetched from the house. They didn't take him inside the manor, because he wouldn't be staying. As soon as the doc fixed him up, Harris belonged at the local gaol in the custody of the constable…and Squire Levington in his official capacity as magistrate. And this time, they'd better keep him.

Within half an hour Doc was working on Harris's leg with Constable Holt standing guard. Lucien, Sherry, and Levington went inside the manor to get the ladies' version of the incident.

"Where are my sisters?" Lady Phoebe demanded the moment she saw the squire.

"Safe with Vicar Potter and his wife. I did not think it proper for them to stay at my home without a mistress to play chaperone."

"Are they all right?" she asked worriedly.

"I think so. Charlotte was in tears. Dora was surprisingly unflappable, sad, of course, but she was the one consoling her older sister."

Phoebe nodded. "I am not surprised. Charlotte was Jasper's favorite, and he wasn't very nice to Dora. I should like to see them, but I suppose it is best if I wait until morning. There is no reason for them to be involved in this matter."

"And you needn't worry about Jasper," Levington said. "I've had the body brought back to the Wheatley home, a neighbor is staying there for now, and we shall make further arrangements tomorrow."

"Oh, thank you. What would I do without such wonderful friends?" she said looking around and threatening to cry.

"Not something you need to think about," Anne said bracingly, "because we are all here for you."

"Perhaps we should dispose of the immediate crisis first," Lucien suggested. "The squire is correct, other things can wait for now."

"While the doctor is looking at Harris," Levington said, "tell me exactly what happened."

Anne sighed. "Everything about our journey was unremarkable until we were only a few miles from Audley…"

As they finished relating the details of the ambush, Lady Phoebe gave a slight shiver. "It was terrifying." She turned questioning, even accusing eyes on Levington. "Harris threatened my child. After he'd set fire to our stables, why didn't you keep him in gaol?"

The squire tried to explain about the law, and that no real harm had been done with the fire. "And he'd been drinking," Levington said helplessly, spreading his hands, but Lady Phoebe didn't look like she was accepting his explanation. "We held him until he was sober. I never thought…" His voice trailed off.

Lucien wondered if this incident was going to put an abrupt halt to their friendship and anything else between them. Mothers were not very understanding when it came to the safety of their children, and at the very least, the squire might have some serious penitence to do. He had plenty of time to win her favor again, however, as Lady Phoebe would not consider marrying again until her year of mourning was over.

Godwin brought an end to the awkward conversation by announcing the doctor had just come up from the stable. Doc was shaking his head as he walked in.

"He didn't die, did he?" Anne asked, her face showing concern.

"He'll live to stand trial."

"Too bad," Sherry murmured.

Doc shot him a sympathetic look. "Yes, well, I daresay he will have a limp, but he was fortunate the bullet didn't shatter a bone or cut a large bleeder. Since he has no one at home to care for him, he is just as well off sitting in gaol."

"He belongs there, until they can hang him," Lucien said. "We'd like to question him before you haul him away, Squire. I'm certain he murdered Audley, and I want to hear him say it."

Phoebe gasped in dismay, cupping her hands over her mouth.

"He is the murderer?" Anne said, her eyes widening. "Then I'm not a bit sorry I shot him."

"How do you know it's Harris?" the squire asked.

"By eliminating everyone else," Lucien said ruefully. "We wasted a long time chasing Ponsonby and Raven."

"Not wasted," Lady Anne protested. "You saved a man's life, stopped a wicked blackmailer, and prevented a scandal that might have shaken the government."

Phoebe had been silent for several minutes. She finally asked in a small voice, "Why did Harris hate us so? Was it over the farm?"

"I'm sure that was the beginning," Lucien said. "But for the full story, we need to talk with him, tonight, if possible, Doc."

"I gave him a bit of laudanum to cut the pain, but not enough to put him out. I think he is fit enough to answer your questions," the doctor said. "As long as I'm there to keep an eye on him."

• • •

Harris was still conscious and complaining to the constable. As soon as Lucien, Sherry, Levington, and the Squire walked in, he grumbled to them about being shot for no good reason. "I din't hurt nobody."

"Way I hear it, you threatened to shoot the ladies, Lady Audley's child, and the coachman," Levington said sternly.

"Jist wanted to scare 'em."

He was slurring his words a bit. Not just from the laudanum. It was obvious he'd over-indulged with spirits, which fit with what William had found. Lucien had sent the footman back to search the scene, and he had just arrived with two empty bottles of cheap whiskey from a trampled area at the edge of the woods. It appeared that Harris had been waiting and drinking, apparently for hours.

"I think you're lying, Harris. You had something more than fright in mind. Otherwise, why did you stop the coach?" Levington sighed wearily, looked at Lucien, and shrugged.

Lucien took a seat on a harness box next to Harris. "You've been angry with Audley for a long time, Jed, since he took your farm. Isn't that so?"

"He wuldn't give me 'nother chance," Harris grumbled. "That's all I needed. Jist one more go at it. Accused me of drinkin' too much, but I's doin' my best. He din't listen, dint care. Took everythin' I had. How's I s'pose to provide for the wife? So she run off. All 'cause of him," he spat with a black scowl and fell back groaning from the effort.

"You wanted revenge."

"Just wanted things they way they was, but you top-lofty nobs control everythin'. No one wuld do nothin'. No one wuld even listen."

"Except Slade. You spent weeks drinking with him and filling his irrational thoughts with your hatred of Audley."

"Why not? He needed to be warned, to see what Audley was doin' to him." Harris's nostrils flared, his deep anger starting to show. "The varlet swindled Slade too. Took his berry patch."

"Is that when you decided to kill him? Was Slade in on it too?"

"In on what? Din't make no plan. I jist saw him drinkin' in the pub in Maidenhead, keepin' his coachman waitin' like it was his right to do so. 'N' it come to me, I could slice the harness, 'n' he wouldn't be so full of hisself then."

"Because he'd be dead?"

Harris shrugged. "Made me no mind. I wulda liked to see *his fancy lordship* take the plunge, but it dint matter, not really. Cuttin' that harness was…a pleasure. And easy when Gordon weren't lookin'. Kinda sorry he died too, but he shuda worked somewhere else." Harris's lips curled in a mocking smile. "Bet Audley's sorry now. I got 'im good 'n' laughed all the way home."

"Egad, Harris," Levington cut in. "That's a frightful thing to say. And today, were you going to kill Lady Phoebe too. And Eliza? And Lady Anne?"

Jutting out his jaw, Harris shrugged again. "Hadn't made up me mind."

• • •

Later that evening, after Harris had been taken away, Lucien and Sherry sat with the ladies and related the important parts of the interview, attempting to answer their questions and make some sense of the whole affair.

"How did Harris know I was returning home today?" Lady Phoebe asked. "Surely he hadn't been out there waiting since I left."

"I dare say he might have done so if necessary, but he heard in the village that the cook was purchasing supplies for your return."

"One of the perils of a small village," Sherry said. "Everyone knows everything."

"It has its good points too," Phoebe said defensively.

"So, Harris had previously ambushed you in the fog outside Maidenhead," Lady Anne said, frowning at Lucien and effectively breaking up the budding argument on village life. "And you never mentioned it to me before now?"

"He just hoped to frighten me into returning to London," Lucien said, attempting to make light of the incident. Lady Anne had just learned of the chase through Maidenhead Thicket during their review of events, and he knew she wouldn't let it pass. Instead of responding to the anger in her eyes, he kept talking about Harris. "He'd become alarmed about my asking questions and followed me to town. The same with the note. And he searched my room at the inn hoping to discover what kind of gentleman was prying into a murder. When he found nothing, it would have added to his growing frustration."

"I understand that feeling," Lady Anne said pointedly.

"We have all been upset by everything that has happened," Phoebe said, clearly missing Anne's meaning. She gave a deep sigh. "It is comforting to know this part is over, and Harris is in gaol. What a dreadful man he is."

• • •

Lady Phoebe was weary and emotionally spent. It wasn't long before Lady Anne made their excuses, and the ladies retired for the night. Once Lucien heard their footsteps on the floor above, he turned to Levington. "So, what happened to Jasper? Did someone shoot him?"

"He drowned."

"Egad," Sherry said. "An accident? I figured his bad habits had caught up with him."

"In truth, they did. It wasn't exactly an accident."

Lucien sighed. "I for one could use a shot of brandy while we hear this tale."

"Excellent idea," Sherry said, going to the sideboard while Levington continued.

"Wheatley was doing his usual, losing money at a gambling table in Maidenhead. When he confessed he couldn't pay, the winner, Jake Ramsbury, took exception to that. They'd both imbibed heavily in a variety of spirits, and I heard Ramsbury threatened to shoot him. He doesn't remember now. Regardless, Wheatley suggested another bet on a horse race. If Wheatley won, the debt would be forgiven. If Ramsbury won, he'd have the deed to the Wheatley farm."

"Good lord," Sherry blurted. "Did Jasper know no shame? What did he think would happen to his sisters?"

"He never thought he'd lose," Lucien said. "Gamblers never do." He lifted a brow at Levington. "I assume Jasper lost, but I still don't understand how he drowned."

"It was a close race," Levington said, "watched by a half dozen witnesses from the tavern. The finish line was the Thames River bridge, but the two men got into an argument over who won. Most of the witnesses sided with Ramsbury, but Wheatley wouldn't accept defeat. He took a swing at Ramsbury, and the argument turned into a fight. Since the witnesses also were foxed, it didn't occur to anyone to intervene before both men fell off the bridge. Ramsbury got out on his own, but apparently Jasper couldn't swim. He was swept downstream, and they didn't find his body for an hour."

"An ignominious end," Sherry murmured, downing his drink in one swallow.

"I regret Lady Phoebe has to hear this story," Lucien added. "I hope Ramsbury is not pursuing the deed to the farm."

"Lord, no. By the time I got there, he was half sober and regretting the entire affair. I kept him in gaol overnight until he was sober and I felt I had the story right, but Wheatley's death wasn't truly his fault."

"No, it was a bloody, jug-bitten misadventure," Sherry said in disgust.

• • •

Jasper Wheatley was quietly laid to rest in the Wheatley family cemetery on the following day with only Lucien, Sherry, Levington, the vicar, and the undertaker present. Meanwhile, Lady Anne and Lady Phoebe set about moving Charlotte and Dora into the Dower House. When they reached the vicarage, they were surprised to find Charlotte in the parlor with John Barclay, a local lad—and he was proposing marriage. As the couple swiftly explained, they had been seeing each over for nearly a year but kept it a secret because Jasper didn't approve.

"We love each other," Charlotte said defensively, "no matter what you say."

Phoebe widened her eyes. "Good heavens, why would I object? You'll have to wait to be married for three months, the proper mourning period for Jasper, but you may stay with me at the Dower House until you're settled."

"You mean it? Oh, thank you, Phoebe, for being so understanding." Charlotte turned to her beau with shining eyes. "Three months from today?"

He grinned. "Capital! Plenty of time to get everything arranged."

And so, Charlotte's future was settled. After the girls and their belongings were transported to the Dower House, Lady Anne and Phoebe climbed the hill to Audley Manor. On the way, Phoebe expressed her relief that Charlotte's future was so easily secured.

"It would be a year before I could take her to town for a London season. Since Charlotte and I rarely agree on anything, I was dreading long months of constant battles. I'm already very fond of John Barclay."

"Other than the vicar saying he's a good lad, how can you be fond of him after such a short acquaitance?"

Phoebe smiled. "Because he wants to marry Charlotte."

Chapter Thirty Two

London, Saturday, 16 April 1814

Lucien, Sherry, and Lady Anne left for London on Saturday. Since it was highly improper for her to be traveling unchaperoned with two gentlemen, they called upon Margret Wycliff on their way into town, and she accompanied Anne home. No one in the earl's household was the wiser, except Jenny, although Lucien wondered if Chadley didn't have his suspicions. It was a testament to the earl's trust in them that he didn't ask.

With Harris's words, "Hadn't made up me mind," haunting him for the last thirty-six hours, Lucien came to a decision around dawn Sunday morning. He sent a note to Lady Anne asking if he might pick her up at three for a ride in the park. He received a reply, smelling faintly of lilacs and stating she would be delighted. He wondered if she meant it or if she was still annoyed with him. Beyond her comments Thursday night, she hadn't brought up Maidenhead Thicket again.

• • •

Promptly on the hour of three, Lucien knocked on the door of Chadley House and was shown into the drawing room where Anne and her maid Jenny waited. Anne looked like spring itself in a muslin gown of primrose yellow and white lace. He bowed over her hand. "My lady, your chariot awaits, and it is a beautiful day."

She smiled and rose. "Good day, Lord Ware. I was in the garden earlier and found it was delightfully warm. Perfect weather for a ride through Hyde Park."

"Then we shall be about it." He escorted her outside and handed her up into his curricle, then leapt up beside her. Finn handed him the reins before he stepped back and did not get up behind.

"Is Finn not coming?" she asked.

"Not today. I do not expect any stops before we return, hence his services are not required. I thought he might have a cup of tea in Chadley's kitchen while he waits."

"He need only ask. Cook is quite accommodating." She peered up at Lucien as though worried the unexpected privacy meant something was wrong. "Has something happened? Is it Lady Phoebe? Or Sherry?"

"They are both well as far as I know."

"Are you being called away on a new assignment?"

He shook his head, his lips twitching with amusement. "Not yet."

She was quiet for several minutes as they entered Hyde Park, a popular spot for the haute ton to see and be seen. They smiled and nodded as they passed friends and acquaintances. At the far end of the park, Lucien allowed his showy chestnuts to stretch their legs, then brought them back to a slow trot on the return trip.

"You're waiting for me to say something about Maidenhead Thicket, are you not?" she finally said.

"I was rather hoping you wouldn't."

She turned to look at him. "I didn't intend to do so."

"Truly?" he asked in surprise.

"Not after I thought about it. If I expect you to treat me as you would Sherry during these inquiries, I must accept the risks you face. I realize my reaction is why you don't tell me things."

Lucien laughed. "Lady Anne, I could never treat you as I do Sherry. He is like a brother to me, and I do not have brotherly feelings for you." He halted the horses beside the path and took her hands. "I thought something unspeakable had happened to you when I saw Lady Phoebe's coach stopped in the road. And then you were covered in blood. That dreadful sight took my breath away."

She tightened her grip on his hands. "I did not mean to worry you."

He let out a long sigh that ended with a chuckle. "You never do, my dear."

"I'm sorry I left London before talking with you. I thought I could handle the situation myself. What more can I say?"

"Say you will marry me, Anne, so I have the right to hold you and kiss you, and yes, even be a bit annoyed, in such heart-stopping moments." He smiled at her tenderly. "You are not going to change, nor am I. One or both of us might be at risk now and then. It's who we are. If something *should* happen, my last regret would be not sharing as much of my life as possible with you."

"Oh, Lucien, are you certain?" she asked, her brows wrinkled. "This proposal is not because of the rather improper carriage ride coming home from Audley, is it?"

Lucien threw back his head and laughed. "Most assuredly not, my dear. If propriety was the deciding matter, I would have had to marry you the first night we met." He wrapped the reins around the handle and bent his head to gently kiss her hands. "I love you, Anne. You *must* know that. I haven't proposed before because I questioned whether I had the right to expose you to an uncertain future. But I finally realized I've been depriving us of precious moments we could have spent together." He lifted one hand to tip her chin up with his finger. "I do not wish to miss another day or night with you."

She blushed, lowering her eyes a maidenly moment before meeting his gaze. "Nor I, my lord. Yes, of course, Lucien, I shall marry you."

Reaching into his pocket, he retrieved a blue topaz ring surrounded by small diamonds. "It was my mother's." He slipped it on her finger. "I hope you like it."

"I love it," she said, her eyes misting.

Lucien pulled her into his arms for one brief kiss, then released her and picked up the reins, belatedly hoping their stolen moment had not been witnessed by others taking the air. If they were to be the subject of the latest on-dit, let it be for their marriage, not an impropriety in the park.

"Thank you for saying yes and saving me from great embarrassment," he said with laughter in his voice. "I already spoke with your father this morning, and he has given us his blessing. Do you want a large church wedding?"

"Is that what *you* have in mind?" She lifted her gaze to smile at him.

"I'd rather not wait to have the banns read, and it seems a waste if we fail to use the Special License from the Archbishop that I've been carrying around for three months."

"Oh, Lucien. Have you truly? I don't need a big wedding, but you must give me a little time to get ready, and I want Margret there."

"How much time do you need? A day, two days? Please don't say more than a week."

"A week from today then," her eyes danced, "I shall become your Viscountess Ware."

• • •

London, Chadley House, Sunday, 24 April 1814

At precisely ten the following Sunday morning, Lucien, Anne, and a few friends and relatives gathered in the Chadley drawing room. The Solemnization of Matrimony from the Book of Common Prayer had undergone little change since 1662, but Lucien and Anne together had chosen the time, the place, and elected to have her father walk her down the aisle. Bishop Sherrick presided at the request of Lord Chadley.

Andrew Sherbourne stood beside Lucien, and like the groom he wore formal attire, complete with a white silk cravat. The bridesmaid, Margret Wycliff, wore a gown of pale blue muslin, trimmed with white silk. Others in attendance included Lord Salcott and Captain Wycliff.

When Lucien caught his first look at Lady Anne on Lord Chadley's arm, he knew he was the most fortunate man on earth. She was beautiful in a white silk gown with an empire waist and embroidered white and pale blue roses across the bodice and the hem of the skirt. A white manteau covered her shoulders and was fastened at the breast by a brooch of blue sapphires and pearls that he knew had belonged to her mother. Her delicate features were surrounded by a halo of fair curls interwoven with blue and white flowers.

They exchanged a private smile as she walked toward him.

The ceremony went off as expected.

"Dearly beloved, we are gathered together…"

"Lucien Simon Grey, wilt thou have this woman…"

"Anne Elizabeth Ashburn, wilt thou have this man…"

"With this Ring I thee wed…"

And finally,

"Forasmuch as Lucien and Anne have consented together in holy Wedlock, and have witnessed the same before God and this company, and thereto have given and pledged their troth either to other, and have declared the same by giving and receiving of a Ring, and by joining of hands; I pronounce that they be Man and Wife together."

For a breathless moment, Lucien and Anne only had eyes for one another.

Following the service, the Wedding Breakfast was held at the Salcott mansion and attended by other friends, among them Lord and Lady Rothe and Doctor Pettigrew.

• • •

Shortly after midday, Lucien and Anne escaped and drove to Hays Mews where they had agreed to live until such time as they were blessed with children. Anne was introduced to the staff, in particular Hughes and Talbot, who both highly approved of their new mistress.

Jenny, who had already taken up residence, awaited her mistress in the bedchamber to change her attire.

"Do you feel any different, Lady Ware?" Jenny asked, as she helped her mistress out of her wedding gown and into a lovely peach-colored muslin gown trimmed in creamy lace.

"My heavens, it sounds so strange to be called Lady Ware. I wonder if those I know well could continue to call me Lady Anne?"

"Perhaps in private, but would Lord Ware object?"

"I doubt it. It's just that Lady Ware makes me sounds so old."

Jenny laughed, her brown curls bouncing. "I think it sounds wonderful. Maybe you'd like it better if I said Lord and Lady Ware."

Anne's eyes met Jenny's in the looking glass, and she nodded. "That has a delightful ring to it." She picked up the brooch they'd just taken off her delicate wedding cape. "I was so pleased to have my mother with me today. I know she would be happy with my choice of husband."

"Who would not, my lady? Lord Ware is so handsome and kind to all of us." Jenny finished removing the flowers from Anne's hair and pinning the curls up so that only one dangled on each side of her face in the style her mistress preferred.

Anne sighed in satisfaction and stood. "I believe I'm ready, and I should not keep my husband waiting. He will be wondering what is taking his bride so long. Thank you, Jenny."

Anne swept from the room to find her husband in the hallway.

"My lady," he said, offering his arm. "May I show you around your new home?"

By the time they'd been over the house, shared a kiss or two while strolling the gardens, and visited the stables—where Anne's favorite mount was already settled—it was nearly time to dress for dinner.

Anne excused herself and lay down for a few minutes, as she hadn't slept much the night before. She understood from talking with Margret that was a fairly common occurrence for brides. She was surprised, however, that she had dozed off, and Jenny had to wake her to dress for dinner.

Lucien insisted on eating dinner in the breakfast room where he could sit beside his wife and not be separated by the length of a dining table. They spent nearly as much time talking and laughing as eating.

Afterward, they spent the evening at a masquerade ball in Vauxhall Garden. Anne enjoyed it immensely, including the new sense of intimacy with Lucien, dancing in the arms of a man who was all hers. At the end of the evening, they went home to Hays Mews to make an early night. Tomorrow they would leave on their wedding trip, beginning with a three week visit to his estate at Waring.

Except for Hughes and Jenny, the servants had retired early. Tonight was for Anne and Lucien alone. After helping Anne into her night dress and combing out her hair, Jenny left to sleep in the attic for tonight with the other servants. Anne was now alone.

She peeked in the looking glass and tweaked a curl, a trifle uneasy about what the night would bring…but she trusted Lucien. She turned as the door to her bedchamber opened, and her husband stood in the entrance.

• • •

Anne awoke with early morning sunlight filtering through the window. Her hand rested on Lucien's bare chest, and a soft smile lit her face. He shifted onto his side, took her hand in his, and whispered in her ear.

"Good morning, my darling Viscountess."

About the Author

After retiring from a legal career with the Juvenile Court System, J.L. Buck published sixteen urban fantasy/paranormal novels under the pen name of Ally Shields. In 2019 she turned her hand to her favorite genre and began working on the Viscount Ware Mystery series set in Regency England (1811-1820).

She lives in the Midwest with Latte, a mischievous Siamese cat, who often attempts to co-author her writing by taking over the keyboard or tries to distract her to come and play. When not writing or running two blogs, she enjoys her eight grandchildren (and a great-grandson), dinners with friends, reading (preferably on a sunny deck), travel (USA—she loves DisneyWorld—and abroad), and binge-watching any sub-genre of mystery shows.

Ms Buck loves to hear from readers and can be contacted through her website or social media (twitter: @janetlbuck or her pen name account: @ShieldsAlly).